THE DOVER DEMON
HUNTER SHEA

Stephen –
The truth is in here!

Hunter Shea

SEVERED PRESS
HOBART TASMANIA

THE DOVER DEMON

For the godfather of cryptozoology and the man who was on the scene in Dover when the strange and unusual came to visit, Loren Coleman.

Cryptid: In cryptozoology, a cryptid (from the Greek κρύπτω, *krypto*, meaning "hide") is a creature or plant whose existence has been suggested but has not been discovered or documented by the scientific community.

The Skeptics Dictionary, Robert Carroll

"It was as if, at moments, we were perpetually coming into sight of subjects before which we must stop short, turning suddenly out of alleys that we perceived to be blind, closing with a little bang that made us look at each other—for, like all bangs, it was something louder than we had intended—the doors we had indiscreetly opened."

The Turn of the Screw, Henry James

On the nights of April 21st and 22nd, 1977, the town of Dover, Massachusetts played host to an unexplained creature that skulked along its darkened roads and piney woods. Several known eyewitnesses reported seeing something so strange, so unearthly, they knew right away their lives would never be the same again.

All of the eyewitnesses were teens, out late with friends and girlfriends during spring break. Both nights were seasonally mild with clear skies. Because Dover was a quaint, rural—and affluent—small town, there weren't many streetlights to obscure nature's own lightshow. Visibility along Dover's roads, thanks to a bright moon and sparkling stars, was relatively clear despite the late hour.

Six teenagers spotted the bizarre, upright being in three distinct locations, all within a two-mile radius. When asked separately to draw what they had seen, the sketches produced were eerily similar. In an age before social media and instant information sharing, the tales told by the unsettled high school students were remarkably coherent and in sync with one another.

What they saw was described as a small, thin, hairless figure, no more than four feet tall, with a large, oval head and eyes that appeared to give off a disturbingly orange glow. Its flesh was almost peach-colored, with a texture that looked both wet and textured, as if pebbled. It had long fingers and toes that it used to steady itself on rocks and downed tree limbs.

In all cases, the creature fled before it could be examined further. The fear it instilled in those that came face-to-face with it was real. A man who would later go on to become known as one of the world's foremost cryptozoologists was in Dover within days of the sightings, interviewing the teens and important figures of the town and police department. Ufologists also came to the town that spring, for the being had the potentiality of being one of several things—it could be an unknown species, possible visitation by something not of this earth, misidentification of a local and potentially sick animal, or outright hoax.

To this day, none of the teens, now in their fifties, have recanted their stories. No one who knows or has interviewed them doubts that they saw something bizarre those spring nights.

There is no disputing that a legend was born over that two-night period—one that lives on, a mystery that is yet unsolved.

That legend is known as...The Dover Demon.

Summer

Chapter One

What a waste of time, Kelly Weathers thought as she took drags from the bottle of whiskey between showering, changing into her dress and putting on her makeup. Def Leppard pounded from the boombox she kept on a shelf in her bathroom. It was the good stuff, not the pseudo-pop crap they churned out after Steve Clark bit the big one. *How can Janie be the only one who doesn't see that Kirk is gay? It's not like she's some dumb kid, and Kirk sure as hell isn't working hard to hide the fact that he prefers a stiff one to a muff. Do I get my gift back if they don't make it through the first year?* She adjusted her breasts so they sat nicely in the expensive bra she'd gotten at Victoria's Secret a couple of months back when 'Janie the hero' set her up on a blind date with one of the groomsman. Yep, he was gay, too.

It was only a mile walk from her house to the Dartmouth Pub where the bachelorette party was being held. No need to drive, so no need to watch what she drank. Before she left the house, downing what was left of the Jim Beam, she admired herself in the full-length mirror by her front door.

"Not bad for a fifty-three-year-old broad," she said to her reflection. Husbands and kids destroyed a woman's body. To that end, she had done her best to defy Father Time and gravity better than most women her age. Staying single was more than a choice, it was a vocation. Makeup hid the wrinkles and dark circles under her eyes so no one was the wiser. Her jet-black hair, aided every other month by a trip to her favorite salon in Boston for a dye touch up, hung in loose ringlets along her shoulders. Her sharp jaw and naturally plump lips made the local gossip queens titter about secret plastic surgery. If they only knew it was just a matter of genetics—her mother had been quite the stunner until Alzheimer's robbed her of her beauty and her spark seemingly overnight. Well, a combination of mom's gene pool and not passing a child through her own birth canal, thank you very much. Just because you're a woman doesn't mean it's your duty to be a mother. She'd been smart enough to realize at an early age that she would never be cut out for motherhood, thereby saving some poor child from a miserable childhood that he or she could use to blame on a host of personal shortcomings as they got older, bending the ear of some overpriced shrink.

Walking down the path from her house, she couldn't resist taking a quick detour to Farm Road. The heel of one shoe got caught between some loose rocks on the side of the road, stopping her in her tracks. It was almost nine o'clock and the midsummer sun had dipped below the massive tree line. Damn trees. They were everywhere you turned.

"I live in the world's capital of trees and horse shit," she'd told everyone who would listen at the Boston accounting company where she worked. They thought Dover sounded just darling and would trade places with her in an instant.

They didn't realize she was a prisoner here. There was no sense trying to explain it to them. Not that they'd give a burning turd anyway.

As she struggled to extricate her foot, she thought she saw something moving to her right. The cool buzz of the Jim Beam fought a war with instant sobriety.

"I see you sons of bitches. What are you afraid of me for?"

Kelly squatted close to the ground, her nylon tearing at the knee as she settled into the gravel.

So now here she was, on her knees like a back-alley whore or Sunday school supplicant, talking to a bush in the dying daylight. The cooling breeze made her eyes water, but she refused to blink. Not yet. She could win a staring contest with anyone—or any*thing*.

It was there, she just knew it. The leaves of the bush riffled. Could have been the wind. Kelly squinted, focusing on the dark spaces within the scrawny limbs of the hearty, untrimmed bush.

"Blink, you little asshole," she said, her thick tongue actually spitting out *asshole*.

She fumbled in her purse for Betty. Her fingers flicked away her makeup bag, wallet, rolls of Certs, spare change and various other debris that had accumulated within its depths. She kept Betty in a zippered compartment at the bottom of the bag. Kelly pulled back the zipper, her eyes never wavering from the bush.

Betty's heavy, icy reassurance jacked up her confidence.

Cocking the hammer back on the .38, she whispered, "Nothing to be afraid of. As long as we all play nice, there's no reason for Betty to make a peep."

The air was preternaturally silent. This time of night, the surrounding woods should have been bleating with the caterwauling of night bugs and the scurrying of nocturnal critters fresh from a day's sleep. That's how she knew she wasn't seeing things. Even the wildlife knew there was something hiding in that bush, waiting for her to flinch.

They were fast—possessing logic-defying speed when it came to hide-and-seek. Kelly knew from experience that if she so much as flicked her eyes away for an instant, it would be gone and there'd be no hope of following it to its hiding place. Natural born hiders, they knew exactly how to keep their presence secret. Unless you were looking for them, you'd never even snatch a blurry glimpse in your periphery.

But, if you knew they were about and you purposefully sought them out, there were times when you could snag them in your sights as they skulked around. Spotting them wasn't easy. Just ask the scores of curious and serious-minded cryptid hunters alike who had come to Dover hoping for their own encounter. All of them had walked away without a story to tell. And the stories they did tell were fueled by delusion or Budweiser or both.

The only people who knew the signs were the very few who had seen them before, larger than life, stranger than a fever dream, a moment in time that could capture you in amber if you let it. Kelly would never have been able to explain the *how* to anyone who asked. It wasn't anything tactile, a triggering of the senses that alerted her to their presence. It was an inexplicable *knowing*, an itch at the base of her skull that could never be scratched.

The problem over the past few years was that her need for a drink often brought on that same itch. The only way to get it to stop was through anesthetizing herself with Jim Beam, Sam Adams, Johnnie Walker and a host of other gentlemen callers that came in a bottle.

On a night like tonight, when that itch should have been nothing more than a Novocained patch of brain matter, it came anyway, luring her to this spot.

The wind shifted, now going from east to west, bringing with it the ever-present musk of horse manure. Farm Road was surrounded by stables. The horses had all been safely tucked away in their barns for the night, but their essence lived on in the fields and soft summer breezes.

It would be easy to just fire a shot into the bush and be done with it. The blast would either scare it away, wound it to the point where she could, perhaps, follow it, or outright snuff the little beast. She was fine with any of the three options.

However, it would also scare the hell out of the people nestled in their pricey homes. Sound out here carried. The cops would be called. She'd have to run home, take off her dress and pretend she'd been watching the television too loud to hear anything if they came to her door.

A particularly sharp-edged chunk of gravel bit hard into the soft flesh underneath her kneecap. She wasn't sure how much longer she could maintain her position. Kelly noticed the slight waver of the heavy gun in her outstretched hand.

Did it just move?

A shape no bigger than the palm of a man's hand, darker than the pitch and shadows of the night, looked as if it had moved just an inch to the left within the bush.

What if it's a scared squirrel or skunk? Kelly thought, her dry eyes stinging.

No way. Squirrels and skunks don't scare the other animals and bugs away.

She took a deep breath, the burning of her muscles in her arms and legs beginning to chip away at her resolve.

No, but people do. I sure did make enough noise clomping over here and cursing like Dad during one of his DIY projects when my heel got caught.

Maybe, just maybe, she could scare it out.

"Hey," she barked, but not loud enough to be heard across the fields to the neighboring homes. "Boo!"

With her free hand, she tossed gravel into the stygian depths of the bush. The pebbles plinked against the lush green leaves, raining down among the branches.

The damn thing didn't even flinch.

"Maybe you're not even there," she hissed. "Wouldn't be my first hallucination, but that usually comes at the end of the night."

The words struck her funny bone. Her cheeks bulged and her lips pursed from holding her laughter in. What the fuck was wrong with her? This wasn't funny. At best, she'd painted a fine tableau of a middle-aged alcoholic training a gun on the local flora. She didn't want to think what the worst of the scenario entailed.

Even Kelly had to admit this was getting ridiculous. She would have stopped if the incessant itch weren't getting progressively worse. She ground her back molars against one another, her body's reflexive response to the itch, a feeble and useless attempt to get it to stop. All it did was bring sharp pains to her temples and jaw.

She heard the rumble of an engine behind her. It sounded like one of those big ass pickups that most folks in town drove, with rear flatbeds ideal for hauling bales of hay or transforming into makeshift motel rooms when the night was perfect like this and one of the dozen 'getting busy' spots in town was free.

The truck's headlights splashed against the stand of trees on the opposite side of the road as it rounded the bend. She couldn't be seen having a Mexican standoff with a bush!

Kelly used her aching knee to free herself and roll to the dry canal cut into the roadside. It was in that moment of clumsily tumbling, the approaching light sweeping across the bush, when she saw the eyes.

Twin, reddish globes blinked once before dashing away.

As she tumbled into the dry weeds, settling on her back, listening to the truck trundle by, she watched the tall grass that had grown atop the culvert sway as something sped through it.

As the noise of the truck faded into the distance, the crickets were the first to make themselves known. Kelly lay still, staring at the stars, waiting for the full chorus of the night music to return. Now she let her laugh break free, a deep cackle that brought tears to her eyes.

She tucked Betty back into her bag and got to her feet, using her hands to assist her rise out of the canal, thanking God for the drought that kept her from taking a full dunk into muddy water.

"Lost again," she murmured, wiping bits of grass and dirt from her dress, shaking it from her hair.

The itch was gone. So was the buzz she'd worked on back home. She used the light on her cell phone to inspect herself for damage. There was a spot of blood on her knee and she definitely looked like someone who'd taken a tumble on a country road. She could go back and change, freshen herself up.

Screw it. Janie's little party wouldn't last all night. Her stockings were already ruined, so she slipped off her shoes and padded onto the paved road. If she did a little power walk, she'd be at the bar in less than ten minutes.

No sense fretting about a missed chance to bag the little bastard back there. They were always around, thinking they could never be seen.

And she was always there, proving to them how wrong they were.

Chapter Two

Sam Brogna looked around his shop, wondering where to start. He'd been so engrossed in a biography on Teddy Roosevelt last night that he'd shut it down without straightening up. All he wanted to do was get home so he could settle into his easy chair and dive back into the book.

Which meant he had to get back to the shop early today and straighten out the racks, re-shelve the graphic novels that had been scattered all over the place by yesterday's browsers, vacuum the place and scrub down the counter. It was in some dire need of Fantastik. He locked the door, making sure the Closed sign still faced the street. Christ, he was tired. On Tuesday nights, Lacy did Skype meetings with her clients in Asia. They usually started around eight, ending well after midnight.

He'd poked his head into her workroom when he got home, catching her between calls. She was dressed all business up top, with sweats and slippers below. No one could see past her chest on the webcam, so why not get as comfortable as possible?

"Did you eat anything yet?" she'd asked.

"I figured I'd make a salad and add some of that chicken I grilled up the other night. You need anything from downstairs? A Coke, glass of wine?"

Lacy brushed her honey wheat hair behind her ears, tapping away on her computer. "No, I'm good. I have a meeting in a few minutes with a development team in Singapore. You know, they're looking for a US team leader with the flexibility of working from home. You'd be perfect for the job."

"I'm done with that kind of life, Lace. You can be, too, if you want. Trust me, the grass *is* greener on this side."

She narrowed her eyes at him. "I don't think I'd be happy reading comics all day."

Sam felt the old argument gaining steam. The muscles in his chest constricted.

Not tonight. I'm too damn tired to go through this again.

For some reason, she partly measured her success by his own. The fact that he had done exceedingly well for the first twenty years of their marriage no longer held water. Having to tell people in their social circle that he still owned and worked in a comic book store physically pained her to say aloud. Which was why she threw herself into her own work, rising in her company to the point where she was rumored to be anointed the next CEO.

"You could do anything you want," he mumbled, gripping the molding of the doorframe so hard his knuckles paled like the underbelly of a fish.

"What?"

He took a big breath and said, "Never mind. You know where to find me if you need me."

She didn't reply. Instead, she connected her call and was all smiles for her clients in Singapore.

The act of preparing dinner, the soft sounds of Norah Jones tinkling in the background and the calming warmth of a scotch and soda settled his nerves. *Why can't she just accept things for the way they are? It's not like we're living in a cardboard box, for Christ sake. Doesn't she see how important this has been for Nicky?*

He chopped the cold chicken with gusto, nearly catching his thumb in the process.

Lacy wasn't a snob when we met. Shit, she comes from an entire family of blue-collar people. Her father was a metalworker. Her mother worked in a department store for forty years. I fell in love with Lacy because she was so different from every other girl I'd grown up around. What the hell happened?

Maybe if he could convince her to take some time off this summer—a couple of weeks, go someplace where the most effort you had to expend was to get up and sip a cocktail. If she took a moment to step back and relax, maybe she'd see she didn't have to run herself ragged proving she was an ideal that was impossible to sustain. He'd start checking travel websites this week and see what he could find. She definitely needed a break.

Some time to wear as little clothing as possible is what we both need. I love her and I'm not going to lose her.

Feeling a little better about things now that he had a plan, he'd settled down with his T.R. book inside his walk-in humidor, smoking a couple of Cohibas while he read. They were Linea 1492, forty-four ring gauge

Corona Gordas, the last two in the box. He'd made a note to get more. By the time he crawled into bed, Lacy was asleep, the TV remote in her hand, snoring softly. When he woke up in the morning, she was gone, wading in the deep end of office politics.

Thinking about the Cohibas as he yanked the vacuum cleaner from the disheveled catchall closet, he wished he had one on him right now. Not that he could smoke it in his own store, in a building that he owned. State law prohibited it. Plus, it didn't look good for kids to walk into a smoke-filled comic book store. That would have been fine when he was a kid, but the world had changed, and he wasn't exactly sure it was for the better. Not that there were many kids these days. Most of his steady patrons were adults. Thanks to shows like *The Walking Dead* and the proliferation of comic-inspired movies ruling the box office, there was no shortage of grown men, and sometimes even women, looking for the next great zombie comic or searching for the history of Captain America or Iron Man.

Running the vacuum over the crumb-riddled floor—he'd fired up the popcorn machine yesterday and was giving it out for free like crack to everyone who walked in the door—he contemplated calling Nicky's cell phone and waking him up. He was supposed to be helping out anyway, but Sam could not get his son to wake up. *Must have been up late playing games online.*

Sam had to squeeze his eyes shut and shake the next thought away. *Or, more likely, he was hitting the porn tubes. God, would I have ever seen the sun if there was free porn when I was seventeen?*

Thankfully, he was rescued from the line of thought by a heavy rap on the front window.

His best friend, Tank Clay, smiled back at him, holding up a brown paper bag sodden with grease spots. Sam switched the vacuum off and opened the door to let him in.

"Special delivery," Tank said, plopping the bag down on the counter.

Sam winced. "Jeez, Tank, I just cleaned that."

Tank opened the bag, dipped his nose inside and took a long whiff. When he looked at Sam, his eyes were glassy, as if he'd just been huffing airplane glue.

He'd gotten his nickname in high school when he'd had a growth spurt for the record books. He was as tall—just under six-four—as he was solid. Even now at fifty-four, he was still in better shape than most college kids. His thinning hair, faint lines of crow's feet and dark patches on his cheeks from years of sun damage were the only things that even gave people a hint he was over forty.

"Did you at least get the sausage gravy on the side?" Sam asked, reaching into the bag.

"Just as you ordered. Six for me, four for you."

Ten of the fluffiest, most golden biscuits ever baked north of the Mason-Dixon line were packed in a greasy cardboard tray. A Styrofoam container of gravy nestled amongst the biscuits. Sam's salivary glands went into overdrive.

"Shouldn't we nuke 'em for a minute or so?" Tank asked—fumbling around the shelves under the cash register to find the stash of plates and plastic utensils Sam kept there. "I got caught in a little traffic jam in Natick. Some woman bumped her Beemer into another woman's Range Rover and they had to stop traffic entirely so they could sort out insurance and wait for the police to tell them to get the hell off the road. There wasn't even any damage. They felt they had to preserve the scene as if someone had been killed. Idiots."

Sam dipped a biscuit into the chunky white gravy, moaning deeply with the first bite. "Without idiots, we can't have smart people. Lacy would kill me if she saw me eating this."

Tank shoved an entire biscuit in his mouth, chewed a couple of times and swallowed hard. "Isn't that the point of eating them here?" he laughed.

Sam nodded. "It's kinda sad. Here we are, two grown, successful men, afraid of what our wives will say if they see us eating something greasy and delicious. Neither of us have even heart or cholesterol problems and we *still* have to face their music."

Already on his fourth biscuit while Sam talked, Tank wiped the corners of his mouth with a tan napkin. "It's the age, Sam. We're at that stage of life where our wives can become merry widows in a flash. They're not ready to take the black yet."

Rolling his eyes, Sam said, "Like Lacy or Steph will ever become little old Italian ladies dressed in black from head to toe. My grandmother was the last to do that in the family. She used to scare the crap out of me with that getup. It was like visiting an undertaker."

"True. Our wives will more than likely use some of the insurance money to go on a big spending spree, take a vacation to some island for a few months to grieve and come home with stories to tell about the twenty-something guy who owned the surf shop."

"Speak for yourself. My Lacy would never shack up with a surfer dude. No, I see her more as the mistress of the local governor."

When they were done with their forbidden breakfast, Tank stayed to help Sam get the shop in order. "Why do you let people take all this stuff out without putting it back on the shelves?" he said, going back and forth along the wall of new comic book holders. Everything was kept in alphabetical order, grouped by publisher. There were sections for Marvel, DC, Dark Horse, Image and so on. Sam would never have been able to afford his comic addiction as a kid with so many titles to choose from. Maybe that was another reason most of his clientele were adults.

"I opened this place to keep it casual. It's not like I have anything else pressing to do. Cleaning up the shop is my way to encounter the Zen in life."

He chuckled when he heard Tank grumble under his breath, "Fucking slobs."

Sam wasn't kidding when he said he had nothing else pressing to do. He and Tank both had retired in their mid-forties from very lucrative jobs in Boston—Sam as the owner of a high-end boat cleaning company and Tank as the fearless CEO of a tech company that at the time was developing quantitative tracking software for social media applications. Sam was the first to cash in his chips, deciding to spend the rest of his life doing whatever he wanted to do and not remaining a slave to money. His own father had died when Sam was young, working himself to an early grave trying to keep up with the Joneses. The last thing Sam wanted to do was follow in his footsteps. He would have rather grown up broke *with* a father than well-off without one. That wasn't going to happen with him and his son. When the time came to sell to a private equity firm headed by a group of stodgy bean counters, he took it without a moment's hesitation.

He hadn't been too keen on the board he'd turned his company over to, so over the course of a year, he'd managed to find better jobs for his former employees. That left his conscience clear and all the time in the world to spend with Nicky and Lacy.

When Tank saw how happy Sam was, stress free and enjoying every day as if it was the first day of vacation, he tendered his resignation a few months later.

Lacy had been none too pleased with his decision. A devout workaholic, she thought he'd had a mid-life crisis nervous breakdown. She couldn't have been further from the truth. Sam's change of course made sure such a thing would never happen. Lacy only warmed to the idea when he explained that he wanted to get closer to Nicky, who was growing into a little man before their eyes. When he asked Nicky if there was any special thing they could do together, his eyes had bulged out of their sockets and he'd said, "It would be awesome if we could work in a comic book shop! We could hang out and read comics and watch movies all day!"

That was seven years ago when Nicky was a ten-year-old in love with *The Fantastic Four, The Flash* and *X-Men.* Granting his wish and going one better, Sam opened their own comic shop, calling it Heroes Welcome. Nicky worked beside him on weeknights and weekends and they did exactly what he'd said. They bonded over those comics and movies in a way Sam could never have hoped for. It was the best decision of his life. Better still, Nicky still loved being in the store…with him.

"Okay, I'm done," Tank said, admiring the ordered stacks of comics on the wall.

"If you want to come back later, we're going to watch *Young Frankenstein* at six. I'm sure all the regulars will be here."

"I'd love to, but I can't. I'm putting the finishing touches on my trip to Belize in the fall."

"Oh, that's right, the Mayan thing. How long you going for?"

"Three weeks."

"Three weeks on your knees with a trowel and soft brush. I'd be crippled."

Tank clapped him on the shoulder. "That's why we keep you here in the store and leave the adventure to me. You forget, I'll be surrounded by pretty coeds in tight shorts. All part of the yin and yang of life."

Tank had decided to use his newfound free time pursuing his lifelong passion of archaeology. Getting his Masters degree in archaeology at Boston University had been his first priority. Then it was on to actual fieldwork, which involved numbing hours spent hunched over dusty digs. Tank loved every second of it. He was like a kid on a treasure hunt. In the past few years, he'd been to Peru, Bolivia, Egypt, Cambodia and even Easter Island. He kept threatening to take Sam with him on one of his excursions. Maybe when Nicky was in college, he'd seriously consider it. Might be nice to visit South America.

"Just be careful. Don't go putting your yin in someone else's yang," Sam joked.

"I seriously think Steph is a witch. I guarantee she'd know it the instant I did anything more than look, even if it was thousands of miles away. She scares me. Truly." His broad grin lifted the full, brown, wiry beard he'd grown over the past two years. Sam thought he spotted some biscuit crumbs clinging to the long wires.

"See you Saturday then. I just got a box of Partagas I know you'll like," Sam said.

"I'm on it."

Flipping the sign to Open, Sam watched Tank lumber down the street.

A young couple passed his old friend, eyes on the Heroes Welcome sign over Sam's head. They were dressed in black T-shirts with horror movie posters—his with *Basket Case*, hers with *The Funhouse*.

Interesting choices for kids who weren't even born when those movies came out, Sam thought.

The boy, his long hair tucked under a Red Sox baseball cap, looked to him and asked, "Hey, is this the place where we can get some Dover Demon stuff? The waitress at the diner pointed us in your direction."

Sam nodded. "Come on in. First customers of the day get a ten percent discount."

Chapter Three

Nicky Brogna woke up at the crack of noon. His pillowcase was stained red. There was a moment of panic as he hands flew to his mouth, searching for—what? Jumping out of bed, he ran to the mirror over his dresser, pulling his lips back and revealing multi-colored teeth.

His shoulders slumped and he shook his head. "Oh yeah, Skittle juice."

He must have fallen asleep chewing on Skittles again. He'd been reading the *Batman, Court of Owls* graphic comic an hour or so before dawn, munching on candy and washing it down with peach iced tea. Next thing he knew, it was morning, or more precisely, afternoon.

Knowing his mother would kill him if she found out he'd fallen asleep with candy in his mouth again—"*One of these days you'll choke to death if you don't cut it out!*"—he stripped the case off the pillow and tucked it in the waistband of his basketball shorts. Nicky dropped the pillow on the windowsill, letting the sun and fresh air dry out his candy-coated drool.

Damn! He was supposed to clean up the comic book shop with his dad today. He couldn't help sleeping in. It was an established scientific fact that teenagers were wired to stay up late and sleep late. He was a victim of human genetics and hormones.

Dialing his cell phone while he stomped down the stairs, he dashed to the laundry room so he could stuff the pillowcase in the washer. His mother had left a bundle of dirty clothes on top, so he chucked them in with it.

"Ah, the son also rises," his father said, picking up on the fourth ring.

"Sorry, dad." Nicky dropped in a cap each of detergent and fabric softener. None of his friends ever had to do chores and he suspected most wouldn't be able to figure out how to even turn a washing machine on. Not so in the Brogna house. His parents both declared as often as he could stand that he'd never be an independent man if he couldn't even do the little things in life. "I forgot to set my alarm."

His father laughed. "Oh, you set it. It just wasn't enough to get you up. I turned it off before I left. What did you think of *Court of Owls*? I saw it on your bed."

"Batman is more badass than I thought."

"This is the summer we expand your horizons. Tank and I have a ton of great DC stuff for you to read."

"I thought you were Mr. Marvel."

"I've more than dipped my toes in the DC waters. Where do you think all those old *Green Lantern*, *The Flash* and *Justice League of America* comics came from? Half the DC section in the store is from my private stash."

Nicky wandered into the kitchen, grabbed three waffles from the freezer and tossed them in the toaster oven. "Yeah, and if you liked them so much, you wouldn't sell them, like all those *Fantastic Four* and *Captain America* comics that you keep in the back room."

"Grasshopper does have a point. You want me to come get you in a half hour or so?"

"Nah. I'll ride my bike over." Pouring syrup on the waffles, he added, "You know, it would be a lot easier for me to get to the store if I had a car."

He could hear his father's grin. "Like I said, you work in the store with me all summer and I'll get you a car before school starts. You're going to have to earn that Subaru."

"Didn't you mean Mustang?" Nicky interjected, syrup dribbling down his chin.

There was a loud banging on the other end of the line. "I'm sorry, I think we have a bad connection. You were talking about some kind of car?"

"Never mind. I'll change and come over."

"See you in a few. Love you, kiddo."

"Love you, too."

Nicky downed a tall glass of orange juice, chasing it with an energy drink. Walking back up the stairs, he had to pause a moment, place his hand on his stomach and let out a belch that could be heard in Boston. If his mother were home, she'd yell at him to excuse himself, muttering that they were raising a pig, not a boy. In a way, he missed not hearing that.

Up until this year, his mother had always worked from home in the summer to watch over him. Now that he was deemed a near-man, she took on more responsibilities at work and was in the office six days a week. The scary thing was, he wasn't even sure what she did. Something to do with sales, but what her company sold was a mystery. He used to think it was strange until, talking with his friends, he realized almost none of them had a firm grasp on what their parents did for a living. They made money, some of them a ton of money, and he guessed that was good enough.

Everyone knew what his dad did—now at least—and he was deemed the coolest parent in town. Well, him and Tank, who everyone assumed was a hulking Indiana Jones. It didn't hurt that his father was always giving Nicky's friends discounted or free stuff at the store and hosting movie nights, complete with refreshments, every week.

Pasting his underarms with deodorant and walking under a mist of body spray, he slipped on a Moon Knight shirt and new basketball shorts. He decided to wear his Converse that had pictures of cheeseburgers on them.

It was a humid day, which would put the body spray to the test. The ride to the shop was a little over two miles. Man, he couldn't wait until he had a car. He'd never ride a bike again. Ever.

Screwing his ear buds in, he selected his *Beebs and Her Money Makers* playlist and headed toward town. Their funky, up-tempo ska beat kept his legs pumping and his brain from fixating on the oppressive heat.

Kelly Weathers fiddled with her radio while trying to munch on a tuna wrap, all while navigating her Escalade around the tight turns of the two-lane road. After calling in sick—there was no way her pounding head was going to make it through a shower—she'd slept until lunchtime. Her stomach was what woke her up. She needed something to eat in the worst way. Her body craved carbs. It would either soak up the remaining booze in her system or make her hurl. Either was fine with her.

That made seven sick days this year and it was only July. The company policy was five sick days per year. Then again, the company was owned by her brother and he wasn't about to fire her.

That's just Kelly being Kelly.

That phrase worked for and against her. She wondered which side the balance tipped to now.

"Shit!"

Kelly dropped her wrap and jerked the wheel hard to the right. The hulking Escalade swerved so much, it almost went on two wheels. The kid on the bike zoomed in the opposite direction, nearly spinning off the road.

She hit the brakes, kicking up dust that enveloped the car. Looking in her rearview as it cleared, she saw the kid pedaling away, un-squashed.

"Jesus fucking Christ," she stammered, her heart beating so fast, her neck and jaw ached.

Tuna was splattered all over the SUV's dashboard and floor. The open bottle of pomegranate juice had flown from the cup holder, spewing its contents everywhere. It looked as though she'd severed an artery.

This is going to be a bitch to clean, she thought, grinding her teeth.

Was that Nicky Brogna she'd almost hit? Jesus, *if she had hit him*. Of all people. That would have been more bad karma than any one person could work off in a thousand lifetimes. Worse still, she'd almost run over the kid when she was stone cold sober. Sober but distracted, as usual.

"Get it together," she said to her reflection in the rearview mirror. She wore a baseball cap low on her head with big, impenetrably dark sunglasses—the uniform of both the rich stay-at-home mom and member of the midweek hangover club. Her hands shook so much, she couldn't put the truck in drive.

Instead, she opened the door and nearly flopped onto the side of the road.

Now the vomit came.

And it wasn't the tuna that did it.

Chapter Four

"Dad, do we have any more Dover Demon books?" Nicky asked, perched on the stool by the register.

Sam was back by the old model kits, changing the prices on the Aurora Universal Monsters collection he'd gotten at a toy fair last month. He had two Draculas, one Wolf Man, three Frankensteins and his favorite, one Phantom of the Opera. Not wanting to part with them yet, he was upping the price so he could admire them just a little bit longer. Hell, maybe he'd open a Frankenstein so he and Nicky could put it together. Sam had assembled the very same kits with his own dad when he was maybe eight. They worked at the kitchen table after dinner, spending hours getting everything just right. Those were some of the scant few memories he had of his dad.

"I'm pretty sure we do. Let me check," Sam said, pulling the curtain aside to enter the back of the store. There were shelves of comics, action figures, models, masks, magic-based card games and magazines.

"Now, where did I put you?"

No matter how hard he tried, the back room remained a mess. He was pretty sure the remnants of the turkey club he'd had for lunch a few days ago was turning into a science experiment somewhere within the mass of stuff. This was Pack Rat City. Some small part of him liked it that way. A little disorder was good for the soul.

"Aha!" He found the box of trade paperback books underneath a pile of *Mad Magazines* wrapped in plastic. Using the box cutter he kept in his pocket, he opened the flaps and grabbed a handful of books. Their glossy covers showed an artist's rendition of the town's famous cryptid in all its glorious paleness, staring out from behind a fallen tree limb. Its orange eyes were the real attention-grabber, that otherworldly gaze snaring more than its fair share of readers.

The majority of Dover's residents despised the fact that they were a cryptid lover's bucket list destination. Outsiders, especially those looking for monsters, were frowned upon. The fact that Sam's store catered to a monster hunter's needs made him the black sheep of the town. Not that he craved their approval. He'd been obsessed as a kid with Bigfoot and the Loch Ness Monster. Back then, he would have loved to have found a place like this to get anything related to the mysterious creatures. So in a way, he was catering to young Sam Brogna, the kid who dreamed about legends.

And these particular books were very special to him.

"Got 'em," he said, emerging from the back. He handed one over to the heavy-set twenty-something at the counter, placing the rest in a plastic stand that he kept by the register.

The potential buyer flipped through the pages. "I promised my friend I'd get him a copy when I passed through," he said, pushing his glasses up the bridge of his nose. He grabbed another copy from the display. "Think I'm gonna take one for myself, too. Is it true the guy who wrote this actually saw this thing?"

Sam nodded. "Oh yeah. Matt Ford lived here for a couple of years in the seventies. I was a couple of years younger, so I didn't really know him. He says he saw the Dover Demon and I haven't found a reason not to believe him."

"But from what I read online, there were only like five or six witnesses. I never saw his name."

Giving the mostly empty store a suspicious sweep, Sam leaned close and said, "Those are the ones who went public. It was spring break and everyone was out those nights. There are more people who saw that thing than will ever admit to it publicly. Believe me, I've lived here all my life and I know."

The guy's face broke into an enormous grin. "No freaking way."

"He's not lying," Nicky said.

"You ever meet Matt Ford?"

"It's been a long time," Sam said. "But he does keep me stocked with his books. No one's written a more comprehensive book on the subject. This is the only place you can get them."

"That's what I heard. How much?"

Nicky replied, "Twenty for both."

The guy dropped a twenty on the counter, muttered thanks and walked out the door with his nose already buried in its pages.

Nicky said, "You know, we could probably make a lot of money selling local maps that highlight the locations where the Dover Demon was spotted."

"The search isn't much fun if it's made too easy. Besides, we already make a good penny on that one book alone. Not to mention the collectibles."

A local artist made Dover Demon models. Each was four inches high and depicted the creature standing along a rock wall, its long, talon-like fingers and toes wrapped around the rocks. Sam had a guy in Worcester who made Dover Demon buttons, pins and bookmarks. If the town was going to be inundated by the curious who all wanted something to take home, why not spread that wealth to nearby craftsmen?

"It would be awesome if we could make our own comic about it," Nicky said. An open issue of *Ghost* lay on the counter.

"If I could draw or write, I would give it a shot. Until then, I'll be the guy who sells them."

"You know that Walt guy from Jay and Silent Bob's Secret Stash?"

"The manager who wears the Devils cap?"

Nicky rocked on the stool. "Yeah, him. He's done the art for some Batman comics."

"That's because he can draw and he has Kevin Smith for a friend. If me or Tank put out the next *Clerks*, I will absolutely get you a Dover Demon comic deal."

Shooing him away, Nicky said, "Then go find Tank and get cranking. I'll run the store."

Sam flicked his son's ear and skipped away before he could reciprocate. When Nicky jumped off the stool, Sam said with a smile, "Remember, no roughhousing in the store."

One of their regulars, a quiet guy in his forties they'd nicknamed Hugh Hefner because he only bought comics with scantily clad women on the cover—like *Vampirella, Red Sonja, Witchblade* and a host of others—came to the counter with his weekly haul. "You have a customer," Sam said to his son.

Hugh made little eye contact and paid with his American Express card. He'd been coming to the store for years and Sam didn't think he'd said more than ten words in all that time. But he did buy a lot of comics, both new and old, so he was always a welcome sight.

"I'll bring a few more books out. Maybe it's time we added a few to the window display," he said. They normally did that in October, when the monster hunters were at their peak, but this summer had shown a spike in Dover Demon interest. It must have been featured on one of those cable shows recently.

Sam squatted over the box, staring at the spines. ""You're a popular man, Matt Ford. I'm going to have to order a couple more boxes soon." He took a moment to savor that special new book smell. E-books could never replace that wonderful odor. Sam had always been a voracious reader, even when he was working like his own version of a Dover Demon in the corporate world. There was always time for books. Reading was knowledge, it was pleasure, it was joy, it was life. Thank God Nicky felt the same way.

The rest of the day was slower than Congress passing a budget. It was hot and sunny outside. Anyone venturing into the great summer outdoors was busy swimming or hiking in the woods or fishing in any of the area's ponds. No one wanted to be cooped up in a comic book store.

Which was all right by Sam. He and Nicky watched *Friday the 13th* parts one and two on the fifty-inch TV he'd mounted on the wall opposite the new comic book displays. They went through three bags of microwave popcorn and all of the bottled water he kept in the mini fridge.

"I don't know how I ever survived working in an office," Sam said when the second movie was over and all of those deviant, pot-smoking, premarital-sex-having teens were taken care of by a vengeful Jason wearing a sack over his head rather than the iconic hockey mask that would come in the next movie.

"Well, without that, we wouldn't have this," Nicky said, sweeping loose kernels of popcorn off the card table.

"You're a wise little man. Now if only you could grow a decent mustache." Sam gave himself a belly laugh. His son's attempts at growing a respectable 'stache were as pitiful as his own at his age.

"At least I'm not losing my hair," Nicky quipped with a smirk.

"I'm not losing it. I've just realized at my age what a hassle it is and have chosen to let it fall out. And any grays you see up top have your name on them, kiddo."

They went back and forth for a while, then decided to close up shop a little earlier than usual. Nicky wanted to meet his friends Roy and Christine and hang at their house. Sam suspected a little something was blossoming between his son and Christine, a retro-punk redhead who was too cool for most any room. The only problem—she was his friend's sister. The Bro-Code was in danger of being broken.

Sam wouldn't mind sitting on the back patio and smoking a cigar with some Johnnie Walker Blue. He'd lure Lacy outside with a bottle of her favorite wine and the soft lullaby of the crickets hidden amongst the lush greenery that surrounded their house.

He'd also have to find out why there was renewed interest in their little demon friend. Not that he'd ever thought it was a demon in the religious sense of the word.

No, he of all people would know better than that.

Chapter Five

Tank Clay put down the book on Mayan potsherds, removed his glasses and rubbed his tired eyes. He'd been studying up as much as he could in preparation for his trip next month. This was his first Mayan dig and he was as excited as he'd been on Christmas Eve when he was a kid with a head too big for his scrawny body. He'd once asked Santa to make him grow and give him real man muscles, the kind his Uncle Al had. Al owned a construction company based out of Framingham and did some amateur wrestling on the side. The man was bigger than Godzilla and King Kong wrapped into one ferocious beast to little Tank—who at the time was still Christopher and years away from earning his nickname.

When Tank saw his uncle last around Easter, the eighty-year-old had shrunken by half and was as fragile as spun sugar.

Well, Santa had granted his wish, robbing Al of the very traits he desired.

It went to show that you can't trust elves. The bastards will put one over on you any chance they got.

Stephanie called out from the other room, "Come in here. You have to see this."

He settled onto the coach next to her. She propped her legs on his lap. Even in old pajamas, she was gorgeous. Unlike all of her friends, she hadn't starved herself in a futile effort to stay young. All of her body's natural collagen was still where it was supposed to be, keeping her shapely face and body beautiful. Her friends looked like lollipop heads with sun-damaged skin and waxen foreheads and cheeks that couldn't move because of the Botox.

Tank ran his hand through her long, auburn hair. "Whatcha watchin'?"

"You'll see when it comes back from commercial," she said, offering him a sip of her wine.

"This better not be another reality show with little people doing weird stuff."

"I promise, no little people."

"And no housewives."

"No housewives. Well, other than the one next to you."

He brought her fully onto his lap. "You're no housewife. You're my MILF."

"I'm going to hold you to that later."

Suddenly, Tank's shorts were a little tighter than usual.

Stephanie took the TV off mute as the commercial faded away and the show's title swiped across the screen.

"*United States of Cryptids*," Tank said. "I think I can see where this is going."

"It's apparently a new show that started a couple of weeks ago. I saw this On-Demand and had to watch."

"Why?"

"Just to see."

The narrator's voice sounded familiar. Must have been one of those character actors that popped up on TV shows and failed pilots from time to time. His gravelly intonation sounded like a dire rumble from the grave. Tank rolled his eyes and sighed. So much for serious, objective reporting. Then again, what did he expect from a show that called itself *United States of Cryptids*?

"*In the world of the bizarre and sometimes unexplained, the state of Massachusetts isn't just home to the infamous witch trials of Salem. In fact, you don't have to go back very far to find purportedly true encounters with the strange and unusual.*"

The iconic sketch of the large-headed, glowing-eyed Dover Demon, its long, pencil-thin toes and fingers draped over a series of large rocks like a lizard, faded into view. It was the sketch Billy Bartlett had drawn for the police way back when Led Zeppelin were rock gods and Jimmy Carter the country's own Mr. Peanut.

"The sketch that launched a legend," Tank said.

"Billy always could draw," Stephanie said.

He felt the muscles along her shoulders begin to tighten.

The Dover Demon segment of the show rehashed everything that had been reported those two nights, allowing a few experts in cryptozoology and zoology airtime to voice their opinions on what it could have been. As usual, no one had a clue.

"*It's my strong belief that these kids were telling the truth,*" some guy in an alligator hat said. His long gray hair was tied in a ponytail, draped down his chest. *"No one doubted them at the time. Not the police. Not their parents or teachers. Not even reporters and investigators who flocked to the scene. It's almost forty years later and no one's story has changed. What did they see that night? I can't tell you. But I can assure you they saw something that wasn't what we would consider normal."*

Tank hit the pause button and kissed the top of his wife's head.

"That was enlightening," he said.

"Truly. If the show is popular enough, maybe it will bring some extra business Sam's way."

"I think it already has. He told me he's had a little run on that book this past week. I'll have to tell him about this." She turned in his lap to face him, her nose inches from his own. Her breath smelled like sweet wine. "You okay?"

She kissed the tip of his nose. "Yeah, I'm fine. You'd think after all this time—"

"At least it didn't turn this place into Loch Ness," he said, chuckling, hoping to lighten her mood.

"Can you imagine how crazy it would make people here if monster hunters set up shop in trailers that never left? I wish people would just let it go and forget about it. I pretty much had until I saw this."

Tank looked at the TV and saw that he had paused it on another artist's rendition of Billy Bartlett's drawing. The full color painting stared at him and Stephanie, the wide, unblinking eyes of the creature attempting to mesmerize them across the gulf of time and space.

He remembered that night at the movies in late 1977, almost six months after everything got momentarily weird in what had always been his quiet, somewhat stuffy hometown. He and Stephanie brought Sam and his girlfriend, Kelly Weathers, on a double date to see what everyone said was the craziest, scariest movie ever: *Close Encounters of the Third Kind.*

The movie was incredible, like nothing they'd ever seen. Steph had squeezed his arm right down to the bone, never letting up, even when Richard Dreyfuss was making mountains out of mashed potatoes. He'd looked over and saw Kelly doing the same to Sam. Tank was so enthralled, he didn't even bother devouring his popcorn. The special effects were so good, he almost believed they had filmed actual space ships as they raced down roads and soared into the clouds, multi-colored machines that looked both like elaborate kids toys and terrifying glimpses of a race far superior to man.

It was all good fun, a perfect date movie that was also a guy's movie.

Until it came to the scene with the exchange.

Atop Devil's Tower, the alien mothership and a dizzying, kaleidoscopic array of incredible UFOs, briefly touch down to give back dozens of people who had been abducted over the years.

When Tank, Sam, Stephanie and Kelly first saw the tiny, child-like aliens bopping around the humans, they held their collective breath. Their hearts stopped when the tall, sinewy 'adult' alien unfolded from the mothership's interior, arms held wide in peace and welcome.

They had seen that creature before.

This was no longer a movie.

Kelly ran from the theater, barely containing her sobs. Stephanie chased after her, though she later told Tank that Kelly simply beat her to a hasty escape.

Sam and Tank stared at one another dumbfounded.

"Sam, how the hell can that be?" Tank whispered, his eyes flicking to the smiling alien.

Sam shook his head. "I don't know. It can't be a coincidence."

That face was still fresh in their memories. It preyed upon their dreams, dragging them kicking and screaming into nightmares.

They all saw it back in April, on the first night when Billy had his encounter. But unlike Billy or John Baxter or Will Taintor, they never told a soul about their encounter. It was one thing to spot that creature as your headlights brushed past it.

What Tank and his friends had witnessed could never be spoken about, not with anyone who hadn't been there. Not even Billy or John would understand. They thought they'd kept it a secret. Now, sitting in a movie theater watching the impossible, they began to question everything.

Stephanie shivered against him, pulling him back to the present.

"I'm going to turn down the central air," she said, placing her palms flat against his massive chest and pushing to get up. "This way I can get in my birthday suit without ruining it with all those goose pimples."

She flashed him a seductive smile and headed for the stairs.

That night in 1977 had done a number on them. They all found their own ways to cope with it. Shows like this brought it all back, but for some reason they couldn't turn away. The world had slit open its veil of secrets and shown them something special. What were they supposed to do with that? You can't run and hide from your own personal experience.

You could try. Stephanie had been the most successful at it.

Tank often wondered if his interest in archaeology was his way of searching for clues to the thing they had seen. Something about it had seemed…primordial. It hadn't just popped up in 1977. Its roots ran much, much deeper. He did his best not to get sucked in by the ancient alien theorists. Sticking to hard science and facts, a small part of him hoped to stumble upon incontrovertible evidence that what they saw was more than just a chance encounter with the unexplainable.

He turned the TV off, staring into space.

"Poor Kelly," he muttered. He'd heard enough about her to know she'd gone off the rails, getting worse as time went on. That night had ruined her.

Sam had done the best he could, exorcizing his Dover Demon in his own way. Of them all, he'd adapted to the mythology that had been born that spring the best. He never was one to run away.

Tank waited a couple of minutes for his thoughts to settle, then jogged up the stairs to his waiting wife.

Chapter Six

The Jaguar in his driveway wasn't familiar. Sam stood outside the house, hands on his hips, looking into darkened windows as if he had X-ray vision. The only light came from the undulating oranges of the fireplace in the den. Even though it was summer, he and Lacy still lit fires, more for the ambiance than the heat.

His mouth was suddenly too dry to swallow, his tongue feeling as if it had grown too big for his mouth.

He was supposed to be home two hours from now. That was the routine, but it was a slow day and Nicky wanted to be with his friends, so why not close up shop a little early?

The temptation to rain blows on the Jaguar with a tire iron was almost too strong to resist. It didn't belong here. He knew what all of Lacy's friends drove. The irritating lilt of *which of these is not like the other* played musical chairs in his head.

Staring at the car, he said, "Who the fuck are you?"

There was no way he was going to stand vigil out here waiting to see who emerged from his house. No, he was walking in to what would most likely be a well-worn country song come to roost in his own goddamn home.

What have you done, Lacy? I know we haven't been on the same page lately, but that doesn't give you the right to destroy our family.

Pausing with his hand on the front doorknob, he wondered who it would be. Was it one of her many clients? A co-worker? Someone from town? A random fuck she'd found on the internet? He tried to steady his breathing. Jesus, he thought he was going to fall back on his ass. Nothing felt real anymore. If he didn't concentrate hard, he'd have an out of body experience. He could feel his essence struggling to break free, to save itself from what was to come. Let his body go through the motions, but protect his sanity.

Sam squeezed his eyes tightly shut. "Maybe it's not what you think," he whispered to his feet.

Right. And maybe men never landed on the moon and 9-11 was a mass delusion.

Lacy had done this before—cheated on him—but never while they were married. They'd met a couple of years after graduating college. They were two young forces of nature who'd worked hard and partied as if their lives depended on it. In the beginning, he was just one of several hoping to win the race to her exclusivity. In fact, at first, he wasn't even sure he wanted to be monogamous with her. She was a little too flirty, too eager to prove that she could have any man she wanted, usually at the expense of the poor schmuck who was paying for dinner that night. Somewhere within that first year of on and off dating and running into each other in the same clubs—hooking up in bathrooms, cars and wherever else the mood hit them—they found themselves falling in love. Before they knew what was happening, they were a couple. When he proposed a year later, she said yes right away. Cold feet had soon settled in and she slept with an old boyfriend from high school she'd run into at a trade show. She'd confessed, he railed, she wept and in the end, he forgave her.

That had been the last of it. Yes, it was almost thirty years later, but deep down, he'd always known what she was capable of. He may not have shown it, but he worried deeply when she went on business trips with other men, powerful men, the kind she longed for him to be once again.

How could they have fallen so far apart? How could it be that his decision to remake his life into one where his family was his primary focus was the very thing that drove them apart?

Cut the shit, Sam. You haven't even opened the door and you're trying to take the blame. There's nothing I haven't given her. If she's in there with some guy, I'm not the one who told her to screw him in my home, in my bed.

His blood ran like a torrent of lava. That last thought swarmed over him, obliterating everything. He turned the handle and kicked the door so hard it banged off the wall and nearly closed back on him.

Lacy's surprised yelp came from the den.

He didn't announce himself with any witty phrase, delivered like a maniacal Jack Nicholson, though he felt very much like him at the moment.

Which one of these is not like the other? Not like the other? Not like the other?

The sound of footsteps on the hardwood floor of the den beat a frantic patter. There was only one way out of that room. Whoever was in there had to come through Sam if he wanted to get to the safety of his precious Jaguar.

Sam could wait for Lacy and her friend to get themselves together, to concoct a bullshit story that would be spoken only to buy them time. Or he could stride into the den right now and catch them at their most rattled.

Fuck it, I don't want to hear a story.

He stood in the den's doorway. A lone Duraflame log burned in the fireplace.

His wife and her lover were in shadow.

Asshole doesn't even know how to make a real fire with wood, Sam thought, his head whirling. Here he was standing before his half-naked wife, firelight casting shadows on her bare breasts, a strange man hopping into his pants, his wild, moussed hair a sweaty curtain that masked his face, and all Sam could think about was the guy's inability to make a fire.

"Sam!" Lacy blurted, covering her breasts with an arm.

For some reason, that gesture, hiding herself from him, her husband, after giving them freely to a fucking stranger, hurt him most of all.

"Care to tell me what the fuck is going on?" he said, though he could barely hear himself talk. The struggling sound of the man's leg trying to find their way into the fabric of his pants was overwhelming.

"Oh, Sam." Tears began to spring from Lacy's eyes.

The man finally looked up at him. His shirt was in his hand. Sam saw bright red welts on his neck and chest, tattoos from Lacy's eager mouth. He was young, maybe in his late twenties, with a douchebag soul patch sprouting under his lower lip. The guy held up his hands. They were shaking. He said, "Look, man, I don't want any trouble."

A disquieting sense of calm washed over Sam.

"Then you shouldn't have fucked my wife," Sam replied. Something was happening to him. He couldn't feel his own body. The edges of his vision began to darken. "Aren't there enough young little whores out there for you? Why bother with some old, married woman?"

He didn't look at Lacy. He prayed his jab at her vanity hurt like hell.

"I'll just go so you can work this out with your wife," he said, his body tensed, leaning forward to take that first step to freedom.

"Please, Sam, let him go," Lacy pleaded. "This is about us, not him."

Now he turned to her. She still kept herself covered from him. Her mascara ran down her cheeks, winding and twisting like the Tigris and Euphrates.

"You shut your mouth," he spat. "You don't have a right to tell me what this is about."

"Get out of the way!" she screamed at the top of her lungs.

Lacy glared at him, her chest rising and falling, an almost feral gleam in her eyes. Sam met her icy stare. He wanted to say, "*Who the hell do you think you are to get angry with me?*"

The words wouldn't come.

He took a deep breath, held it, exhaled.

"You're right," he said, stepping aside. His head swiveling to her lover, he said, "It's best you go. Now."

The gesture had the effect of deflating all of the anger, indignation, surprise and fear that had held his wife together. She collapsed into a chair, burying her face in her hands.

As the man passed, he said, "Hey, I'm really sorry, bro."

Bro. As if they were long lost friends.

Sam had no control over the hand that shot to the man's throat. His numb fingers tightened as much as muscle and sinew would allow.

Somewhere, Lacy screamed, "Sam, stop it! You're choking him!"

For this one moment, he gave her what she wanted. He let her lover go.

By throwing him in the fireplace.

Nicky, Roy and Christine sat on separate chairs in the downstairs billiard room, each engrossed in their iPhones. Roy was watching a movie, Christine was texting three of her friends at the same time and Nicky was using a graphics editing program to turn a picture of the three of them taken at the baseball field last week into a cartoon. His laughter over what he was doing to their faces, exaggerating their features with brushes of his fingertip, didn't even make them glance up from their phones. New Year's Day's latest download blared from the room's Bose sound system. Their hard, crunching metal sound didn't make a dent in their concentration.

Roy suddenly said, "You should hang tonight. I found some awesome old horror movies on Netflix we can binge on."

"Sounds cool," Nicky said, saving his work.

"You ever hear of Hammer films?" Roy asked, pausing his movie.

Nicky nodded. "Yeah, my dad told me a little about them. They made like a bunch of Dracula flicks and had a lot of chicks with big, heaving boobs in old English clothes. He says you know a Hammer movie just by the way it sounds. I tested him once. He could actually tell from the way they recorded the audio for people walking if it was a Hammer movie or not."

"That's freaking weird," Christine said, her thumbs flying over the screen. She'd dyed her light brown hair rose red the first day of summer vacation and, despite her new goth inclinations, spent as much time as she could in the sun. Her skin was Doc Savage bronze.

"It's his super power," Nicky said.

"Yeah, well, I added *Horror of Dracula*, *Count Yorga, Vampire* and *The Vampire Lovers* to my list. I hear the last one has hot lesbian vampires in it."

"Gross," Christine snorted. "You two gonna jerk off in the same room or something?"

Roy shook his head in mock contempt. "The only gross thing here is where your mind automatically takes you."

"Right, it's *my* mind that's choosing a lesbian vampire movie to watch with *my* friend."

"Why are you even here? Shouldn't you be in a tanning bed or something?"

Without looking at either of them, Christine got up from the chair and walked from the room. Nicky couldn't help but watch her walk away. The seductive sway of her hips and ass within the tight, denim shorts almost made him fall off his own chair.

"Jesus, what's the matter with you?" Roy said.

Nicky's cheeks bloomed crimson. He'd assumed Roy had gone back to watching his movie.

"What?" he replied.

"She's my sister, you dumbass."

"What does that mean?"

"It means you shouldn't be looking at her like that."

"Like what?"

"I'm not stupid, I know you and every other guy in school is crushing on her. I get it. But you have three strikes against you."

"Oh yeah, what's that?"

Roy held up his hand, his middle finger extended. "One, you're my best friend. It's your job to help me get guys to *stop* looking at her. You're not allowed to be part of the problem. Two, you're a fucking dork. Christine thinks her first boyfriend is going to be Chris Motionless or Rob Zombie."

"Rob Zombie is like as old as our dads," Nicky said.

"That's besides the point. And three, I repeat, you're my best friend. Best friends don't leer at, touch or date their best friend's sister."

Nicky knew he was right, but the way his insides got twisted up whenever Christine was around didn't care about the rules. She was only a year younger than them. At sixteen, she already had grown into her woman body, skipping the awkward, skinny, pimply high school stage as well as the freshman fifteen, college body and mind fluctuations that were still years ahead of her. What made her even more intriguing was the fact that she possessed the air of someone older, wiser and already apathetic to a world conquered. Yes, all the guys in school wanted her. But none were as lucky as Nicky, who got to spend so much time actually with her, so close he could smell the light touches of perfume she dabbed behind each ear. Sneaking into her room one day, he'd found that her favorite perfume was called Beach. When he'd gotten her a bottle for her sweet sixteen, she'd squealed as if he'd bought her a new car, giving him a tight embrace he still dreamt about. Roy gave him the same look then he was giving him now.

No matter how he felt, there was no way he was going to try to explain everything to Roy. His friend would knock his teeth out before he finished his first sentence.

"I wasn't looking at her that way," he protested weakly.

"Yes, you were." Roy hit the Play button on his phone, his signal that this conversation was over.

Nicky switched subjects. "I'll call my dad, let him know I'm staying."

The phone rang four times and went to voicemail. He tried his mother's phone and got the same thing. He called his father back and left a message.

"That's weird. My dad always answers the phone."

Roy flashed a wry grin. "Maybe they're doing the nasty."

"Oh, come on man, that's my mom and dad."

"Exactly, just like Christine's my sister."

"Okay, you win, asshole!" Nicky said, tossing a pillow at Roy's face.

"We should probably put the finishing touches on our demon hunting plan tonight," Roy said. "You know Tom and Bill are in. Maybe your dad can put us in touch with that Ford guy, the dude who wrote that book you guys sell. I bet he'd know the best places to look."

"What's the point? If there was ever something here, it only stuck around for a couple of days forty years ago. All we're gonna find are some horses and raccoons. This town is boring as hell."

"Did you read that article I sent you about the guy who said he killed a bunch of skunk apes in the Everglades? I bet he didn't think he'd find anything either."

Nicky smiled. "Oh yeah, I did check that out. Loved his name— Rooster Murphy. If he killed them, then why can't he produce the bodies?"

Roy shrugged. "I don't know. Maybe he didn't get all of them and they take care of their dead, just like us."

"Or maybe he was full of shit."

"Come on, Nicky, you know it'll be fun to at least try. I've been sneaking cans of beer here and there from my father's stash for months. I have enough to get us all wasted that night."

Dover Demon hunting was a rite of passage for all teens in town. Of course, most of the hunts devolved into drinking until they fertilized the woods with urine.

Nicky laughed. "I bet we'll all be seeing Dover Demons then."

"Better than pink elephants."

Chapter Seven

Sam's first thought when he saw the young asshole spring out of the fireplace, his hair and back of his pants engulfed in blue flame, was *I hope it hurts, you motherfucker.*

Lacy ran to pat out the flames while he wailed like a cat in a wood chipper. Sam stood his ground, motionless, deciding if he should toss him in a second time for good measure. It had been a long, long time since Sam had placed his hands on another guy in anger. The situation justified it this time. What gave him pause as he watched spirals of smoke rise from the schmuck's hair was how good he felt inside. Yes, he was sick to his stomach by his wife's betrayal, in their own home, no less. But the endorphin rush that swept him out like a riptide when he launched her lover into the fireplace was too good to ignore.

Rein it in, Sam. Don't black out now.

He'd thought the blackouts were well behind him. The years of brawling at the slightest provocation ended when he accepted his college diploma. They had to end. If they didn't, his future would have been bleak.

"Go, go!" Lacy pushed her lover past him while Sam stood collecting himself. The guy was bleeding in several places where his exposed flesh had scraped against the fireplace stones. The stench of burnt hair made him cringe.

"I'm calling the goddamn cops!"

Lacy begged, "Please, please don't. I'll take care of it. Promise me, you won't call. It'll only make things worse."

Sam heard a door slam and the Jaguar pull away.

Lacy returned to the den. Whatever pleasure she'd gotten from her tryst was long gone. She looked as if she'd aged ten years. Good. That was a small price to pay for deception.

"You should have told him to go to the cops. I'm sure my cousin would have enjoyed the story he had to tell," Sam said. The need to lash out physically had drained from him. He had other ways to feed the awakened beast.

"Are you insane? You could have killed him!"

The words exploded from his mouth. "Do you think I give a shit about your boyfriend? What if Nicky came home early instead of me? How were you going to explain that to him? Hell, how are you going to explain it to me? What does he do, fuck you on a dare from his fraternity brothers? I can't believe you'd stoop so low!"

Lacy spluttered, "I didn't mean for you to find out this way."

Sam huffed, gripping his hips to keep his hands at bay. "How were you going to do it? Send me a picture of the two of you on Instagram? How about writing it all out in a nice Hallmark card? One of those cards that plays music when you open it. How long have you been seeing him?"

She fell onto the sofa, tugging the sleeves of her shirt. The tears were coming hot and heavy now.

"I…it's only been a few months," she said, not daring to look him in the eye.

A few months. My God, I've been made a fool of for months!

There were so many awful, terrible words he wanted to sling at her. Too many, in fact, to even form one coherent sentence. He looked at the wreck of his wife, of his marriage, of his damn life, and could only say, "Why? Why would you do this to me? To Nicky?"

She surprised him by screaming, "Because I'm not happy! I work hard. Is it too much to ask for a little happiness every now and then?"

Sam closed his eyes, shaking his head. He felt as if he'd been punched in the gut by an elemental sadness. "So you think screwing a kid is the best way to make yourself happy."

Lacy didn't reply. Her legs jittered up and down and her hands trembled. Sam felt as if his heart might simply stop. The rage that had boiled the blood in his veins seeped out of him like steam from a launder's press. He walked past her on legs that didn't feel like his own.

Before he left, he said, "You have whatever time is left to make yourself happy now."

There were footfalls on the linoleum. He turned to see her standing in the dining room, holding a chair to keep her balance.

"Sam, please."

He held up a hand. "You have until tomorrow morning to get your stuff out of the house. If I find you here, I'll have every cop in Dover escort you out of the goddamn town."

There was a small Victorian table by the door whose only function was to hold a ceramic urn that had been in Lacy's family for generations. Sam swept it off the highly polished table, shattering it into hundreds of pieces.

She gasped, her mouth frozen in an O, eyes locked in disbelief.

"Don't forget to clean that up before you go," he said, softly closing the door as he left.

Kelly Weathers thought for sure she was seeing ghosts.

She leaned back on her barstool, in danger of tipping over. It was a slow night in the Dartmouth Pub—just a few regulars and a couple from New York if she was any judge of accents. George Strait was warbling on the jukebox, one of those new ones that was connected to the cloud and could play every song known to man. Kelly was on her fifth bourbon and Coke when the door opened, bringing a gust of the humid night air into the cold tavern.

"Sam?" she said, her eyes squinting.

The visitor, most of his face in shadow, seemed lost in his own thoughts. He stood by the entrance, seeming to decide whether to sit in a booth or at the bar.

"Sam, is that you?"

He took a step forward and his face came into the dim light of the pub. His lips were pulled into a tight, painful line. A dark aura hovered over him like a tethered storm cloud.

"Kelly," he said flatly, as if they ran into each other every night. She couldn't remember the last time they had actually spoken to one another.

"Is everything all right?" She put her drink on the bar, splashing some on her wrist. She hadn't seen Sam in the Dartmouth in decades. Why was he here now? Something had to be wrong. Sam Brogna *did not* come to the Dartmouth, and he most especially did not talk to her.

To her surprise, he settled onto the stool next to hers. He said to Luke, the bartender, "What's the oldest Macallan you got?"

Luke thought for a moment and said, "I ran out of the eighteen a couple of nights ago, but I have a bottle of fifteen."

"It'll do. I'll take a Sam Adams, too."

Kelly sat in silence. Sam downed the scotch and drank half the beer. He motioned to Luke for another Macallan. For a moment, she wondered if he was going to finish his drinks and leave without saying another word.

She was too afraid to speak herself, lest her words break this strange spell that had put Sam just inches away from her.

He took the second scotch slower, but finished the beer. Head down, eyes closed, she watched the steady rise and fall of his back. He was breathing hard, as if he'd run to the bar. She almost rubbed his back, pulling her hand away before it could get too close.

It felt like hours before he turned to face her, though it had only been minutes filled with apprehension and confusion.

"It's been a long time," he said. His voice sounded scratchy, as if he'd been cheering on the Sox in a playoff game.

"Sam, what are you doing here?"

"Having a few drinks while an old friend catches flies," he replied without a hint of humor.

Kelly hadn't realized her mouth was partly open. She filled it with a long sip from her glass.

"You haven't been in here since, Jesus, since we were kids."

"They were always lax on the whole drinking age thing," he said, ordering another beer.

The booze was going down awfully fast.

"Something had to have happened. People don't drink like that to celebrate. I should know."

Sam sucked his teeth, pushing back from the bar. "You could say that. I did just throw a guy into a fire."

A fire? Before she could ask him to elaborate, he looked at his phone and put it to his ear. Nodding, he returned it to his pocket.

"Sorry. First good news of the night. My son is sleeping over his friend's house."

"You just said you threw someone into a fire, Sam. Is he hurt? What kind of trouble are you in?" Kelly's pulse raced. Whether it was for concern about an old friend or the rush of being so close to him after three decades of silence, she couldn't tell or care.

He gave a short laugh. "I hope he's hurt. His hair isn't quite so perfect anymore. He may need to buzz it tomorrow. I can still smell it. Am I in trouble? Depends on how you look at things."

"This may sound crazy, but why did you throw a man in the fire?" The ice in her glass clinked as the bottom cube shifted.

When Sam looked at her, she almost gasped. A crimson rage flared in his eyes.

"Because I caught the fucker sleeping with my wife," he said, loud enough to be heard over the music. A couple of people and Luke looked their way.

"Lacy? I can't believe it," Kelly said, lowering her tone, hoping he'd get the hint. Gossip traveled faster than a bullet train in this town and the Dartmouth was the central station.

"You know what?" Sam said. "I'm so damn blind, I don't think I would have believed it if I hadn't seen it with my own eyes. But I did, and it's done. All of it. Twenty-five years in the fucking toilet." Tapping the bottom of his beer glass on the bar top, he added, "I should find him and finish the job."

This time, Kelly did reach out, wrapping her fingers over his tense forearm.

"No, don't do that. Think of your son."

His jaw pulsed and he drew a few long breaths. Kelly relaxed when he slumped forward, asking for another scotch. "Hit me while you're at it," she said to Luke.

"So, what are you going to do?" she asked.

"For now, I'm going to sit right here and have a few drinks. You're welcome to stay or leave. I'm not going to be good company."

Leaving was never an option.

Kelly stayed. They closed the Dartmouth together. He was so drunk, he could barely walk. He explained with a tongue thicker than a pillow that he hadn't been drunk, really stinking drunk, since his honeymoon. When he wanted to walk home and confront Lacy, Kelly convinced him to stay with her. The booze made him very compliant. She knew what could happen if he started things up with his wife, especially in this state. There was a time when Kelly spent countless nights extricating her boyfriend from scuffles large, small and downright frightening.

That one night had changed him, changed all of them. From afar, she'd admired his ability to put it behind him and create an enviable life.

Looks like things weren't as perfect as they seemed. Nothing ever is, she thought, helping him into her house. He made it as far as the couch, collapsing face down. She turned his head to the side and placed a large bowl on the floor under his mouth.

Kelly shut out the lights and padded upstairs to her bedroom.

Sam Brogna is in my house.

She fell asleep wondering if she should show him the study in the morning. What would he think? Would he even be here when she woke up?

Chapter Eight

When Sam first woke up on the strange couch, panic gripped him to a cellular level. His head felt as if it had been slammed off a curb repeatedly.

Where the hell am I?

He spotted the puke bowl on the floor and grimaced. Thankfully, it was empty, though his stomach was wishing otherwise.

No matter how hard he tried, he could not remember how he'd gotten here. And no matter how much he surveyed the room, expensive furniture, not a dust bunny to be found, the obvious handiwork of hired housekeeping, he couldn't recall ever being here before.

Then the realization of what had happened at his house, Lacy's betrayal, crashed down on him. His head pushed as far back on the pillow as it could go. His guts churned when he recalled her and her lover, half-naked, struggling to get their clothes on.

He was going to be sick.

Sam rolled off the couch, stumbling into an ottoman and slamming his shin.

Was anybody even home?

There were no pictures on the walls, other than a few paintings. He staggered down a long hallway. Spotting a door, he turned the knob, praying it led to a bathroom. He wanted to throw everything up—the booze, the pain, the image of his wife covering her breasts.

Feeling for a light switch on the wall, he stared at the floor and saw carpet, not tile.

"Damn it," he cursed.

Then he looked up.

For a moment, the pain and nausea settled into a muffled roar. The walls were canvassed with clippings from newspapers and magazines, printouts and pictures, index cards and crude drawings.

In the center of the room was a desk piled high with books, a laptop and tablet. The windows were covered by heavy black curtains. A large, square hump, covered by a sheet, sat in a corner of the room. His feet did a slow shuffle as he made a 360 degree turn, taking in as much of the riotous mural as his dry eyes and pounding brain could stand.

In that moment, he knew.

He spoke to the empty room.

"What the hell have you been up to, Kelly?"

Winter

Chapter Nine

This time, the story came from an outsider. And because no one really trusted him, and the fact that he was a lone witness, it was easily dismissed. Nicky Brogna saw the man's picture in the blog post and recalled his face. He'd come into the shop a few weeks ago carrying his own well-worn copy of Matt Ford's *Dover Demon: Nights of Terror*. He was accompanied by an exceedingly attractive woman. She wore a baseball cap, her long, golden hair flowing from under it. She had striking blue eyes and the body of a Victoria's Secret model. She never spoke, just looked around while the man talked to him.

He'd asked Nicky if Matt Ford lived in town and if it was possible he could have his book signed. Nicky told him he'd never met the man himself, even though this was the only store that sold the book.

"Where did you get your copy?" Nicky had asked.

The wiry man with the hawk's nose and downturned eyes looked at the cover, coffee rings across the title, and said, "Got this puppy off of eBay for fifty bucks. As you can see, I've read it more than once." He'd smiled but there was no humor in his eyes. He thanked Nicky for his time and left. The woman followed in his wake, but not before flashing him an unsettling glance. It was a look that said, *I see you staring at me. I know everything you're thinking. Don't even bother dreaming, kid.*

And that was it, until the Internet posts.

Nicky had created a Dover Demon Google alert a couple of years ago so he was notified of anything being posted about their hometown monster. The man from the shop—he called himself Lando Solo—wrote a series of blogs about his visit to Dover and a brief encounter with a strange hominid during the snowstorm they'd had the Saturday after Thanksgiving.

In the post, he wrote that he'd tried to report it to the police and was quickly shown the door. He called a few local papers and they rejected his story. So he turned to blogging about it. His posts got picked up by other blogs and though it wasn't exactly viral, it was picking up momentum.

Roy jostled next to him on the cafeteria bench. He craned his neck to see what Nicky was reading on his phone.

"Is that the Star Wars guy again?" he said.

Nicky smirked. "Dude, he's got like over two hundred Likes on this blog alone."

"You think he saw anything?"

"I seriously doubt the credibility of anyone who calls himself Lando Solo. But if you read it like fan fiction, it's pretty cool. He says the creature looked like a gray alien, but it was on all fours. When he locked eyes with it, the demon, who was caught running between two large rocks by Upper Mill Pond, melted into the ground and disappeared."

"That's the crazy part. If it was really there, it wouldn't melt. It's the Dover Demon, not the friggin' Wicked Witch," Roy said, breaking out his lunch of three ham and cheese sandwiches.

"Maybe he lost it in the snow and it just looked like it melted," Nicky said. His own lunch of leftover, cold pizza and an energy drink were untouched.

"You wanna go there this weekend and check it out?"

"I do, but I have to work at the store."

"Tell your dad he can handle it alone." Roy took a huge bite out of his sandwich.

Nicky drank half the energy drink. "He needs me there."

"I think he can handle it."

"That's not what I mean."

They ate in silence, cocooned from the raucous uproar that came with every senior lunch period. It was way too cold outside for anyone to venture into the courtyard, so the cafeteria was packed solid.

Since his mother had moved out, he'd been afraid to step too far away from his dad. Neither had told him the exact details of what had happened that night. What he knew he'd learned from the town grapevine. People were saying terrible things about his mother. She'd been caught hosting swingers' orgies while his dad was at the shop. She was having an affair with her company's board, which explained how she'd gotten all those promotions. She'd skipped town to be with another woman.

The rumors got worse from there. Whenever he'd asked his parents about it, they shut him out. His mother lived in a nice apartment in Boston overlooking the Harbor now. He went there every other weekend. She doted on him as if he were a little kid and his days and nights there were suffocating.

"She's obviously overcompensating," Christine had once said to him.

Yeah, but overcompensating for what?

Meanwhile, his father had grown distant, but not so much that he didn't look pained every time Nicky said he would be out with his friends or especially on the Fridays when his mother came to get him.

Tank spent a lot of time at the house, trying to get his Sam out of his funk. So far, it wasn't working. When Tank wasn't around, his father would slip out to the Dartmouth. Nicky rarely stayed up waiting for him to come home.

Whereas his mother seemed as if a weight had been lifted off her, his father was now carrying what'd she'd shed. Nicky wanted to hate her, but he couldn't fully commit without really knowing why.

When his father wasn't with Tank or at the Dartmouth, he was Nicky's shadow in almost every sense, including the silence. It was as if Nicky were a roaring fire, and his father, alone now, needed to stay close to keep warm, to hold on to the thinning thread that was their family. They still had movie nights at the comic book shop and had started bringing in comic book artists for appearances. Those days were especially busy, the store filled with comic book fans from neighboring towns. But the light that radiated from his father's eyes had dimmed. He went through the motions, but nothing brought him joy.

When the Dover Demon stuff had sold out, his father stopped replacing it. When Nicky asked if they could at least order more of Matt Ford's book, because they were getting requests every week, his father's mood turned dark. "I'm tried of this being the place for ridiculous monster hunters to hang out," he practically shouted. "We're here to sell comics and have some fun, not be the way station for every fool that thinks he'll find the demon. I think I've pissed the commerce board off enough over the years, encouraging it. For once, I'd like to have a little peace, at least on one front that I can control. Forget the books, Nicky. If people ask, tell them it's out of print."

And that was that. He could tell from the unflappable cast of his father's face that there was no arguing the point. No books, no models, no nothing.

The hard part was, the more Nicky had to tell people no, the more interested he himself became in the Dover Demon. He knew it was childish to gravitate toward the one thing his father had deemed off-limits, but he couldn't help it. He and Roy and Christine had done their own ghost investigations in a couple of cemeteries over the fall. Roy asked for and was given a great night vision camera and they tried their hand at digitally recording EVPs. Nothing really came of it, but they considered the ghost thing practice anyway.

Should we retrace Lando Solo's steps and go see for ourselves one night? Nicky thought. *It's too cold for other people to be out now trying to do the same thing. This is probably our best shot at it, the way his posts keep growing in popularity.*

Roy was finished with his three sandwiches before Nicky got to the crust of his one slice of pizza.

"You in a rush to go somewhere?" Nicky asked.

"Yep. Look what I got."

Roy dug into his backpack, plucking out a Blu-ray and waving it in front of his face.

Nicky grabbed his arm. "Hold still, ass, I can't see what it says. *Fire in the Sky*. All right. You have an alien abduction movie we've seen like ten times. I think I'm missing something."

His friend jabbed at his crotch, just pulling up short from a damaging nut shot. Nicky didn't flinch. He knew the penalty for flinching was the real deal.

"Open it, man," Roy said.

He popped open the Blu-ray case. Inside was a shiny disc that was far from an alien abduction flick. Nicky shut the case quickly.

"*Double Penetration Party Girls*? Really?"

Roy laughed. "We both have free period after this. I figured we could sneak into the media lab and check it out."

"Dude, if I want porn, I can get it free at home and not have to worry about being caught and kicked out of school."

"Bro, this is vintage 80s porn. No one has this stuff. It'll be a blast. We're talking pre-bush whacking!"

Nicky barely gave it a thought before saying, "Fine. Just let me finish my lunch."

When he got right down to it, he wasn't all that concerned about getting caught. Maybe something as traumatic as possibly being expelled in his senior year would be enough to jolt his father from the purgatory that held him hostage.

While Nicky and Roy made their way to the media room, Kelly Weathers printed out Lando Solo's latest blog post. She noted that it had been retweeted fifty times in just the last hour. Taking a sip from a can of Modelo, she filed one copy of the post in a folder marked CURRENT and tacked another copy to the wall on her left.

Reading the countless posts on the walls from right to left was like viewing a timeline of articles on the Dover Demon mixed with what would seem a ragtag array of true crime and missing persons reports. Kelly had started her secret project in the early nineties, right after her soon-to-be ex-husband left citing irreconcilable differences. It was a polite way of saying they could no longer stand one another.

As the collage grew and took over the room, Kelly still managed to keep track of every minute detail and the tree branch connections for each item she added. She knew it had the appearance of a textbook psychotic or conspiracy theorist's private lair. Not that she gave a shit.

She wasn't crazy. And there were select people who would attest to that, even if reluctantly.

Settling back behind her desk, she picked up her tablet and tapped on the link for *The Lowell Sun*. The town of Lowell was less than thirty miles from Dover. It was what she called a Red Flag Town, so she checked their online paper several times a week. Scrolling down, she tapped the headline for a story about a woman who had been missing for several days.

Kelly spoke aloud, a habit that had evolved from living alone the past twenty years. "Maria Sanchez, let's see if they tell us your age. Fifty-seven. Vintage year. Okay, you were last seen in Boston going to a movie with a friend. You parted ways at ten o'clock, but you never made it home. Hubby is offering a reward for any information of your whereabouts. That doesn't necessarily mean he's not responsible, but it is a step in the right direction."

She swiped through several screens, gleaning out the important bits of information like teasing seeds from a delicate flower. Opening up her spreadsheet, she opened the Search function and typed in Maria Sanchez in quotes. In a split second, a pop up box returned stating : No Results Found.

"Okay, let's try this."

Next, she typed in Maria. There were nine hits in total. None had the last name of Sanchez.

"I know you're married, so let's find out your maiden name."

First she went to LinkedIn, the professional social media site. If Maria worked in the corporate world, odds are, she'd have a profile there. Searching for a Maria Sanchez resulted in dozens of matching profiles. A picture of the missing woman had been listed in the newspaper's article. Maria was a pretty, mature woman with light brown hair in a bob and a round face. Kelly minimized it so the image was at the top corner of her screen and worked her way down the various Maria Sanchez profiles on LinkedIn. Only two bore a resemblance to the Maria Sanchez she was looking for. One lived and worked in Sacramento and the other in Canada.

"No dice," Kelly said, popping the top of another beer. She kept the room pretty chilly, so the beer was still cold.

Next was Facebook. There were even more matches there. "Why couldn't you be named Agnes Higglebottom?" Common names were a bitch to research and often led to dead ends.

This wasn't one of those times.

"Maria Benson-Sanchez. Lived in Lowell your whole life. Married to Richard Sanchez. Three boys. You and Richard made some good-looking kids." The most recent pictures showed a beaming Maria standing next to a tall man-boy in a red cap and gown. She closed the Facebook window. If she pried too much into the happy times chronicled of Maria Sanchez's life, she'd have to hit the hard stuff earlier than usual.

"Now I know who you are. Let's see if we get a match now."

Going back to her spreadsheet, she typed Maria Benson.

There was one Maria Benson. In the notes next to her name was a brief description of a sighting Maria had had of a strange craft hovering over her family's house on a crisp autumn night in 1981. Quite a few other people in the neighborhood had seen the same thing—a glowing orb that hovered in the clear sky for several minutes before whisking away at an impossible speed. Maria had the presence of mind to try and snap a picture of the object on her Polaroid camera. The image was less than sharp. It could have been anything. She was interviewed in a now defunct paper, and the article was republished by a now defunct UFO magazine fifteen years after the incident.

"Now I've got you," Kelly said.

The feeling of satisfaction was fleeting.

Looking at the woman's face, she felt an overwhelming urge to cry.

Where have they taken you, Maria? Your family will never be the same.

Kelly printed the *Lowell Sun's* article and tacked it under Lando Solo's blog. She stared at it for a long time, wishing to hell she wasn't so alone in this. Some days, like today, were more than she felt she could take.

Chapter Ten

"I think we should close early tonight," Sam Brogna said to his son. "The weather guy just changed the forecast. Snow is supposed to start in the next couple of hours."

As he said it, a dark chill ran down his spine. The last time he'd closed up early, his marriage went to shit.

Nicky was busy putting out the new comics that had come in earlier. "Fine by me. Maybe we can stop at the supermarket on the way home and get something good to make for dinner."

"You sure you're not in the mood for Chinese? I've had spicy orange chicken on the brain all day."

Nicky dropped the new *Buffy The Vampire Slayer* issues in a clear plastic holder on the wall. "Fine," he said, his tone screaming that he was far from fine.

Sam turned off the TV and stepped outside to check the skies. Enormous, marble clouds scudded under a slate gray background. Lighting up a Paul Gamiran Torito cigar, he thought about going to the supermarket. While they were there, he could also pop into the liquor store and pick up a bottle of Grey Goose. They were supposed to get walloped with snow over the next twelve hours. It would be smart to get something in the house. They couldn't live on the dregs in takeout containers.

But if he started to drink the Grey Goose, he knew he wouldn't stop until the bottle was empty. Nicky didn't need to bear witness to that. It was bad enough he was there to see him all those morning afters when he knew he looked as bad as he felt.

As much as he wanted to finish his cigar, it would take too long and it was too damn chilly out. Using his cigar cutter, he snipped off the lit end, letting it drop on the sidewalk. He'd save the rest for home in his warm humidor.

He went back inside and flipped his car keys to Nicky. "I'll finish that up. You go get whatever you think we need." He handed him his debit card. "Just make sure you're back before the snow starts. You're a good driver, but you haven't had to slog through snow yet."

Nicky's face lit up. A car and a debit card. Every teenage boy's dream. Now if he threw in a pretty brunette and fake ID, he'd have hit for the cycle. Not that that was even an option.

"Cool," Nicky said. "I think we're down to a Pop Tart and can of cream of mushroom soup at home." He was out the door before Sam could say anything else, even make a special request.

That was his own fault. He spent most days walking around like a mute, as if he was afraid starting even the most benign conversation would lead to his ranting about Lacy. The last thing he wanted to do was destroy the boy's mother in front of him. That wouldn't be fair.

So he kept quiet, haunting the store and their home like a phantom made corporeal.

The snow fell in earnest by six o'clock. Sam and Nicky locked up the store and made their way home, easily passing by a couple of Toyotas that slipped and slid along the snow-slick streets. Once a couple of powdery inches settled down, the streets would be easier to drive, at least until things hit the six or seven inch mark. The town's main roads were filling with cars as people dashed to their homes.

In the backseat, the contents of the grocery bags shuffled loudly as Sam made a wide turn around a car trying to pull out of a space.

"I bought a couple of rib eyes," Nicky said. "I also got a bag of potatoes. What's that stuff that they serve in the good steak houses?"

Keeping his eye on the road, the windshield wipers flicking fat snowflakes left and right, Sam said, "You mean creamed spinach?"

"Oh man, I got creamed corn instead."

"It'll do. I was never a big fan of spinach anyway. And to do creamed spinach right takes more skill than you or I have. Now, opening up pizza boxes or digging into containers of Thai food, that we can handle."

Nicky edged away from him, slumping against the door, his head resting on the frosted window.

Why did you have to do that? Sam scolded himself. *Yeah, Lacy was the chef, but that's no reason to take it out on him by driving home that we can't cook for shit and are stuck eating take out because she left us.*

He thought of that night, Lacy's concern when he threw loverboy in the fire, her decreeing that she wanted to be happy. His hands gripped the wheel and he pushed the accelerator down. Before long, he was pulling into the oncoming lane to swerve around anyone who wasn't driving as fast as he'd wanted them to. The back end of the car swerved to the left as he hit an icy patch. He cut the wheel into the slide, straightening the car out.

"Aren't you going a little fast?" Nicky said, now sitting straight in the seat and holding the dash with one hand.

Sam's sudden swell of anger burst and he eased off the pedal.

"I was. Just trying to get us home and away from these people with all-wheel drive cars and no clue how to drive them."

Damn you, Lacy!

The rest of the short drive was slow but uneventful. They carried all of the bags into the house, shaking the snow from their heads and coats in the mudroom. It looked like Nicky had bought enough to get them through the winter. Good kid. Maybe he'd keep the shop closed tomorrow and they could just hang out and talk, maybe play some video games. Plus they had to go through those college applications.

Watching his son put the groceries away, he said to himself, *Try, just try to be a normal dad for one day.*

As much as he wanted to start up some silly conversation right now, within the warmth of their kitchen, a beautiful white spectacle unfolding outside the windows, he forced himself to retreat to his humidor. Thinking about Lacy had gotten him all wound up. When he got like this, it physically pained him to open his mouth and flex his jaw muscles.

Squatting hard into his reading/smoking chair, he pulled out the remains of his cigar from earlier and lit it with a wooden match. He puffed on it with the urgency of a man with an axe to grind.

Tank Clay got off the phone with his wife and leaned back on the couch. She was still at her sister's house the next town over. Even though she had a truck that could plow through the Arctic, she said she might just stay the night. Have a girls' night in.

"You can have the whole place to yourself," she'd said. He could tell she'd had a few glasses of wine. He encouraged her to stay there. Wine and snow were not a good combo.

The damn snow. It wasn't even Christmas and they'd already had a season's worth of the stuff.

He looked out the big bay window. It was a whiteout.

Now what to do. Just heat up some of Steph's lasagna, have a few beers and watch that Nova special on the North American mound builders.

Sitting up, Tank stretched his long arms and yawned. It would be so easy to settle into his cocoon. Cold nights like this made his bad shoulder ache and his knees were none too happy either. He wasn't sure which *itis* was flaring up at the moment. Pain was pain. It was the price one paid for playing every sport known to man, and playing them like there were no tomorrows.

Tank stomped to the kitchen, took out the lasagna and a beer. He stared at the beer bottle.

I wonder if she'll be there. Tonight's the perfect night to find out.

He put the lasagna in the microwave, but stopped himself from setting the cooking time. Taking it back out and rewrapping it for the fridge, he chugged the beer.

She'll be there. She can't help herself.

"Screw it," he said.

Shrugging into his heavy winter duster, he pushed what he called his Indiana Jones cap onto his head. It had seen its fair share of sun and dust and dirt—just none of the adventure that Indy went through.

The biting wind and snow attacked his face the moment he opened his front door. His knees practically screamed at him, willing his legs to turn back into the house.

"Shut up," he barked, plodding into the snow.

This weather was no match for his olive green Range Rover. He hopped in the SUV and took to the roads as if it were a clear spring day. The streets were empty. Everyone was home and it was too early for the street cleaners.

There weren't any cars outside the Dartmouth Pub, but there were plenty of scattered footprints on the sidewalk. Tank pulled up to the door and went into the bar. It was loud inside with the voices of revelers out to celebrate another storm.

He spotted Kelly Weathers sitting in a booth by herself, a glass filled with amber liquid and ice between her hands.

"Hey, Tank, long time no see buddy!"

"How's it been Frank?" he said, patting his old friend on the shoulder. He and Frank had gotten their start in corporate America in the same company when they were fresh out of college. Frank in no way resembled the young man he'd been back then. His hair was gone, his belly was big and his multiple chins wiggled when he talked.

"Still slogging along. They pay me so much, I can't bring myself to leave." He and the man with him laughed thickly.

Tank said, "You should take the plunge. It's worth it." Before Frank could lock him into a real conversation, Tank stepped away, making a beeline for Kelly.

He collided with a tall woman carrying a martini glass. A little splashed on his shirt.

"I'm sorry," he said.

She smiled at him. "No, it was my fault. I didn't think this place would be so crowded."

"I'll be happy to buy you another. Looks like I'm wearing most."

Her cobalt eyes held him like a tractor beam. God, she was pretty. And young. And probably attached. And, of course, he was happily married. He didn't remember bumping into attractive women like this when he was single. Then again, he'd been married so long, it was hard to ever remember being single.

"No need," she said, her finger running along the wide rim of the glass. "I should watch how much I drink anyway. I'm the designated driver."

The way she looked at him, he expected her to ask him to join her. That wouldn't be good. So, he said, "I'm sorry again." It hurt to break her gaze, but he did it. He noticed that he'd gotten Kelly's attention and eased himself away, angling between a couple talking over beers.

She looked up from her drink when he squeezed himself into the booth, his knees accidently hitting into her own.

"Oh, hi, Chris," she said. For some reason, she was the one person who had steadfastly refused to call him by his nickname. Even his wife called him Tank. He'd always wondered if she did it to irritate him.

"What are you drinking?" he asked.

"Jim Beam on the rocks."

Tank motioned to Rosie, the bar's lone waitress. She'd worked there forever, having served Tank's father when he was young. Rosie's dyed black hair framed a face etched with long, deep lines. Even on a cold night like tonight, she wore a black skirt. For a woman older than the hills, she had the legs of a much younger woman. "Two Jim Beams," he said to her.

"Got it, Tank," she said, darting back to the bar. He hadn't been in the Dartmouth for at least ten years and she didn't bat an eye, acting as if he were a regular.

Kelly stared at him nervously. "What brings you here? Where's Stephanie?"

He rubbed his massive hands together. "At her sister's. They were making plans to go to Florida next month when the snow hit."

"Do her parents still live in Naples?"

"Her father passed away a couple of years ago. Her mother lives with a cousin now in Tampa. Safety in numbers."

Kelly nodded. Rosie delivered their drinks. Tank took a healthy sip to drive away the cold.

"I'm gonna get right to it," he said. "What's going on with you and Sam?"

Her brows knit together. She ran a finger over the rim of her glass. "What do you mean?"

"You know what I mean. Sam's in a bad place right now. There's a lot of stuff going on in his head."

"I'm not sleeping with him."

"That's not what I'm talking about."

He had to admit, for someone who drank as much as she did, Kelly still looked great. He could see how Sam would be tempted. And after what Lacy did to him, he deserved to get a little revenge sex.

But sex with a long ago ex was far from his concern.

Kelly downed her drink, slamming the glass on the table.

"Did you really come out in this weather just to harass me?"

"Actually, yes."

"I can't stop Sam from coming here, Chris. Sometimes he'll sit with me and we'll talk. That's it. I promise I won't steal your precious friend from you."

The word precious came out sideways. She'd been at the bar for a while.

Tank leaned across the table. "My concern is *what* you're talking about. He doesn't need you filling his head with all of that shit."

Kelly's face darkened. "All that shit? You of all people know better. Don't you dare try to rewrite history."

"That's my point. It's history. Let it go. If you want to piss your life away living in a moment, that's fine by me. But I won't have you dragging Sam down with you."

She leaned back against the booth. "Sam say anything about me?"

"No. In fact, he hasn't even told me that he comes here. I got that from other people who've seen him come and go. But I see how he acts, and I know it can only be because of you. So please, just back off."

"You can't hide from it forever," Kelly said.

"Hide from what?"

To his surprise, she reached across the table and grabbed his hand. "It's all coming back. No matter how much you try to tuck it away, it's coming for us."

He jerked his hand away as if he'd touched a hot stove.

"Now you sound like a bad horror movie. Jesus, you're a mess."

She smiled an icy smirk that chilled him to the core. "I might be a mess, but I have my eyes open. No matter how much you hate me, I'm going to do what I can to protect you. It'll be easier if you open your mind and let me show you everything. Because the way I see it, you, me, Sam and Stephanie are living on borrowed time."

Chapter Eleven

The snow didn't let up when the weather woman said it would the night before. In fact, the eye of the storm shifted, hovering over the town instead of skimming past. By three A.M., the blizzard intensified, dropping five inches during the next hour alone. When Nicky's alarm went off at seven, there was a foot of snow outside. He checked his iPod, searching for school closings. Sure enough, all classes were cancelled.

He went to the window and saw how snowdrifts obliterated the patio table and hid the covered gas grill. Frozen wave patterns were carved into the soft blanket of snow, forged by the wind.

It was still coming down, but not as hard as it had when he went to bed seven hours earlier.

"See you at lunch," he said to the snow. He crawled back under his comforter and prayed his father would have enough sense to realize school was cancelled and not try to wake him up.

Sam had stayed up late reading a collection of M.R. James stories and working on a new box of aged Dunhill cigars. He'd also made a sizeable dent in a bottle of Glenlivet 18 he'd forgotten about. It seemed the perfect combo for a stormy night—good smokes, medium flavored Dominican cigars and classic horror stories that inspired Stephen King. After a dinner where they ate watching TV, saying very little to one another, Nicky had gone to his room and Sam to his walk-in humidor. In other words, aside from the poorly home-cooked meal, it was business as usual.

He'd gone to bed early in the morning and saw the blizzard in its full fury. Turning off his alarm, he settled in for a nice, long sleep.

He awoke to a distressing burn in his throat. Sitting up, he gagged on the taste of bile that had pooled in his mouth. Drinking and smoking late always aggravated his acid reflux. He stumbled to the bathroom, drank a cup of tepid water then rinsed his mouth out with mouthwash.

"You look great," he said to his pallid reflection.

Returning to his bedroom, he sat on the edge of the bed, listening for signs of Nicky moving about. The house was as silent as the grave, the snow absorbing all outside sound, the usual flow of people and cars taking a day off.

Lying back on the bed, he promised himself today would be a good day. He just needed a couple more hours sleep. No hiding away. No cigars and especially no booze. He and Nicky needed to talk. And he would. Just after some sleep and this damn headache went away.

Sam closed his eyes and was snoring in less than a minute.

Kelly Weathers had walked home just when the storm was kicking into high gear. The ends of her hair were actually frozen by the time she'd walked stiffly through the front door. Her face felt as if she'd rubbed it on dry ice. Dropping her coat on the floor and kicking off her boots, she shivered all the way to the wet bar in the living room. She poured a little brandy into a snifter and drank it down, bringing her core back up to a survivable temp.

Fucking Chris. How dare he come into my bar and make accusations and demands! He thinks he's got it all figured out but he doesn't know shit.

Settling onto her couch, she turned on the plasma screen TV, flipping around until she found a rerun of *All in the Family*—Archie Bunker yelling at Meathead that if beauty was in the eye of the beholder, stupid was in the head of the Polack. For a brief moment, she actually laughed out loud.

"You'd never pull that off today," she said to the television.

She hadn't been exaggerating to Chris that everything was coming full circle. She tried to tell him about it, explain the connections. He'd looked at her with utter contempt, dropping a twenty on the table before rushing out of the bar.

It was a long shot, trying to cram everything in at once. She'd been stupid. If she wanted to get him to see the truth, he'd have to be eased into it. Even better, Sam would have to be the one to convince him.

What the four of them witnessed that night was more than a chance encounter. Kelly was convinced that a hell of a lot more had happened. The worst parts had been swiped from their memories.

It was really ingenious. Leave behind the images of something so terrible, so frightening, and you would never think to search for more.

But it was there, and parts of it were coming back.

Yes, Sam had been coming to the bar frequently, but the only time he was receptive to her was after he'd had a few. He'd seen the room and had questions at first. She tried her best to answer them succinctly, keeping a level head. She didn't want to scare him off.

To his credit, he'd listened, but she could tell he didn't believe her.

Something *was* getting through. She'd heard that his store—*Praise the Lord*, many of the other local businesses sighed—was no longer carrying Dover Demon memorabilia. The monster mecca was no more.

Deep down, his belief was changing, and it scared the hell out of him.

Now they were both scared. And they both drank.

If it weren't so serious, she'd leave Chris and Stephanie out of it. She wasn't offering them a future of fun and leisure. They'd have to be brought to the truth kicking and screaming if necessary.

Kelly passed out, the glass still in her hand. When she stirred at noon, she called into the office only to get the auto-attendant.

The snow clung to the windowpanes. No one was out, not even the early shovel brigade.

She went to her study and did something rare—she opened the heavy curtains that protected the room from prying eyes. The sun blinded her. She had to shield her eyes and turn away. They were running out of time. For once, she wanted the office bathed in daylight while she searched for more pieces to the puzzle that had ruined her life.

Chapter Twelve

The constant pinging text alerts woke Nicky from a dream about his ninth grade math teacher. The moment he opened his eyes, the specifics of the dream shattered into dust and floated away on the slip currents of consciousness. He just knew the statuesque, young and exceedingly hot Ms. Manelay had been a big part of it. His painful morning wood confirmed it.

A dull whine buzzed one long, irritating note. He rubbed his ears, trying to make it go away. It felt like something had popped in his inner ear, momentarily disorienting him. Nicky shook his head. The whine slowly dissipated, but there was a pulsating ache in the center of his head.

The sun was out, made brighter by its reflection on the snow covered world outside his window. He rolled over to check his phone. More texts came in while he read. They were all from Roy.

KILROY : *yo, u up yet?*

KILROY : *dude, wake up*

KILROY : how bout now?

KILROY : *come on, let's do something*

KILROY : *wake up princess*

KILROY : *GET UP LAZY ASS!!!!!*

KILROY : *hellllooooooooooooooo*

Nicky squeezed the remnants of sleep from his crusted eyes. He texted back without looking.

DANICK : *cut it out asswad. I'm up now. Give me a sec to pee*

He got up and flicked the chiming phone on his pillow. His warm pillow where he wished his head was right now.

"What the hell time is it?" he said aloud. When he was done, he checked his phone. Almost eleven. That was ten hours of sleep and he still felt tired.

He texted back to Roy.

DANICK : *wanna come here and hang?*

KILROY : *b-o-r-i-n-g*

KILROY : *let's go outside*

DANICK : *and do what? Make a snow fort? Have a snowball fight?*

Roy didn't answer right away. Nicky feared whatever his active little mind was devising. He was suddenly very hungry. Passing by his dad's room, he heard the old man snoring away. It was his new, I've-had-too-much-to-drink snore—deep, gravelly, with disturbing stops and starts.

Nicky froze when he heard his dad mumble, "It's time. It's time. I know."

"Dad?" he said, peeking into the room. His father was lying on his back, head buried between two pillows, talking in his sleep.

"It's time," he repeated.

Time for what? Nicky thought. *Maybe he's thinking about making up with mom. They've been apart for months but neither ever says the D-word.*

He could only hope that was the case. This new family dynamic wasn't working for him. But his mother seemed so happy. His biggest worry was that she would have to be dragged back to Dover.

Closing the door, Nicky trotted down to the kitchen and ripped open an energy bar for starters. His phone chimed.

KILROY : *u tell me what u wanna do for once*

Nicky's eyebrow lifted. This was a shocking turn of events. He had long ago accepted the role of blind faith follower in their friendship. Roy was always bursting with ideas and things to do. Nicky found comfort in leaving all of the planning to his friend. That way, if the idea sucked, only Roy was to blame.

He poured orange juice into a beer stein and sat at the kitchen table, looking out at the pristine alabaster yard.

"What the heck can we do in the snow that won't make us look like ten-year-olds?" he said, leaning back in the chair.

"Ahh."

The whine returned, along with an intense burst of pressure on his eardrums.

Is that coming from outside?

The noise and the pain stopped at the same time. He poked his fingers in his ears, feeling for crusts of wax or anything that could explain them. It had been at least ten years since he'd had an ear infection—too long to remember if this is what the start of one was like.

His eyes drifted to his open knapsack on the counter. The manila folder where he kept the Lando Solo posts and other things related to it peeked out from the darkened bag. Everything clicked into place.

DANICK : *how about a demon hunt?*

KILROY : *where?*

DANICK : *Upper Mill Pond. The place where that Solo guy saw it*

KILROY : *where he 'says' he saw it…that's a hike, bro*

DANICK : *u got 2 snowmobiles*

KILROY : *still*

Nicky chugged his orange juice and threw some English Muffins in the toaster. Today would be the perfect day to do it. No one in their right mind would be around and the snow would betray any weird tracks.

KILROY : Chris just saw and wants in

Nicky couldn't stop the smile from spreading. That was more than fine by him, but he'd have to play it off so he didn't piss off Roy.

DANICK : *seriously? Tell her it's cold as hell out*

KILROY : *she's bored and says she's going…we'll be over in like a half hour. I don't wanna be out there when the sun goes down and freeze to death*

DANICK : *OK. I'll wait for you at the mailbox.*

Nicky darted back to his room after wolfing down the toast. This had all the makings of an awesome day. No school. Finally going Dover Demon hunting. Maybe having Christine holding on to him on the snowmobile, feeling her face and breasts pressed against his back. If they got trapped outside, they'd have to find shelter. If there was no fire, they'd definitely have to strip down and cuddle together to survive the night. Well, he and Christine would. Roy didn't figure into his fantasy.

Slipping on several layers of clothes—and cologne—he scribbled a quick note for his father and left it on the kitchen table.

What he didn't notice when he closed the front door was the cold breeze that slipped through the opening, lifting the letter of the table and depositing it under the refrigerator.

When Sam opened his eye and looked at the digital clock he jumped out of bed. The unwavering blue numbers—1:17—stared back at him with accusatory LED. The last time he'd slept this late must have been back in college. He may have retired from the 9-5 world, but he still took pride in getting up relatively early each day and knowing what day of the week it was. He'd met plenty of retirees who couldn't tell you whether it was Tuesday or Saturday.

He went to the bathroom, splashed water on his face and brushed his teeth. His breath was offensive, even to him. Pulling a Michigan sweatshirt over his head, he went downstairs, calling out, "Hey Nicky, I'm sorry I slept so late. I must have blizzard fever. How about I make us some lunch before we shovel?"

Nicky didn't answer.

Sam stopped in the living room. "Nicky?"

There wasn't another sound in the entire house. He went to the front window and pulled the blinds open. A pair of footsteps went in a straight line from the door to the street. The plows had come overnight but there was still a good amount of hard packed snow on the street. Studded tracks crisscrossed over the snow remnants in the street. Dover was a winter wonderland to some. Probably half the town had snowmobiles now, especially after the string of rough winters they'd experienced the past five years.

Sam wasn't one of those people.

He couldn't picture Nicky trudging through waist high snow just to get out and enjoy the biting, fresh air. It wasn't an indictment of his son. It's just that being outside for the sake of being outside was not one of the trademarks of Nicky's generation. Sam was pretty sure his was the last to embrace those kinds of notions.

Then he remembered that Roy's father had bought some snowmobiles a couple of years back.

"Have fun with Roy," he said. He'd have to shovel alone. It was a weak penance for pulling away from his son these past months.

Ever since Kelly's realization that something very bad was making its way back to Dover, she'd installed a state-of-the-art security system. There were some elements of the Dover Deon mystery and the related phenomena that she'd tied together that told her they could walk through any security system as if it wasn't even there. But there was an entirely separate aspect that the cameras and tripwires would stop in its tracks.

It was all so sensitive that she'd drunkenly set it off several times, twice forgetting the password to stop the police from coming out. One more time and she would have to pay a fine.

As she drank her coffee standing by the kitchen sink, looking out at her yard, she knew she had to check the recordings from last night. She ran to her study, accessing the security log. Nothing had been tripped overnight.

Of course not. Sirens designed to wake the dead would have pierced the silence of the neighborhood if the perimeter sensors had been breached.

So what had left those footprints in her yard?

Whatever it had been, it walked on two legs.

The wind's constant shifting had obscured the tracks, but she could discern the basic outline.

They were about the size of child's, but not rounded and with a heel as if someone with a small foot had wandered into her yard, wearing boots.

To Kelly's horror, each print left the distinct impression of several, long toes.

Who the hell would be walking in a blizzard in sub-freezing weather without their shoes?

She looked outside the study's windows. There were more, just inches from the side of the house.

What the hell? How did I miss them before?

Holding her tablet with the security dashboard enabled, she went from room to room opening curtains and blinds, searching for more footprints. By the time she was finished, her heart pounding so hard her ribcage ached, every downstairs window was bursting with morning light.

Those strange footprints made a perfect circle around her house.

She went upstairs, repeating the process. She had to find the direction from which the prints came, and more importantly, where they left. Flinging windows wide open, oblivious to the cold, she held on to the sill and stretched her body out as far as she could without falling.

In the back yard, there were only the odd prints hugging close to the house.

The same went for the sides of the Victorian home.

Hands shaking, she had a difficult time prying the windows open in the bedroom facing the front. When she did, the cold nearly froze the tears as they welled up in her eyes.

It was as if whatever had stalked her home had dropped from the sky, then after making its round, been yanked back up.

"No, no, no, no!"

She ran back downstairs, having forgotten to close the second floor windows. The temperature in the house plummeted.

In her study, she booted up her laptop and accessed the recordings from the security cameras she'd had installed around the house. Some looked out, others directly in at the house. Selecting all of the cameras, she clicked Rewind. All of the videos scrolled backward at the same speed.

Kelly held her breath as day marched back into dawn, then night. The images changed to the green screen that the system employed for night vision. With a few commands, she was able to slow the rewind rate. Her eyes danced across the eight video output squares that filled her screen.

"Where are you?" she said, her teeth clenched.

Nothing was showing up. The time stamp showed it was just after five in the morning. The prints were there, barely touched by the lightly falling snow. As the recordings rolled backward to 4:45, they were suddenly gone.

"What the hell?"

Kelly hit Stop. Clicking her mouse, she went forward, searching for the exact moment the prints appeared, frame by frame.

She froze when the frame went from a shot of undisturbed snow to the track of deep prints that wound around her house in the time it took to record one frame of video. That was impossible! Something made those tracks. There was nothing in the laws of physics that would allow for it to happen that fast.

Kelly pushed back from her computer table, gripping the chair's leather armrests. She felt like crying. She wanted a drink. An arctic breeze whistled into the room, making her shiver.

"Oh Jesus, the windows."

A part of her was grateful for the distraction of going upstairs and closing all the windows. The images of those prints suddenly appearing from nowhere rocked her. Before stepping back into her study, she grabbed a bottle of bourbon from the wet bar and a tumbler. Her hands shook as she gave a healthy pour, bringing the firewater to her lips. It took her a few more sips before she could sit down and look at the security camera images again.

How did you do that? she thought, staring at the screen. She had been concentrating so much on the outdoor cams that she'd neglected the two that had been set up inside the house. One showed her bedroom, her nightshirt draped over the bed.

The other was a still image of her living room. There she was, passed out on the couch, the room bathed in light from the television. One leg and one arm hung off the couch.

What she hadn't seen before was the dark figure standing behind the couch, looking down at her. It had a thin neck and large, oval head. Somehow, the television's light stopped just short of the figure, keeping it bathed in shadow. All except for the flesh of its long, tapered fingers, bone white and needle thin, as they touched her breast.

Kelly screamed until her throat was raw.

Chapter Thirteen

By the time Nicky, Roy and Christine got to Noanet Woods, their faces were as red as Stop signs and felt as if their skin was on fire. Nicky's fantasy of driving the snowmobile with his secret crush at his back had been quickly dashed. Instead, he'd been forced to hug Roy's waist the entire trip.

The snowmobiles were loud and fast and Nicky was sure Roy was trying to tip them over. It was no wonder he'd failed his road test twice. His best friend was a madman behind the wheel.

"That was some sick driving," he said to Roy, removing his goggles.

"That's the fun of it," he said. "No rules. I obviously wasn't crazy enough. Christine was able to keep up."

She kicked snow at him. "You wish you could drive like me." Turning to Nicky, she said, "So, this is where that guy saw the demon?"

Before they left, Nicky had printed a map of the Noanet Woods—it was a popular place for hikers in nice weather—and did his best to estimate where Lando Solo had his encounter. They'd driven down an unplowed Old Farm Road, taking it as far is it could go, before getting into some heavy off-roading. What was once a picturesque location for taking in all of the wonders of nature in full bloom was now a never-ending alabaster blanket. The only thing that broke through the snow were the trees, their branches cloaked in powder.

He remembered playing catch with his father out this way when he was a kid. His mother had packed a lunch of PB&J sandwiches, cheese and apples. His parents drank from a bottle of wine without using glasses. At the time, it had seemed to Nicky that they were breaking some kind of cardinal adult rule. His mother even took the mitt from him at one point, tossing the baseball back and forth with his dad. They laughed a lot that afternoon, especially when his father had to run after the balls Nicky was pretty sure his mother intentionally threw over his head. She had a wicked good arm. Better than Nicky's, at least until he got a few years older and started to fill out. He couldn't remember the last time he'd seen his parents happy like that, even before the breakup.

Nicky pulled the map out of his pocket with stiff fingers, unfolding it for Christine to see.

"He said it was by the pond. By the way we came, it's a straight shot through the woods to Upper Mill Pond."

"Dude, it's cold as shit out here. I'm not walking through those woods. It'll take forever without snowshoes anyway. Why couldn't we just go to the places it was seen originally? At least they were on roads that I'm sure have been plowed," Roy said.

"Because that was like forty years ago. This was a month ago, dumbass," Christine replied, giving Nicky a quick smile.

Nicky's heart did a triple beat. That smile would be locked away in his memory, recalled when he was far from Roy.

Roy said, "Nicky, even you said a guy with a ridiculous name like that can't be trusted. This makes no sense. I had fun riding out here, but I'm not down for freezing to death."

"The trees aren't that close together. I bet we could ride around them if we took it slow," Nicky said.

The way ahead was choked with innumerable thin-trunked white pine trees, their branches drooping with snow.

"I don't know, man," Roy said, shaking his head.

"Come on, chickenshit," his sister cajoled. "If you won't do it, I'll take Nicky. What else are you gonna do? Go back home and watch your old pornos?"

Roy's eyes bulged out of their sockets. "What the hell are you talking about?"

"I bet if the double penetration party girls were at the pond, you'd be halfway there by now."

"What did you tell her, Nicky?"

Nicky raised his hands up. "I didn't say a thing, but you just kinda told her everything she needs to know now."

He and Christine laughed while Roy did a slow burn.

"Okay, fine. I'll go. Hop on, Nicky." He revved his snowmobile.

With Christine close behind, they entered the grove of pine trees, making a serpentine route to the pond. Nicky turned back to give Christine a thumbs-up.

He didn't see what threw him off the snowmobile, sending him crashing into Christine's windscreen.

Sam was sweating out every last ounce of booze as he shoveled a path in his driveway. Thankfully, the frigid air kept the sour stink of his pores jettisoning the poison from assaulting his nose. The snow was too high for the snow blower. This was going to be a manual job. Normally, he would have been plotting how to punish Nicky for leaving him high and dry like this. Considering everything, he decided to let this one slide.

Besides, the exercise was good for him—as long as he didn't stroke out.

As he added to the nine-foot pile on the plot where he was pretty sure his lawn once lay, his phone began to ring. He stuck his shovel in the snow pile and pulled a glove off with his teeth, fumbling with his other hand to find his phone. Sam hoped it was Nicky checking in.

He looked at the incoming number and paused before swiping to answer.

Kelly Weathers.

I am not meeting you at the Dartmouth, he thought. Maybe not ever again. Since the incident with Lacy, he liked being around other drinkers. Drinking alone had a whole set of miseries associated with it. The Dartmouth was the only bar in town and the only place to drink in walking distance, which was its biggest appeal.

At first, it had been kind of nice to reconnect with Kelly. Life had not been easy for her, despite her trust fund baby status. She was the poster child for 'money can't buy happiness'. When they were teens, they'd dated seriously for three years. He had been the first one to say 'I love you' when they were making out in her father's horse barn the first night of summer vacation. That had been a lifetime ago, and it was nice, in a nostalgic way, to reconnect with that part of his life through Kelly.

But the things he saw in her room, and the crazy stuff she talked about when she thought he'd had too much to drink. At first, he listened, placating an old friend who had lost her way. Lately, though, she was getting edgier, her theories wilder.

"Pretend you never saw it," he said, steam billowing from his mouth.

The phone stopped ringing and in a few seconds the voicemail alert beeped.

Why is she calling me today of all days? I know she's lonely but she's not blind. She can see the mounds of snow everywhere. I bet even the Dartmouth is closed.

He stuffed the phone back in his pocket and slipped his glove on. There was still a ton of shoveling to do.

Bleeeep. Bleeeep. Bleeeep.

It was Kelly again.

What if she's hurt? Even though she's always at the bar, no one other than Luke the bartender talks to her. Does she have anyone close by she would call in an emergency? God, have I become that person in her eyes?

There was no way he could ignore her call now. He answered the phone, slipping it between his wool hat and ear.

"Kelly, are you all right?"

She was crying on the other end. Jesus, he was right!

"Kelly, tell me what happened. Are you hurt?"

"I need you to come here," she said, sniffling.

"What's wrong, Kel? Why are you crying?" His heartbeat accelerated. He was never good at handling distress calls. That had always been Lacy's thing. Throw a business-related shit storm at him and he'd dive in headfirst. Personal, touchy-feely stuff with people who were not his immediate family had never been his strong suit.

"I…I have to show you something. It's bad, Sam, real bad."

"Kelly, there's about a foot and a half of snow on the roads. It's kinda hard to get to your house right about now. Tell me what's going on."

"No, you have to see it. I have to show it to you and if you wait too long, you might miss the most important part. Please, I would never ask you if it wasn't serious."

Sam's brain riffled through all of the possible things that she could want to show him. It could be serious, or it could be crazy. There was no telling with her lately.

"I'll have to walk to your house," Sam said, eyeing the sun as it slipped behind a passing cloud. Walking to her house wouldn't be bad. If she kept him there long, the walk back minus the sun was going to feel like a march in a meat locker. And whatever snow still waited for him would start to freeze over. He'd need an ice pick just to get through the top layer.

"Please, come as fast as you can. But before you do, look at the snow around your house. If you see anything strange, take pictures with your phone."

Sam closed his eyes and sucked in a great breath. What did the snow around his house have to do with anything? "You're not making any sense."

"Just do it. And call Chris. Ask him to do the same thing."

He pulled the phone away from his mouth and groaned. Not this shit again.

"Sam? Are you there?"

"Yes, I'm still here."

"Do this for me, and if nothing comes from it, you never need to speak to me again," Kelly said, desperate.

"Look, it's not that I never want to talk to you. We have a history. It's just this other crap that you can't seem to get over."

She came back on the offensive, "Walk around your house, call Chris, and come here."

Before he could reply, she hung up.

Holding on to the shovel's handle, he turned around, inspecting his house. It looked like something straight from a Norman Rockwell painting. The three-story Victorian was bathed in the finest sheen of powder, icicles glinting like jewels.

What the hell would I even look for?

He glanced at the shovel jutting from the mound of snow and the unfinished path. At the very least, it would be a break from the backbreaking work. Spring would be here in four months. He could always let nature clean up its own mess.

Trudging through the thigh-deep snow, he walked around the front of the house. Snow. Nothing but snow had buried all vestiges of his property. Somewhere down there were the pottery frogs he, Nicky and Lacy had made five years ago, waiting for the garden to return to life.

Ribbit, ribbit, hop into spring!

His lungs burned from the cold as he awkwardly made it to the side of the house, wondering out loud if he'd lost his mind.

He looked up at Nicky's window, then down at the ground.

His muscles clenched.

Sam twisted his body so he could see to the bend leading to the back yard. The tracks seemed to start here. Right under his son's window.

His numb fingers had a difficult time getting his phone to work.

"Hey, they plow your street yet?" Tank answered.

"Tank, I need you to look outside your house. Take your phone. When you're done, meet me at Kelly's."

"What the hell are you talking about?"

Sam stared at the alien footprints.

"I don't have a fucking clue. But I think Kelly does."

Chapter Fourteen

"Oh my God, Nicky, are you all right?"

Christine hit the brakes as hard as she could, the snowmobile swerving to avoid running over Nicky's tumbling body.

Nicky was stunned but not hurt, at least as far as he could tell. He rolled to his side and raised his arm. "I'm good." He didn't want to look like a crybaby wuss in front of her. Even if his leg had been severed, he would have said he was good.

Christine hopped from her snowmobile and shouted, "Roy!"

Her alarmed tone shocked Nicky from his daze. His friend's snowmobile was upside down, covered in snow. Roy was nowhere to be found. Christine ran over, calling for her brother. Nicky got up with a slight groan. His shoulder hurt like hell where he'd hit the windscreen.

"Roy!" he joined in. Where the hell could he be? It had all happened in an instant. There hadn't been enough time for Roy to wander off.

Nicky paused. *What the hell* did *just happen?*

Christine suddenly dropped to her knees and began shoveling snow with her hands like a dog burying a bone. Nicky saw Roy's gloved hand sticking out of a huge fresh pile of snow.

"Help me!" Christine barked. He ran, sliding next to her, digging blindly.

In seconds, Roy's snow-flecked face appeared. His sister brushed as much of him as she could. He spit the rest away from his mouth.

"Holy crap, that hurt," he moaned.

Nicky worked on getting his arms and torso free while Christine helped raise his head a bit.

"That tree dumped like two tons of snow on you," she said.

They all looked up at the now barren pine tree limbs. The weight of the snow combined with the grating whine of the snowmobiles must have created a mini tree avalanche. Poor Roy had taken the brunt of it. All Nicky had seen was a blur of white and felt a force push him off the snowmobile.

He gave his friend a hand and pulled him into a sitting position. The exertion sent bolts of pain from his shoulder to his neck. Nicky plopped on his ass and leaned against the flipped snowmobile.

Roy rolled his neck, making tiny pops. "We could have been killed, dude."

Christine took off Roy's hat and smacked it against her leg, clearing the snow from it. "That was crazy. One second you were there, and the next, it was like a curtain coming down and you were gone. It hit Nicky so hard, he flew backward into my windscreen."

"No friggin' way," Roy said.

Nicky pointed at the cracked windscreen. "Way. Those spider cracks are from my shoulder."

He started to laugh, if for no reason other than to be grateful that no one was seriously hurt. Here they were, out in North Pole weather looking for a monster and they almost bit the dust. Soon, Roy and Christine were laughing as well.

"Freaking crazy," Christine said. "When you hit into me, I almost went headfirst off my snowmobile. It reminded me of the time I did that on my mother's horse when I was like ten. I broke my arm then. I could hear the snap this time like it was going to happen again."

"Lucky it didn't," Nicky said. God, his shoulder was going to need half a bottle of Motrin later.

Getting to his feet, Roy said, "Help me get this turned over."

They were lucky in that the snowmobile had come to rest at an angle against the mound of powder the tree had dumped on them. The three of them got it back on its tracks easily.

"Well, this was fun," Roy said, straddling the ice-cold seat. "Time to watch YouTube and veg out. Hop on, Nicky."

Before he could, Christine pulled him back.

"Wait, we haven't even gotten to the pond where that guy saw the demon," she said.

"Yeah, that's because the woods made it pretty clear we're not wanted here," Roy shot back, shaking his head with incredulity.

"I still wanna check it out," she said, ignoring his jab. She turned to Nicky. "Don't you?"

The faint whine from earlier filled his ears. This time, the noise made sense, considering he'd just had his bell rung.

Nicky knew the logical answer was to say no. Another mother lode of snow could easily drop on them again.

But there was no way he could follow logic. Any time spent with her was worth the risk.

"You know, I still want to see it for myself," he said. Roy narrowed his eyes at them both.

"You're both idiots," he said. "My balls are ice cubes. I'm heading back. It might take me a week to warm up."

"We won't be long," Nicky said. "I'm freezing, too. We came this far. It's not much farther to the pond. We'll be back before you know it."

He was struck by an urge to yawn. When he did, there was a tiny pop in the center of his head and once again, the annoying sound was gone.

Roy looked like he wanted to protest, but his body deflated. "You got your phones?"

"Yeah," Christine said.

"Call me if you need me. And please, don't need me."

He motioned for Nicky to come over. Leaning close to his ear, he whispered, "Dude, do not think you're going to try anything with my sister."

Nicky thumped him on the arm with his fist. "We're just demon hunting. When we get back, we can swing by my house and sneak a few beers and chill."

Roy huffed, smoke bursting from his lips. "I am so chill right now, I should have penguins living on me."

He smiled, gunned the snowmobile and took off, riding in the tracks they'd made on the way in.

Turning to Christine, Nicky said, "So, you want me to drive?"

Christine gave him a smile that warmed his body by several degrees. "You're the navigator. I'll drive, you give directions."

Sam waited outside the long driveway to Kelly's house. His toes had gone numb from the walk. He looked over at the two million dollar Victorian home. He knew every nook and cranny of the place. Her parents had left it to Kelly and her brother when they'd passed away ten years ago. Both had died from liver cancer within a year of one another. He used to find it hard to believe that Kelly could still drink after watching her parents fade away like that.

Now he wasn't so sure.

He spotted Tank in his enormous black pea coat trudging clumsily in the deep snow. No matter how cold it got, Tank always wore the relatively thin coat. *I guess giants are their own furnaces,* Sam thought, smiling for the first time that day.

"I saw them, Sam," Tank said as they shook hands. "They were right outside our bedroom window; six prints, but nothing leading to them. I even checked the roof to see if something had jumped down from it. How did you know?"

"I didn't. Kelly did. She had me look around my house and asked me to call you, too."

"This can't be that thing from when we were kids. What the hell did it do, hibernate for four decades? It doesn't make sense, but those prints look a hell of a lot like it."

"What we saw back then didn't make any sense. I know you don't like to talk about it, but it wasn't a hallucination. We saw what we saw."

Tank stood with his hands on his hips, contemplating something Sam wasn't privy to. He waited a moment before saying, "Let's go inside and hear what she has to say."

As they walked, Sam said, "She said there's something else we have to see, besides the prints. Something that will make it impossible to ignore." He'd called her during the walk to her house, prying for more information. She gave hints, promising the rest when he got there.

"I'm almost afraid to ask."

Kelly flung the door open before they could knock. She wore a long T-shirt and sweats. She looked terrible—older, tired, frightened. Her eyes were red and puffy, as if she'd been crying.

"Come in, guys, it's freezing." She crossed her arms over her chest, kicking the door closed behind them.

"The place looks real good," Tank said. He'd been there quite often himself back when they ran in the same pack. Sam remembered the time Tank had broken some kind of commemorative dish when he was reenacting a wrestling move from the meet earlier that day. Somehow, he'd flipped himself sideways, caroming into the wall. The plate landed on his head, shattering. Sam and Kelly had laughed until they cried. Tank sat on the floor, blood trickling down his forehead, trying to piece the plate back together.

"Bet you were expecting a rundown shithole," she said. "I may be a drunk, but I can still afford a maid."

Sam interjected, "That's not what he meant, Kel."

"Actually, it kinda was," Tank said from the side of his mouth.

This whole situation had the potential to derail in a hurry. Sam could feel the tension between Tank and Kelly. After their shared experience, the two had retreated to opposite ends of the spectrum. Sam would have to be the mediator here.

"Let's agree to be civil," he said. He showed Kelly the pictures on his phone. "This was the only set of prints by my house."

Kelly and Tank looked at the display and the long, narrow footprints.

Tank said, "They could have been normal prints at first that got longer and deeper as the sun melted the edges."

"So how did they just appear there, under Nicky's window, and nowhere else?" Sam asked.

"Let me see yours, Chris," Kelly said. She chewed at her left thumbnail. Sam smelled the faint odor of whiskey on her breath.

Tank pulled his phone out of his pocket with a dramatic sigh. There were more prints by his house, but they looked exactly the same as the ones Sam had taken.

"Follow me," Kelly said, slipping on a pair of boots. She walked through the first floor to the back door, pushing hard to open it against a snowdrift. "Look, they're everywhere."

Sam and Tank each took a step into the yard. She was right. It was as if someone or something had taken great pains to study every inch of her house, creeping by windows like a pervert or a thief.

"Could be an animal," Tank said.

"Now this," Kelly said, ushering them inside.

She went ahead of them into her study. Sam stopped his friend before they went in. "Just play it cool when you go in there. Don't say anything," he whispered.

"What, is there a body under the floorboards?"

"You'll see."

Sam had seen, the day after his marriage flew the coop, and stumbled into her secret room or command center or whatever she called it. If it had shocked *him,* it would absolutely bring out Tank's ridicule reflex in the face of absurdity.

There were even more postings on the walls. Natural light streamed in through the parted curtains. Faces of strangers were plastered everywhere. That odd shape was still in the room, hidden under a large sheet.

To his credit, Tank remained impassive.

"When you guys see this, there's no turning back," Kelly said. Sam noticed her hand trembling slightly as it hovered over the wireless mouse.

"That's a matter of opinion," Tank said, stepping behind her chair. They stared at a blank computer screen.

"A while back, I flooded the house and property with security alarms and cameras," Kelly said, easing them into her big reveal. "I've been following a bigger story for a long time now—bigger than what we even saw, though it was an important part of the overall picture. If I hadn't experienced it, I couldn't have connected all these dots." She motioned to the patchwork timeline on the walls. Sam's stomach tightened. Whether it was from pity or tension, he wasn't sure.

"After I saw the prints today, I immediately started checking my systems. None of the alarms had been tripped. They're sensitive as hell. So I went through each camera's recording of last night. Outside, the snow is perfect, untouched, and one frame later, the prints are there. In fact, in that one frame, they were everywhere. We're talking less than a second. And there's nothing that I can see that made them."

She showed them the video, taking it frame by frame across multiple shots.

"Holy shit," Sam said. "How can that be? I mean, how long does it take to go from one frame to the next?"

"Less than a second," she said.

"Then something's either wrong with your cameras or the timer," Tank said.

"I'll buy one camera malfunctioning, but all of them, at the same time? I'm not that stupid," Kelly said.

Tank said, "So we all have strange footprints outside our homes. Okay, even I can't deny that. What does it mean?"

The tremor in Kelly's hands intensified. The on-screen pointer poised over the image of one of the security camera feeds. A still image of her living room was bathed in ghostly green. Kelly was asleep on the couch. The TV was on.

"It means this," she said, so softly the words barely made it to their ears. She clicked on the small square, enlarging it to fill the entire monitor.

One moment she was alone, passed out, judging by the empty glass by the couch.

In a flash, a being cloaked in shadow hovered over her.

"Fuck me," Tank said, stepping back from the screen.

Sam's head spun, blood rushing to his ears, a pounding surf frothing with dread.

It may have been dark, but he'd seen that thing before. The Dover Demon had returned. Except this time, they didn't just happen upon it.

The demon had come specifically for them.

Chapter Fifteen

Christine and Nicky took it slow as they wended through the trees. Upper Mill Pond wasn't much farther. As the sun weakened, the bone-cracking chill grew more and more threatening. Even with long johns underneath his jeans, Nicky's legs were growing more numb by the minute.

Not that he cared. With his body melded to Christine's back, all was right with the world. He kept on the lookout for more snow-dumps, his eyes scanning every passing tree branch.

"I think I see it," Christine shouted over the engine and whistling wind.

He looked around her shoulder and spotted the clearing.

"That's it," he said.

The pond had frozen over and was coated with snow. It may have been cold as hell, but he wasn't sure the ice would be thick enough to stand up to the weight of the snowmobile. He remembered the water being pretty deep for a little pond. He tapped Christine's arm to stop.

As much as he didn't want to break his embrace, he was comforted by the fact that they had a whole ride home ahead of them.

"Roy was right, we are nuts," Christine said, shivering as she slipped off the snowmobile.

"If you want, we can turn back now, go to your house and load up on coffee."

She smiled. "No way. I'm in this for the long haul. So, where did this weird guy say he saw the demon?"

Extracting his Lando Solo printouts, made difficult by his thick gloves, Nicky unfolded a picture on the snowmobile's cooling seat. "This is one of the pictures he took. He was standing right about there, I guess," he said, pointing to a spot fifty yards to their right. "He snapped this picture right after the demon disappeared."

"When it just sank into the ground, right?"

He nodded. "Yep, that's what he said. The best way to find the exact spot is by comparing the trees. See this one over here? It has a huge gouge taken out of its trunk. We need to find that tree."

Christine scanned the trees across the pond, using her hand as a visor to block the meager sunlight from her eyes. Spirals of smoke were coming off her neck and face.

"That's not gonna be easy. The snow is on them like a winter coat," she said. "They all look the same."

"I'm pretty sure if I get close enough, I'll be able to find it. Come on, let's go. At least the walk will warm us up."

His heart almost stopped as he strode toward the opposite end of the pond. Christine's hand was suddenly in his!

"You're going to have to help keep me up," she said. "I'm like four inches shorter than you and this deep snow is not easy to walk in."

Was that a slight glimmer in her eyes? He squeezed his hand around hers, guiding her along the way. "Just step into my prints. It'll make it easier," he said.

Thank you thank you thank you, he thought. *I don't know what made me want to come out here so bad today, but man, it's worth it.*

When they made it to the area he suspected the picture had been taken, he began dusting the snow off the surrounding tree trunks.

"Here, let me help," Christine said. She had a hard time pulling her feet out of the snow because it was even deeper on this side of the pond.

Nicky waved her off. "I've got this. No sense getting your hands any colder than they already are."

You're not being very subtle, are you?

Riding below the current of his attraction to Christine was the knowledge that he may be standing exactly where the Dover Demon had last been spotted. How freaking cool was that? He wondered if there was a time when his dad would have been just as excited. After all, he was the one who made the deal with Matt Ford to sell his books and make the comic book shop a destination for any curious cryptid seekers.

But that was the pre-separation dad. He probably wouldn't give a fiddler's fat ass now.

Nicky went from tree to tree, swiping off the snow to reveal the icy bark beneath. These trees were oaks with bare branches, so he wasn't worried about pounds of snow tumbling down on his head.

Using two hands, he raked the snow down on a thick-trunked tree. Christine yelled, "Hold it! I think that's the one."

He'd given her the picture to hold and compare to the scenery. Stumbling to her side, he looked at the picture, then the tree he'd just exposed.

A slit ran down the side of the tree for almost four feet, right down to the roots. It was as if the tree had been filleted at one time, the raw ends long since healed over but the guts of the tree forever exposed.

"That's the one," Nicky said, excitement raising his voice an octave.

"Cool. He said the demon looked back at him, then just disappeared like it was going down an elevator or melting into the ground."

"Makes no sense, right? I mean, there isn't even a depression around where you'd think an animal or creature could slip down into. At least I don't think there is. Hard to tell with all this snow."

Christine pocketed the picture. "Only way to find out is to check. Let's stomp around and see if we sink any deeper."

Holding hands again, they crunched through the snow around the tree, laughing from the absurdity of it all. Here they were, freezing, and instead of going home, they were looking for Dover Demon gopher holes.

"I'm beginning to think Lando Solo was full of shit," Nicky said, the cold air gnawing on his lungs.

"Probably toked up before he came out here," Christine said, hopping through the snow.

Nicky stopped to catch his breath, leaning against the wounded tree. "I think we can say this place is demon free, at least for today. If it's an intelligent monster, it has more sense than us."

Christine pushed a lock of hair that had escaped from under her hat away from her eyes. With her red cheeks and a radiant smile, all Nicky could think about was rushing over and kissing her. Roy would kill him. Christine might slap him or even worse, kiss him back but feel nothing— no fireworks, zero attraction.

She said, "At least we can say we made it. We've stood where the Dover Demon last hung out."

"Allegedly," he reminded her.

Just do it. Walk those two steps and kiss her. This is the best chance you're ever going to get. Deal with the consequences later.

"Let's get back to the snowmobile," he said, moving forward, his hand outstretched.

"Yeah, before we get frostbite."

As their fingertips touched, Christine let out a small cry. Her hand slipped away from his grasp.

"Nicky!"

Before he could react, Christine was pulled into the snow. In a flash, she was gone, as if she'd fallen into a camouflaged pit.

He dropped to his knees, digging like a possessed man, shouting her name. His gloves scraped at the cold earth under the snow. It was hard as a rock.

"Christine! Christine!"

Something tugged at his ankle. Nicky jerked his leg back. His knees gave way. The snow rose up to swallow him whole.

Kelly had poured three fingers of scotch for all of them. They stared at the image of the shadowy figure looming over her on the couch.

"Tank, even you have to admit it looks just like it," Sam said. No matter how much scotch he drank, his mouth remained parched, as if he'd been in the desert for days without water.

His friend, normally unflappable, was pale. "In a way it does, but it's bigger. Taller than I remember."

"It doesn't have to be the same one we saw when we were kids," Kelly said. She paced around the room. "It's not like we saw the last of the line. If there's one, there are others. Since we know they're being protected—"

"We don't know that," Tank said.

Kelly shook her head. "Yes, we do."

The scene from that night, their spring break double date, flooded Sam's memory. It had been a fun time. They'd gone to Boston to catch a movie. It had been *Annie Hall*. It was no *Sleeper* or *Bananas*, but that was sometimes the price one paid if they wanted to feel under a bra later. Stephanie and Kelly had loved it. Sam and Tank tolerated what would later be known as a Woody Allen classic. They had grabbed a late snack at a diner in Framingham, then headed out to their spot to make out for a while. Plans were made to head over to Cape Cod the next day, maybe spend the afternoon in Provincetown.

Driving to their spot, the car's headlights caught the impossible in their twin beams, and all thoughts of Cape Cod were vaporized.

"Sam, what do you think?" Tank asked.

His eyebrows rose as he stored the memory away. "I think we'd be stupid to ignore what's right in front of our eyes. I just don't know what the hell it means."

If the creature had been both outside and inside Christine's house, had it done the same to him and Tank? Had they slept last night, unaware that some strange creature was watching them, just inches away?

"Kelly, by the looks of things, you're probably the only one with a clue as to what's happening," Tank said. Sam was relieved to hear how his friend's tone had softened toward her. Maybe she wasn't crazy after all. If so, they needed her now. "How can something make prints like that without seeming to walk to or from our houses? And how did it get through all the security and inside your house? Most importantly, what is it and why the hell is it here, now, after all this time?"

Kelly finished her drink. She stared hard at Tank. "You're scared. Good. You should be. I think I know what it is. I don't know the full extent of its abilities or intentions. I do know that we're in serious danger."

"Hold on," Sam said. He left the study and grabbed two chairs from the dining room and the bottle of scotch. Setting them behind the desk, he said, "I think we're going to need these." He poured them each another finger of scotch.

"Let's take it one at a time. Kelly, I know everyone calls it the Dover Demon, but what exactly is it?" Sam asked.

"I can tell you it's not anything anyone has theorized it to be," she said. "Unlike the book, *Dover Demon: Nights of Terror* says, it's not a misidentified animal in the throes of some kind of disease." She caught Sam's gaze and wouldn't let go.

"What?" Sam said.

Kelly said, "I know you wrote it, *Matt Ford*. Did you think I'd forget that was the name you used to register us under at that little motel?"

Sam knew there was no sense arguing.

"I told you to use a better pseudonym," Tank said.

The only people Sam had let know about his little writing endeavor was his wife, Tank and Stephanie. He'd never stopped to think that his distant ex-girlfriend could have easily tied him to the book. Those days and nights they'd shared had been tucked away in the cobwebbed recesses of his mind's attic.

"You wanted to be a reporter when we dated," Kelly said. "Aside from your off-base conclusion, the book was really well written."

"Okay, we've established I'm Matt Ford and I was wrong. I needed to put some theory out there. If I said the truth, I was afraid someone would figure out I'd written it and then I'd be in deep shit. It was a chance to try my hand at writing and get some free therapy."

"You were right to end it the way you did," Kelly said.

"So what is the damn Dover Demon?" Tank said, his arms crossed over his chest. His left leg bounced up and down rapidly. "All this time, Steph and I assumed it wasn't from here. Remember when we saw *Close Encounters*, Sam? And then everything else that came after it in the media. It's like what we saw was the beginning of some kind of subliminal disclosure. I wouldn't tell another soul I believe in aliens but it's been hard to convince myself otherwise."

Kelly turned to Sam, placing a hand on his knee. "And you've thought it was some kind of unknown animal, haven't you?"

"Animal, experiment gone wrong, I don't know. It was terrestrial to me."

Kelly closed her eyes and sighed. When she opened them again, she said, "I think you were both right."

"How can that be?" Tank said.

Kelly got up from her chair, striding to one of the walls papered with news clippings, pictures and printouts. "I think what we saw is alien, or better yet, *was* from someplace other than earth. They've been here a long, long time, but they're no longer coming from other planets or dimensions. They've probably been here as long as we have, a fact that would make them, by now, a terrestrial species. But oh, they're alien all right."

She pointed to pages that looked as if they'd been cut from textbooks and Bibles. "If you go back to the earliest written histories, strange stories of men from the skies, giants and beings with incredible technical abilities are everywhere from the Sumerian texts to the Old Testament and Bhagavad Gita. Rock petroglyphs and ancient cave art all depict beings that look eerily similar to what we call our Dover Demon."

Sam said, "We've all watched *Ancient Aliens* and have heard the theories."

Tank nodded. "I can easily debunk all of their horseshit with rock solid facts. It comes with the archaeology degree. But I can't deny that some things have made me shake my head and wonder."

"I'm a little surprised," Kelly said.

"How can you be, after what we experienced?" Sam said.

She rubbed her temples. "I don't know. I guess because you both went on to live normal lives, I just assumed you'd put it out of your minds. I mean, I know you took some interest because of the book, Sam, but I just assumed it was a way to make money at your store. You have to admit, you've always known how to make a buck."

He almost laughed. "Oh yes, the comic book shop is rolling in the black. That book helped me get it all off my chest. I couldn't very well sit with a shrink and spill everything. They would have had me on a ton of meds or committed."

"So tell us what you know about what's going on now," Tank said, rising to study her walls. "There's a lot of stuff you posted that covers the past five years. If this is some kind of alien race that's been here for centuries, why all the modern missing persons stuff?"

Kelly sidestepped to the older posts. "They've been called many different names in the past: fairies, gnomes, goblins, even leprechauns. But I think the fairy folklore is closest to the mark. We're not talking Tinker Bell fairy time. The true fairy legends depict them as much bigger than winged grasshoppers and they could be frightening to say the least. Elves and trolls are also part of the mix. Over time, maybe because of the different gravity here than on their originating planet, they've evolved from large beings, our early giants, to much smaller beings, like what we saw. Or maybe they can will themselves to change in order to remain hidden, like chameleons. It's hard to keep a low profile when you're some large-headed, eight-foot tall biped. No matter their size, the one thing all of the legends have in common is that they're terrifying."

Pointing to magazine articles with headlines shouting about alien encounters and abductions, she continued, "Each continent and time period has their version of what I'll call Dover Demon lore. I think these creatures have a way of projecting their appearance to us, making us see what they want us to see. By doing this, they create an evolving folklore that instills fear and guarantees their secrecy. Here in the US, that folklore became the rise in UFO and alien sightings that started with Kenneth Arnold's flying saucer encounter in the late 1940s. Since then, the UFO mythos has exploded, moving from casual sightings to intense forced abductions and even suspected murders."

Sam got up to read some of the articles. Tank had slipped his glasses on and was speed-reading through the postings.

"But you said these things aren't coming from space," Sam said.

Kelly slammed her empty glass on the desk. "You're right, they're not. But they've found a way to use the UFO illusion to keep us looking up when we should be looking down!"

Chapter Sixteen

When Christine came to, she was alone. She looked up at the earthen ceiling. Roots dangled above her like arthritic fingers.

There was no wind or snow and she felt remarkably warm. Her head pounded with each beat of her heart. A sulfuric tinge coated her tongue. She scraped it against her top teeth, hoping to peel the awful sheen away.

Sitting up was a chore. Hugging her knees, she stared down into a dark tunnel.

"Where am I?" she said. It was comforting to hear another voice, even if it was her own.

It didn't take a rocket scientist to realize she was underground, but where exactly? And how did she get here? Closing her eyes, she tried to recall the last thing she remembered. She'd awoken to her brother knocking on her door telling her school was closed. Then she went back to sleep for a while. It had been very bright outside her window when she woke up again, hungry for breakfast.

A small landslide of pebbles rained down on her. Christine's eyes flew open and she rolled to the other side of the tunnel. The pebbles and dirt settled onto the floor.

Wait! How can I be underground and see everything?

She found that she could stand with a few inches to spare. The way ahead was dark, but there was a glow of light coming from somewhere behind her, illuminating this section of the tunnel.

"I know which way I'm *not* going," she said. Her words were absorbed by the hard-packed dirt. She turned toward the lighted end of the tunnel, the fingertips of her right hand gliding over the surface of the wall, keeping it close in case she got dizzy. Her head wasn't quite right. It felt a lot like the concussion she'd gotten in field hockey last year.

Maybe that's why I can't remember how I got here, she thought.

Another reason she felt she might have a concussion: she should be so freaked out right now, she'd be a bawling mess. She mentally knew how she *should* be reacting, but that part of her brain wasn't in touch with the rest of her body.

"Hello," she called out. There was no returning echo.

Who would dig a tunnel out like this? And why?

"It can't be for anything good," she said, spitting out the rotten egg taste that coated her mouth.

"Hello, is anybody there? Hello!"

Just keep walking. Find out where that light is coming from and take it from there.

Christine's legs almost buckled when a wicked case of the spins cycloned through her head. She stopped for a moment to regain her balance.

Had her brother left her down here as some kind of joke? Where the hell did he find this place?

No, she was obviously hurt. Roy would never go that far.

"Hey, anyone, I could use some help."

There was no reply.

With concentrated effort, she put one foot slowly in front of the other.

Tank's patience was wearing thin. In a way, he felt sorry for Kelly. What they'd seen had obviously unhinged here. The booze didn't help matters any. If she didn't find a way to unify the insanity she was showing them, he was going back home—with Sam in tow whether he liked it or not. So far, she'd spouted enough wild theories to light a thousand conspiracy fires.

"Kelly, you're not making much sense," Tank said. "So we have creatures from someplace else that have been here for maybe as long as humans. Now you tell us they've created the entire UFO phenomenon as a sleight of hand. But what does that all have to do with these people you have around this room?"

Kelly walked around the room, briefly touching the photographs of each missing person.

"This is why we need to be worried," she said. "Every single face in this room has had an experience with a UFO, or a close encounter with what they described as an alien. Every one of them. For some, it happened when they were kids, others in the very recent past. That's when they were marked. The second trait they all share is that they've disappeared without a trace. In fact, all of them have gone missing within the past five years, with a huge spike this past year." She stopped at the section of the wall with the most recent posts.

Sam tugged at his chin. "Wait, you said they were marked. Marked how?"

Kelly shrugged. "I don't know. But something in their experience with that they thought was a UFO or alien set the stage for them to be abducted years later. You've heard of screen memories, right?"

"Of course I have," Sam said. "I had to do a little research on it when I wrote the book, especially on that section linking theories that the Dover Demon was an ET. In abduction folklore, it's like when people report seeing owls or deer in their yard and outside their window. When they submit to deep regression hypnosis, it turns out the owls and deer are actually strange beings. The implication is that the alien visitors used their own hypnotic methods to implant screen memories, so people couldn't recall what happened to them."

Tank sat back into his chair.

To think we were once prominent CEOs, he thought, swirling the remaining scotch in his glass. *Now we're running the X Files.* He looked at the still image of the bizarre, shadowy shape watching Kelly sleep. A chill gripped the base of his spine and wouldn't let go.

"Exactly," Kelly said. "As fantastic as what we encountered seemed, there's a good chance we're not remembering it the exact way it happened. Or, if we are, there may be more that we haven't been allowed to recollect. I don't know how people are marked, whether it's through the implant of a device or psychically, but when people come across these things, their fate is sealed. They're going to disappear one day.

And I think with everything we've just seen, we may be next."

Tank said, "Are there cases where some of these other people had warning signs?"

"Who's to know? They're not around to ask," Kelly replied. "I'm sure if they did see something, it was so strange, they kept it to themselves. Remember, these are people who had already been through the ridicule mill once before—once bitten, twice shy."

Holding up his hands, Sam said, "Let's pretend everything you're saying is true. Me, you, Tank and Steph were all marked back in 1977. Now these, *things*, have come back for us. Aside from asking why now, we should be thinking of ways to prevent it."

Kelly walked across the room and cradled his face in her hands.

"Sam, think back to that night. Do you remember everything?"

"How could I not?"

"If what we saw wasn't a screen memory, you know why things are happening now."

Tank watched them, saw Sam's mind go back. As much as he himself had avoided that particular trip down memory lane, he forced himself to relive it all over again. His stomach coiled, writhing with the snakes of fear that had festered in him for years afterward.

There was a reason they never spoke of it, even if it would have supported the stories their classmates reported to parents, teachers and police.

No one, not even the ones who had just witnessed the demon themselves, would have believed them.

Chapter Seventeen

April, 1977

Tank wound the 1974 Dodge Dart with a lead foot down the dark, two-lane road. The boxy car wasn't much to look at, but the V8 engine was killer. He wished it had better suspension so he could take the turns even harder.

"Slow down, Tank. Jesus, are you trying to get us killed?" Stephanie said, rolling her window closed. "You're gonna make my scarf blow out the window." She made sure the silk paisley scarf she had tied on her head remained tightly in place. Her long hair flowed from the scarf, ending in pretty waves at the middle of her back. Tank knew that if he wanted to get any action tonight, and he most assuredly did, he'd better do what she said.

He spotted the glowing orange orb in his rearview mirror. Sam took a long toke off the joint and passed it to Kelly.

"That is the last chick flick we're seeing for a long time," he said, coughing the smoke out and smiling with glassy eyes. "Next time, me and Tank pick out the movie."

Kelly cuddled closer to him, resting her head on his shoulder. She had blue and red feathers clipped in her hair. A third clip attached to pink feathers was being used to hold the joint steady in her hands.

"Oh, come on, Sammy, you know you liked it. I heard you laughing a few times," she said.

"Sometimes I laugh at the news. That doesn't make it fun to watch."

"What the hell do you laugh at on the news?" Tank said. He figured they'd be at their private makeout spot in five minutes. Steph looked exceptionally hot tonight. Sure, they couldn't go all the way, not with Sam and Kel in the car, but he could cop a feel of her stupendous boobs. Just thinking about them, heavy and round and remarkably high on her chest, with thick nipples that called out to him like twin sirens, he grew uncomfortably hard in his tight jeans.

"Mostly I laugh at the hair of the anchors. Kill me if I ever cut my hair, man."

Unlike Sam, who hadn't cut his hair since ninth grade, Tank's was buzzed Marine-style every other week. His coaches—football, baseball and lacrosse—absolutely forbid hippies from playing on the team. Those hypocrites had probably dropped acid at Woodstock and screwed whatever muddy girl passed by.

"I wouldn't have to kill you. That's where your strength is. Cut it and you'll just drop dead," Tank said.

"I'd kind of like to see what you look like with short hair," Stephanie said.

"Not me," Kelly said. "I don't date squares." She took a drag and pulled him in for a kiss. Smoke seeped from their lips.

Stephanie plucked the joint from Kelly's fingers. "This stuff is weak. Where did you get it?"

"This guy who plays for Nattick. I hung out with him after the game. He had a whole glove compartment full of nickel bags," Tank said.

"Well, next time, let him keep his stuff," she said, toking and holding her breath as long as she could.

When she finally let the smoke go, Tank said, "Steph, you gotta open your window." He swatted at the smoke billowing in the car.

"It's cold outside," she said.

"Yeah, but I need cross ventilation to clear the smoke. I can't drive if I can't see."

"Fine, but I'm not opening it all the way." She cranked the window down to the halfway mark.

Sam sat forward, resting his chin on the seat between Tank and Stephanie. "You guys going to that spring church picnic tomorrow?"

"My mom says I have to go, but I'm doing it under protest," Stephanie said, giggling.

"I've got practice," Tank said with a huge grin. "The only church my father cares about is on the baseball diamond. Or a football field. So, unlike my sisters, I am exempt from all holy activities."

"Lucky bastard," Sam said. "I know Kelly's out, so I guess it'll be me and you tomorrow, Steph."

Stephanie turned back in her seat to face her friend. "You're so lucky, Kel. Your parents don't make you do anything. I mean, we're old enough to legally be called adults but I still have to hear, 'As long as you live under my roof, you'll do what I say' from my mom and dad. Your parents are so cool."

Kelly said, "I wouldn't exactly call them cool."

As the last of the smoke filtered out the open windows, Tank spotted a dark figure in the road. "Holy shit!" he exclaimed, slamming the brakes as hard as he could. The Dart swerved hard to the right, kicking up bits of asphalt. Stephanie and Kelly screamed with everything their lungs could give. Only Sam stayed silent, hands gripping the bucket seat in front of him, eyes fixed on the bizarre scene as they spun past, just missing the object in the road.

Tank fought to maintain control of the car and keep it from flipping off the side of the road. He let out a string of expletives that could never be recalled or repeated. The brake pedal shuddered beneath his foot. The steering wheel fought to free itself from his grasp. He held on, his fingers deathly white, knee locked in place.

The Dart came to a sudden stop, tottering left and right, the shocks wailing.

They were now facing the opposite direction, a sitting duck for a head-on collision. The motor sputtered and died.

"Is everyone all right?" Tank screamed. He couldn't control his own voice. His nerves were tingling.

Stephanie held the side of her head where she'd hit the window. "I think I have a lump already."

"Hold on, honey, let me see," Kelly said, leaning over the seat to tenderly touch Stephanie's head.

Tank flinched when Sam spoke close to his ear, pointing outside the front windshield. "What the hell is that, man?"

Following Sam's finger, Tank stared ahead. Just within the fading glare of the car's headlights, something stood with its long, tapered hands on its knees, glaring back at them. It was as pale as a fresh tombstone, hairless with flesh covered in a sheet of sweat or water. Its head was huge in comparison to its sticklike body, with a thin line for a mouth and large, orange eyes. It had orange fucking eyes!

His body still humming from the near miss, Tank fumbled with the door handle. Sam pulled back on his shoulder.

"Don't go out there! You don't know what that is."

Kelly and Stephanie caught their concerned vibe and looked to where their boyfriends were transfixed. Stephanie's hand flew to her mouth. "Oh my God, what is that?"

"Is that what we almost hit?" Kelly said, sidling next to Sam to get a better look at the creature.

Sam said, "I don't think it's real. Look. It's not even breathing. It should have run when we just missed it. It hasn't moved yet. Maybe it's a statue or something."

"Yeah, a statue that someone just happened to stick on the side of the road to scare the shit out of people driving by," Tank said, anxious to get out of the car and confront what had nearly killed them. If it was an animal, he wanted to put the fear of God into it. If it was a person thinking he had played a hell of a practical joke, he was going to put the fear of Tank into him.

He tried for the door again. This time, Steph gripped his arm.

"Sam might be right," she said. "It's not moving at all."

"But those eyes," Kelly said, sounding as if she were in a trance. "They're looking right at us. Can't you see it? Those aren't fake. It's like it's studying us."

Tank tried to start the car. The carburetor must have been flooded. It wouldn't turn over. Still, the weird thing out there remained stock-still. "Look, I gotta move the car off the road. But before I do that, I'm going to see what the hell that thing is."

"What if it bites you?" Stephanie said. "It could be some diseased animal. Why else would it look like that?"

"What kind of animal stands on two legs?" Sam said. "That sure as hell isn't a bear."

Tank slipped out of the car before anyone could stop him. He opened the trunk and took out one of his baseball bats. The car rocked for a moment and Sam was at his side. "Here, take this," Tank said, handing him his fungo bat. "Just in case."

As they walked past the car, Stephanie pleaded, "Please, don't go over there. Let's just push the car away from it. Maybe it'll run off into the woods."

"Maybe I don't want it to run into the woods," Tank said, his breath forming wispy vapors.

Kelly got out of the car, too, walking close behind Sam.

"Get back in the car, Kel," Sam said.

As they approached the strange creature, its eyes remained fixed on the car and Stephanie. Tank didn't even see it twitch. If it was a living thing, it would have to sense danger. He knew he was an imposing figure, especially with a weapon in his hand.

"I'm going with you," Kelly said.

"Well, then stand back a little. If I have to swing this, you're gonna get hit," Sam whispered.

Why is he whispering? Tank thought. *It's not like we have the element of surprise.*

Kelly moved to Sam's side, giving him plenty of arc room for the bat. They walked in a straight line in lockstep. The night was utterly silent. Usually, night critters made a racket. Something had scared them away.

Could have been the car with the brakes and girls screaming.

Tank flexed his fingers on the bat handle, just like he would when he was waiting for a pitch to come in. If he had to, he would knock this thing's head clear over the trees.

The orange eyes of the creature appeared to be full of moving clouds, almost like a snow globe that had been shaken hard. Tank tensed. *What has eyes like that? This has to be some kind of setup.*

Stephanie muttered something from the car but he couldn't make out a single word. Every fiber of his being was concentrated on the pale thing in front of him. The closer they got, the stranger it looked. One thing was for sure, it was no animal. Nothing like this existed in nature, or at least the Massachusetts outdoors.

Sam eased the bat down and huffed.

"Nice costume, man," he said to the still creature. "Too bad it's gonna cost you a beating." He turned to Tank. "We should just tackle him."

Something about the wet sheen of its puckered flesh repulsed Tank. Even if it was just a costume, he wanted no part in touching it.

Kelly stopped. "Guys, I think I just saw its eyes move."

Tank said, "What? I didn't see anything."

Sam laughed. Carrying the bat at his side, he broke from their advancing line, rushing forward.

The thing started to scream.

Broken from its paralysis, hands still grasping its narrow knees, the creature turned its head and locked its terrifying gaze on them. Its mouth opened wide. It had no teeth, just a black open space. The screech it let out flash froze Tank's blood. They jumped back, Kelly gripping both boys, breathing heavily.

Stephanie screamed, "Come on, get away from it! Let's go!"

Tank wanted nothing more than to jump in his car and pin the accelerator as far as it would go. The creature had changed positions, but was once again still, the ear-splitting cry ceasing.

Sam mumbled, "I think I just shit my pants."

Kelly gasped, pointing at the beast. "Oh my God, look!"

They watched in horror as a brown, ovular object slid from between its legs. Encased in a gelatinous slime, it touched down softly onto the road. Tank's stomach recoiled.

It was an egg!

"What the fuck?" Tank said, hoisting the bat high.

"Step back, step back," Sam cautioned, his arm protectively over Kelly's chest.

There was a wet pop, then a squish, and another egg slid down its thigh, settling next to the first.

"Kill it," Kelly said, her voice shaking.

"Don't go near it," Sam said. "If it's laying eggs, it'll kill you if you get too close."

Tank looked down at his friend. "Are you an expert on these things?"

Why couldn't he listen to his instinct and just run?

An awful stench wafted from the creature and its insidious eggs. They had to cover their mouths and noses. It smelled like old meat and overripe onions.

The creature moved, crouching down, its orange eyes narrowing. Another egg began to fall.

It was Kelly who broke the spell. Yanking on Tank and Sam's jackets, she pulled them back with strength Tank never knew she had. "We have to get the hell out of here and call the cops!"

"Tank, please!" Stephanie wailed in the background between sobs.

Sam caught his eye. "They're right. I don't want to be here when it stops."

They ran for the car. Something went plop behind them. Tank didn't need to see to know another egg had been squeezed out. The pungent smell intensified. He slammed his knee into the car door, ushering Kelly inside.

Stephanie had moved to the back seat, clutching Kelly. The girls were in tears. Sam looked like someone in shock. They were all in shock.

"Please start," Tank said, turning the key. The engine jumped to life. There was no way he was going to even drive past that thing. Slamming the gear into reverse, he looked back at Steph and Kelly and said, "Get down so I can see."

Before he could gun it, Sam cried out, "Holy crap, look!"

The creature was now in the middle of the road, standing straight and glaring at them. At best, it was five feet tall. But now it had company.

Men in black overalls knelt down by the eggs. They wore dark ball caps. It was difficult to see their faces, even though they were so close Tank should have been able to spot any moles or freckles. Each man was carefully lifting an egg. Once the eggs were cradled in their arms, they dashed into the wooded area along the country road. They never once looked at the teens in the Dart.

"Were…;were those people that just took that thing's eggs?" Sam sputtered.

"I don't fucking know," Tank said, finally hitting the gas.

The creature let out another bowel-watering shriek as they sped away. When Tank had driven in reverse for a quarter of a mile, he rolled into a driveway and straightened the car out. He drove in silence, the only sound in the car being the occasional hitching sobs from the back seat.

Chapter Eighteen

Nicky woke up with a splitting headache. It was so bad, he was afraid to open his eyes. If there was any light around him, the shockwave would absolutely make his head explode. Even touching the sides of his head felt as if he were driving spikes into his skull.

It was best to try to fall back to sleep, though he wasn't sure how he'd manage that through the thickening haze of agony. How could he dream when all he saw was red and white sparks flickering like lightning in his brain?

Wait.

If I'm in bed, how did I get here? I was at the pond with Christine. We found that tree where the demon had been spotted. The rest was black, an empty space that absorbed all sound and light.

As much as he didn't want to do it, he had to open his eyes.

Slowly, his lids fluttered open. Mercifully, there was very little light.

But this wasn't home. That wasn't his white ceiling. The so-called bed was made of, of dirt or something. It smelled strange. Like potting soil and burnt matches. He tried lifting his head. A fireworks display shot off in the center of his cranium, walloping the breath from his lungs. He lay back down, squinching his eyes shut.

Nowaynowaynoway. It hurt too much to move.

He wanted to feel the ground around him, because he was certainly not in his bed, but first he had to get his gloves off. Groaning, he lifted his hands so they rested on his stomach. Slowly, he pulled each finger free from the thick, insulated gloves. Just that simple act compounded the piercing pain. He let his arms fall to his sides, his open palms coming in contact with…dirt?

Did I fall in a sinkhole? But then, I'd be able to see the sky above me. Maybe I hit the ground and rolled a little bit. That would explain why my head hurts so much.

His heart fluttered when he considered the possibility that he was seriously injured. Did anyone know where he was? Of course not. If they did, someone would at the very least be calling down to him. He had left the note for his father. Maybe he hadn't seen it yet or it was too early in the day to be concerned. There was no sound down here, not even the persistent whistling of the winter wind.

Why can't I remember?

Despite his growing panic, a pervasive numbness tingled its way from his feet to his aching head.

Something brushed against his leg!

He tried to roll over.

The flaming ache in the center of his skull went supernova. Nicky was pulled back into the impenetrable darkness, and all of his pain and confusion was forgotten.

Tank walked over to the shrouded hump in the corner of Kelly's study. "What's under there?" he asked.

She shouted, "Don't!" when he grabbed a corner of the sheet.

Sam said, "Kelly, if it's in this room, I'm sure it has something to do with all this stuff." He waved a hand at the walls and computer.

"You'll really think I'm crazy," she said.

Tank gave a short laugh. "Too late for that. Besides, at this point, I think all three of us are nuts. Come on, what can you possibly be hiding under there?"

She turned away from them both.

Just let them see. Who cares what they think? It sure as hell won't change Chris's opinion, she thought.

But Sam's. Well, for some reason, that still mattered.

"Look, if you don't want to show us, it's okay. I know all of this has been difficult," Sam said.

She looked to him and saw the honest concern in his eyes. They had loved each other at one time—deeply. That night had changed the courses of their lives. She wasn't sure if they would have gotten married like Chris and Stephanie, but there were many nights she wished for the chance to see how things would have been if she could just make that trip home from the movies disappear.

She sighed and said, "It's fine. Go ahead, Chris."

Tank pulled the sheet away and cried out, "What the fuck? Please don't tell me you're kidnapping people."

The square steel cage had a hinged entrance locked with the thickest padlock she could find. Each corner of the cage itself was bolted to the floor. Within the five by five foot cage was a mattress, folded blanket, jugs of water, canned food, silver pot with a lid, flashlights, matches, a butcher knife, shotgun with a box of shells and her .45.

"What is that for?" Sam said.

No sense holding back now, she thought. Her chest felt heavy and she needed another drink.

"It's my anti-abduction cage," she said so softly they almost didn't hear her.

"Your what?" Tank said.

"Look, I know for a fact that something is going to try to take me. It's been building for several years now. I've even spotted them lurking around at night. They think I can't see them, but I know they're there."

Sam held a hand out to her. "Wait, if these things are already around us, why haven't they taken any of us?"

"The ones I've seen are small, almost like children. They're not the ones we need to worry about. I figured I would have a sense when the time was getting closer. After what I saw last night, that's where I'll be spending my nights. I don't know if it will work, but I'm not going without making it hard as hell for them."

"Whoa, whoa, whoa," Tank said. "Go back. You've been seeing things like the Dover Demon for years now?"

She nodded, taking a swig of whiskey straight from the bottle. "I see them out of the corner of my eye sometimes. Or behind the brush. I think they were just there to watch me."

"You sure you're just not seeing things after having one too many?" Tank said.

Until the video proof last night, Kelly had been on the fence about her supposed experiences herself. Any doubts she had were now erased.

"They were real. Just like the footprints and the thing in my living room. I know it looks crazy, but I'm betting that they're not used to people resisting them, especially not like this." She stared at the cage, dreading spending her nights inside, waiting for the inevitable.

"So you're going to lock yourself up and shoot anything that come near you," Tank said, squatting to better look at the provisions inside.

"Yes."

"Sam, how the hell are we supposed to process this?"

"I don't know," Sam replied, staring at the still of the creature that had stood over her the night before. "I can't shake the feeling that the cage and those guns wouldn't even slow them down. Kelly, you mind if I use your bathroom?"

"Not at all. It's right down the hall."

He left the room pale as flour.

Kelly hoped to hell she hadn't said and shown too much. If there was ever a time when she needed a friend, it was now.

Sam splashed some cold water on his face and sat on the closed toilet lid, thinking. As much as his rational mind wanted to reject everything Kelly had shown them and spoken about, a growing part of him was becoming intensely worried. Looking at the photos of the prints from his own house weakened his resolve against rationality.

Although, maybe at this point, fighting it was the *irrational* thing to do.

That night in 1977 was so bizarre, he'd never even told Lacy about it. She knew about his writing the book, but he'd never spoken a word about his encounter. To her, it was just another one of his childish diversions. Secretly self-publishing the book about the Dover Demon legend was the closest he'd ever come to disclosure. And even then, writing under a pseudonym, he'd refused to even hint at the high strangeness they'd witnessed. Instead, he'd pretty much rehashed the story his braver classmates had told, embellishing it with opinions from outside sources.

Did their return have something to do with the eggs? And why come back for them? It didn't add up.

But those prints were right under Nicky's window. He wasn't even a thought when we saw that thing. Why would it choose his window of all the ones in the house?

Nicky!

Sam jolted upright on the toilet, gripped with panic. He burst from the bathroom, stalking into the study. Kelly and Tank froze when they saw him. He had his phone to his ear.

"Sam, what's wrong?" Tank said.

Sam held up a hand. After four rings, he got Nicky's voicemail. He dialed their home number. Again, after four rings, it was picked up by their answering machine. He'd forgotten to erase Lacy's recorded message:

"You have reached the Brognas. We can't come to the phone right now so please leave a message at the beep."

Damn it!

He tapped a quick text to his son.

NICKY…WHERE ARE YOU? CALL ME.

Turning to Kelly, he said, "You told us that you think we were marked. Would that mean my son is marked, too?"

The color drained from her face. "Oh my God."

"What's happened to Nicky?" Tank said, knocking the chair over as he stood. Nicky was his godson and the child he and Stephanie never could have. He looked like he was ready to murder anyone or thing that brought harm to him.

"I don't know. Probably nothing. I haven't seen him all day. I slept late and he was gone by the time I got up. I assume he's with one of his friends. He's not answering his phone or texts, though."

Tank said to Kelly, "Tell me there's no way Nicky could be involved in this."

She shook her head. "I…I can't. There are cases where the children of people who have had these experiences have disappeared."

"How could he be marked when he wasn't even born?" Tank exploded.

Sam kept one eye on his phone, waiting for a return text.

"Look, I don't know how everything works. These are all just theories. I don't think the same creature we saw in 1977 is the one coming around now. I'm pretty sure what stalked us last night could be what's come out of those eggs. Those men, or whatever they were, took them away to care for them. I get the feeling it takes a long time for them to hatch and mature. Maybe they can sense genetic transference. I can't be sure. No one can."

Sam grabbed his coat. It was going to be dark soon. "I have to find Nicky."

Tank put his on as well. "I'm going with you."

Kelly called out, "Wait, take me with you. I'm afraid to be here alone."

Sam didn't have time to protest. All he wanted to do was get moving. Movement meant progress. He was shocked when he saw her stuff a pistol into her pocket.

"I call it Betty," she said. "I don't leave my house without it."

"Do you have any of his friends' numbers?" Tank asked. The temperature had dropped considerably. Pretty soon, all of the remaining snow on the roads would be ice.

"Yeah, I have a few. I'll call Roy first."

He stopped at the end of Kelly's drive when Roy answered the phone. Tank and Kelly stood at his sides.

"Hey," Roy said. "Did Nicky tell you how I got dumped off my snowmobile?"

Sam's stomach dropped. "No, Roy. I haven't seen him."

"Oh, I thought he was back at your house with my sister."

"Where were Nicky and Christine when you last saw them?"

Cold fingers tightened around Sam's spine as Roy recounted their trip to the pond.

"So you left to warm up and they said they'd be back soon?"

"Yeah. I know my sister. She hates the cold. I didn't think she'd be able to stand it much longer," Roy said, concern creeping into his voice. "Maybe I should go out and look for them."

"No, you stay home in case they come back. If they do, tell Nicky to stay put and call or text me. I'll go out to the pond with Tank."

The pond. Why the hell was he out there? If they took a snowmobile out on the ice, it might not have been thick enough to support them. Visions of his son's blue face looking up at him through thin ice made him shudder.

Don't go there. Just don't go there.

Roy added, "I didn't think it was the best time to go Dover Demon hunting, but Nicky kinda insisted. He's following the path that guy Lando Solo blogged about."

Dover Demon hunting. Placing his hand over the phone, he said to Tank, "Roy said Nicky went Dover Demon hunting by the pond at Noanet Woods."

"In this weather?"

Sam shook his head. "Roy, tell me how to find this guy's blog."

Kelly tried to hold his arm but he pulled away. *This isn't her fault.* But maybe, if she hadn't been so obsessed, this somehow would never have happened. It didn't make sense, but then nothing was making much sense today.

When he hung up, Tank said, "We'll go to my house and get my Range Rover. We can be at the pond in fifteen minutes."

"I want to stop at my house before we go to the pond," Sam said.

They walked to Tank's house as fast as they could, the frigid air stinging their lungs with each breath.

Sam prayed. *Please be home and doing what teenage boys do with girls when they have a house to themselves.*

Christine battled a surging rush of tears. Crying wasn't going to help. She'd never felt so lost and helpless in her life. It appeared that she was in some underground maze, lit intermittently by LED lights recessed into the walls. In some spots, everything around her was nothing but solid dirt. In others, there had been attempts to lay wood boards for walls, with solid two-by-fours supporting lintels. In every respect, it was as if she'd fallen into a mine, except it couldn't be a mine. The floor and walls were way too smooth. And as far as she knew, there had never been any mining done in Dover, even in past centuries. She'd gone on enough class trips to the historic Benjamin Caryl House to have a pretty good working history on the town. Whenever they'd gone to the old, tiny, two-floor homestead on Dedham Street, they'd had to sit through talks from visiting historians and learn about life in Dover from the mid-1700s until the turn of the twentieth century.

As much as she'd dreaded those trips, she'd give away her iPhone and entire music collection to be there right now.

The fuzziness in her head had started to clear and she remembered being with Nicky just before everything went to a foggy hell.

"Nicky! Where are you?"

What had they been doing? Had they fallen into some kind of pit and she'd hit her head? That wouldn't explain this tunnel system that was obviously created and maintained by someone. It was cold down here, but not as bitter as it had been when they were on the snowmobiles.

Thank God for small favors.

The toe of her boot jammed against an unmoving rock. Christine pitched forward. Her hands bore the brunt of impact, saving her face from greeting the floor.

Now you can cry!

Hot tears leaked from the corners of her eyes, ran down the edge of her nose, dripping onto the smooth earth, making miniscule mud puddles.

"Roy! Nicky! Somebody help me!"

She knew she wasn't hurt, but she couldn't deny that she was scared as shit. Shifting so she sat leaning against the wall, she let the tears come.

There had to be a way out. She couldn't be buried alive. If someone was keeping the lights on, there had to be a way out. Christine thought about the catacombs under Paris, miles and miles of tight channels, some fortified from floor to ceiling with skulls and bones. People had been lost down there forever. Quite a few had died from dehydration, having spent days wandering in the darkness, searching in vain for an exit.

"This isn't Paris," she said, wiping her tears away with the sleeve of her coat.

There were no mines or catacombs in Dover! End of story.

She'd been with Nicky. He had to be close by. He'd never, ever take off and leave her. They'd been flirting more and more lately and she knew he liked her, just as she liked him. If it weren't for Roy and their stupid bro code, they'd probably be boyfriend and girlfriend by now. Instead, she had to wait for little moments like today when they shared her snowmobile. Even though she knew it was dangerous, she didn't care.

"Nicky! Nicky can you hear me?"

Get up and start walking. Nicky could be down here, too, and hurt.

Sniffling back her tears, she moved ahead, pausing at bends in the tunnel, wary of what lay in wait around the corner.

After one of those bends, she saw a long, straight passageway. It went so far, she couldn't see where it ended.

"Nicky!"

She paused to listen for any kind of response, even if it was the slight shifting of soil. Nothing.

Mustering up her thinning courage, she headed down the deep tunnel. Maybe Nicky was wandering, too. The ground absorbed sound like the foam walls of a recording studio. He could be just ahead of her, following the light.

She called his name out one more time, picking up her pace, nearing a slow jog. If her mind wanted to take things cautiously, her legs wanted out.

Her boots padded along the dirt floor.

Chuh-chuh-chuh-chuh.

Her heart froze when she heard another sound, overlaying her rapid footsteps. It was softer, an animal's skittering keeping in step with her own.

Christine stopped.

So did the sound at her back.

Please, please, please don't let there be anything behind me.

Her chest heaved. In another minute, she'd be hyperventilating. If she didn't turn around, her imagination would run wild and she'd faint. It had happened to her before. If she cracked her head down here, she was up a creek.

Biting so hard on her bottom lip she tasted old pennies, Christine slowly turned around.

The tunnel was empty.

"Thank you," she sighed, feeling her heart rate decelerate.

Her breath erupted from her lungs as something heavy hammered her square in the back. Her face banged off the ground. Christine screamed as hands pulled at her hair and legs, dragging her down the dimly lit tunnel.

Chapter Nineteen

Kelly caught her reflection in the full size mirror in the foyer. Her face was red as an apple, her eyes bloodshot. She stayed with Sam while Chris stormed deeper into the house, calling for Stephanie.

Sam leaned against a wall, eyes locked on the phone in his hand.

"Still nothing?" she said.

"No."

She didn't want to tell him about the dozens of reports of the children of supposed UFO experiencers who had vanished over the years. To her, it was almost as if the passage of time between the initial experience and the return had changed something in the person that had been marked—like they had gone bad, passed their sell-by date. The creatures then went for the next best thing that also shared the same biological traits—their children. Explaining it to Sam now would send him over the edge. Plus, she couldn't prove anything, to herself or Sam. Everything she thought and said could be dead wrong. The only things that were right were what they had gone through as teens and the footprints and video of the thing in her house now. Trying to get everything to make sense had nearly driven her insane for over thirty years.

"Nicky's going to be fine," she said.

Sam tapped the back of his head against the wall. "I know. I know. We've been having a tough go of it lately. I haven't been leading the pack for Dad of the Year. I wouldn't blame him for ignoring me. If it weren't for everything today, I wouldn't even think twice. But now…"

They heard Stephanie and Chris talking in a room upstairs. There was a lot of moving around as Chris's heavy footsteps paced back and forth.

"What?" Stephanie exclaimed.

"Listen, just sit down for a second. I haven't got much time," Chris replied with a tone that offered no resistance.

"Come on, Tank," Sam muttered, squeezing his phone so hard, Kelly thought it was going to snap.

Kelly couldn't make out what her ex-friends were saying now. What concerned her most were all the coincidences that had lined up. If those creatures were back, whatever they were, and spying on them, why didn't they just take Nicky last night? Lord knows, they had the ability to snatch people from their home without even the family dog noticing. She'd long believed that there was a large element of mind control that came with experiences with these things.

Kelly was startled by a loud rush down the stairs. Chris was back with Stephanie close behind. She hadn't seen Stephanie this close in years. At best, she'd spied Steph from a distance at the supermarket or driving through town. Where had all the years gone? She'd been her best friend. Now they may as well have been strangers. Stephanie's brows were knit close together, her mouth pulled tight. She couldn't tell if Stephanie was worried or angry.

"I'm coming with you," she said to Sam and Kelly.

"It's better if you stay here with Kelly," Chris said.

Kelly blurted, "You may need me. I'm going with you, too. In fact, there may be strength in numbers." She gave Stephanie the same conspiratorial glance they'd used to great effect back in the day when they had Sam and Chris do their bidding. Teenage boys were so pliable.

It was as if all those years apart had never happened. For at least one day, Kelly had her old friend back.

"It's probably nothing," Sam said. "I just need to check it out and Tank has the only truck that can get us to Upper Mill Pond."

Stephanie laid down the law. "If Nicky's in trouble, there's no way I'm sitting here waiting for the news." She grabbed a heavy white coat from the closet, gloves and a wool hat. "We don't have time to argue, so let's go. Come with me, Kelly. We can get to the garage from here."

Kelly turned to see Chris take something out of his pocket and show it to Sam.

It was a gun. He handed it to Sam, which meant he probably had his own as well.

That made three of them with firearms. They may just need them. These creatures were real, flesh and blood beings that would bleed if shot. The color of their blood was debatable.

They speed-walked through the kitchen into the heated three-car garage. A coal-black Range Rover took up one and a half of the spaces. It looked as if it could go *through* a mountain as easily as it could *over* one. The garage door slowly opened. There was very little sunlight left. Sam grabbed a pair of heavy-duty handlamps from a shelf of tools and household accessories. Chris threw a bundle of rope in the backseat, along with an ice pick.

Kelly thought of all the possibilities and felt a tremor go through her body. She needed a drink to straighten out. As they hit the icy road, she realized with deepening dread that it may be a long while before she had access to a glass of bourbon.

Tank drove the Range Rover to its limits on the slippery roads. Twice they almost fishtailed into a snow bank. Sam pulled up the Lando Solo blog on his phone, reading it twice. They'd made a quick stop at his house for him to confirm with lead in his gut that Nicky wasn't home. Now, with the sun just about gone, they were headed for the most remote part of the town.

"I can't believe we're all following the route taken by a guy who calls himself Lando Solo," Sam said.

"Does it say he lives in Cloud Fucking City?" Tank said, slowing to take the next turn. His headlights turned on automatically, twin daggers stabbing the road ahead of them.

"Why would Nicky even give this thing the time of day? It's ridiculous," Sam said, scrolling to the top of the blog post.

Kelly said, "If they had blogs back when we were kids and one of us happened to write about what we saw, can you imagine what people would have said about us?"

"That's different," Tank said.

"How?"

"We weren't looking for a monster in the woods. This guy is an opportunist who may have led a couple of kids to a very dangerous place."

Sam knew that tone. He turned around to give Kelly a warning look. There would be no arguing with him. Not now.

Stephanie, sensing the same thing, said to Kelly, "Tank only gave me a few details. Can you tell me the rest?"

"You won't think I'm crazy?" Kelly asked.

"Then I'd have to think all three of you are crazy. After what we've been through, I can believe anything, even if I don't talk about it much."

A rush of words poured from Kelly's lips, including showing her the screen captures she'd loaded onto her phone. Sam watched Stephanie's expression turn more and more grave.

"It was at our house?" she gasped.

Kelly replied, "All of ours last night. Look, it was actually *in* my living room!"

Sam braced himself as the Range Rover hopped a curb at a dead end street.

"I'm gonna follow those snowmobile tracks," Tank said. "It might get a little bumpy. I have to keep moving so I don't get stuck, so everyone hang on."

He wasn't kidding. Tank drove the SUV like a man possessed, plowing over the pair of treads leading to the tree line. At one point, Sam was lifted off his seat and his head hit the padded roof.

Everyone shot forward into the seatbelts across their chests when Tank hit the brakes. The Range Rover slid another fifteen feet. Sam thought for sure they were going to wrap themselves around the trunk of a fast approaching pine tree. The SUV came to a merciful stop a foot from the tree.

"We'll have to go the rest of the way on foot," Tank announced, opening his door. The wind had picked up and was as bitter as the draft from a freezer.

Sam grabbed a handlamp, making sure Stephanie had the other. Tank snatched the rope and ice pick.

"It's best if we walk in the snowmobile's tracks," Sam said. "I'm sure they have to belong to Nicky and his friends. This way, we'll follow their every move and the snow will be packed enough so we don't fall through to our hips. Follow me."

The bright light from his handlamp bobbed along the path ahead of them.

"It's freezing," Stephanie said.

"All the more reason why we have to hurry," Tank said. "If the kids are hurt, they could freeze to death out here."

Sam tensed, then felt Tank's reassuring hand on his shoulder.

"We're going to find him and he's going to be fine," Tank said.

All Sam could do was nod and continue on. The snow crunched under their feet. It wasn't an easy trek. At points, each of them stumbled, taking a knee and needing help getting back up. Night had fallen but the sky was clear with a nearly full moon. They came to the point where Roy must have turned around. There was only one set of tracks to follow now.

"The pond isn't far ahead," Sam said, recalling far nicer days when he and Lacy would bring Nicky out here for picnics and nature walks. *My God, how will Lacy react if something's happened to Nicky? It would kill her.*

Sam wasn't sure it wouldn't kill him as well. He loved that boy more than anything in the world. He'd rearranged his entire life just to be closer with him. Swallowing hard to keep a bubble of vomit from breaking free, he trudged on, willing himself not to break from the group and run as fast as his legs would take him.

"Nicky!" he shouted. His son's name echoed in the darkness.

Tank bellowed, "Nicky! Christine! Shout if you can hear us!"

Years of barking plays on the gridiron had conditioned Tank's voice to where it was a thunderclap not to be ignored. Sam was glad that despite decades away from commanding the field in college, his friend still had the gift.

"There," Kelly said, pointing ahead through the V of a pair of ash trees. "I think that's where the pond is."

"She's right. Come on," Sam said, picking up the pace.

They stopped short when they came upon Christine's snowmobile. A light dusting of swirling snow blanketed the vehicle. Tank removed his glove and placed his bare hand on different parts of the snowmobile.

"It's ice cold. The engine hasn't been on for a while," he said.

"Why would they leave it behind?" Sam asked, his heart pulsing in his throat. Sweeping the area around the pond with the handlamp, he saw nothing but snow.

Stephanie said, "Let me see your phone, Sam."

Recalling the link to Lando Solo's blog post, she read it aloud, her words mashing into one another. When she came to the picture he'd posted, she said, "It looks like this guy was over there."

Kelly pointed her handlamp at the ground. Two sets of boot prints went from the snowmobile to the pond's edge, then followed the bank to the other side. "They got off and walked the rest of the way. Look."

Sam sprinted, his eyes locked on Nicky's size eleven boot prints. "Tank, check the pond," he called over his shoulder. A searing slash of white light skimmed the surface of the snow-covered pond. Thoughts of finding a break in the snow cover or the footprints veering onto the pond made Sam's chest tighten.

He heard the scrunch of snow behind him but didn't bother to see who was following. Having to slow down to keep from getting trapped in waist high snow on the far side of the pond, he had to carefully walk in his son's footsteps. Christine's own tracks were very close to his Nicky's. They had stayed close to one another, Nicky leading the way, guiding her through the drifts.

"Sam, wait up," Kelly cried out.

He ignored her request. If she had a child, she'd understand. Nothing and no one else mattered, not now.

A harsh gust of wind threatened to rip the breath from his lungs. It felt like microscopic icicles had been thrown at his face, in his eyes. Blinking hard and fast to stanch he pain, he was forced to stop. He'd come to the end of the tracks. Boot prints meandered in a small circle, following the tree line but not venturing past it.

Kelly pulled to his side, breathless.

"This is where they came, but there's nothing leading out," Sam said, feeling hysteria clawing for control. He swung the handlamp from left to right, exposing a mishmash of tracks.

"Stop!" Kelly barked.

"What? Why?" Sam said. The beam trembled.

Grabbing his arm, Kelly directed the light to a spot in the center of the prints.

"What is that?" she said, smoke flowing from her mouth and obscuring his vision.

Then he saw it. Sam dropped the handlamp.

"Tank, over here!"

He reached into his coat pocket, clutching the barrel of the pistol.

Chapter Twenty

Nicky woke up choking.

Chest hitching, he spasmed into a sitting position, desperately trying to draw a breath. Something was in his mouth.

His diaphragm twitched. A flow of hot bile dislodged from his throat, spilling onto his lap. The acrid taste made him wince.

It didn't matter that he was covered in puke. He could finally breath. His throat burned like hell. Pulling in breath after breath of cool air helped it a little.

Coughing up anything left clinging to his throat and mouth, he turned his head and spat. He saw that he was no longer on a dirt floor. A thick band of spittle hung from his lower lip, stretching to what looked like a steel-coated floor.

He was in a bed atop a very thin mattress. His coat, hat and gloves were gone.

Nicky looked around the room. It was small, just large enough to accommodate what appeared to be a hospital bed. There were no windows or doors. The entire room was made of some sort of smooth, polished steel. A lone light bulb hung from a chain over the bed.

Confusion made his head spin.

"Where am I?"

To his relief, he found that he wasn't strapped to the bed, for this place had the look and feel of a solitary confinement room in a utilitarian psych ward. Swinging his legs off the bed, he tried to stand. Instead, he fell back onto the bed. What had happened to him? It felt as if he'd been drugged.

Christine!

He remembered being with her at the pond, then waking up in some kind of dirt tunnel. Now he was here. What had happened during those periods of missing time? If he was here, in this cube of a room, where was Christine?

Planting his feet on the floor again, he gripped the edge of the bed and stood slowly. His head retained some semblance of equilibrium this time. He could shuffle around the bed while keeping hold of it and still touch the surrounding walls. There wasn't even a seam he could see. How the hell did he get in here? Through the ceiling?

Nicky pounded on a wall.

"Hello! Can anyone hear me? Somebody please let me out!"

No one answered.

There was no way he got here by accident. Someone intentionally brought him to this room. There had to be someone on the other side of these walls. He would have started to panic if he didn't feel so woozy.

"Hey! I'm awake now. Where am I? I want to get out now."

He had to lie down. If he didn't, he was going to be sick again. Resting back, he continued to kick at the wall.

The bulb flickered for a moment, threatening to cast him into complete darkness. He stopped kicking. The light in the room stabilized.

"What the?"

Nicky gave the wall one hard kick. The light dimmed and the bulb made a sizzling noise. He removed his foot from the wall. The wattage returned to normal.

Someone's messing with me. That means they can hear me.

"I promise to stop kicking the walls if you'll just open a door. Please. I...I don't know how I got here."

Nothing happened. All he could hear was his own breathing. He took the sheet off the mattress and used it to wipe the vomit from his shirt and pants.

And suddenly he remembered everything before the tunnel. He and Christine were at the spot where the Dover Demon had last been spotted. Something sucked Christine into the ground, just the way Lando Solo said the demon seemed to melt through the earth. Next thing he knew, he was being dragged down as well. How was that even possible?

"Where's my friend?" he said, holding his head in his hands. "I want to see her. We both fell into a sinkhole or something in the same place. Her name is Christine. I want to know if she's okay."

The light switched off. Nicky flinched. He couldn't see a thing. Bringing his palm to the tip of his nose, he couldn't even make out the outline of his hand.

For the first time since he was a little kid, he wanted to cry. He thought of his father, wishing him to magically appear.

He did cry, wondering if whoever was outside the room was happy that they had broken him so easily.

Christine licked her lips and tasted blood. Pushing herself up with her hands, she rolled onto her butt. She was no longer in the tunnel system.

Whatever had grabbed her had brought her to a cavernous room filled with wooden crates. Wire mesh covered the old time lamps dangling from the ceiling. It was like some kind of military storage room.

Standing, she felt as if she'd done three rounds of kickboxing. Her arms and legs ached where she'd been roughly manhandled. The small of her back throbbed. Her ribs barked every time she breathed in.

"Hello?"

She wished she'd gotten a good look at who had tackled her. There had to have been at least two of them. They'd kept her facing the floor as they dragged her down the tunnel. Neither had spoken a word. At one point, her head had bounced off the floor and she'd gone kind of fuzzy.

An iron door with a spoked wheel you'd find on a bank vault was to her left. They had thrown her in the room and slammed the door. She pulled at the handle, not surprised that it didn't budge. Christine tugged at the wheel, but it felt as if it was frozen in place by decades of rust.

"Asshole!" she shouted at the door, immediately regretting it. What if they came back in and roughed her up again? She backed away from the door, ducking behind a stack of wooden crates.

To her relief, they didn't come barging through the door.

But odds are, they would again at some time. She had to find a weapon. In this enormous storage place, there were plenty of places to hide. Maybe she could find a way to lie in wait and sneak out the door. She'd need something to defend herself with in case things got bad in a hurry.

"Let's see what's inside," she said, lifting the top off the crate she hid behind. Inside was nothing but brittle packing straw. It smelled mildewy, bordering on toxic. She quickly replaced the lid.

She carefully walked among the haphazard rows of crates, lifting the lids of the ones that weren't nailed shut, finding nothing but straw and shredded paper. Some of the crates looked like little coffins, the kind you saw in old western movies. There was no way she was going to look inside those.

If they brought you in here, maybe they did the same with Nicky.

She whispered his name. "Nicky, are you in here? Nicky."

Considering the way she'd been handled, she imagined how much worse they would have been to a boy. Maybe he was unconscious somewhere. On every turn, she called out for him softly so as not to alert whoever had dumped her in this place. Tears streaked down her face. Every crate was empty, Nicky never answered back and she couldn't find anything that even remotely resembled a weapon.

A part of her wanted to blame Roy for leaving them. If he'd been there, maybe he would have seen what happened to them and rushed for help. "Damn you, Roy."

She came upon a square box with a lid made of multiple slats of wood. Slipping her fingers under the lid, she pulled hard, popping it free. This time, she didn't even care to see what was inside. Propping the lid against another stack of crates, she kicked through its center, shattering it. One of the slats broke free with a jagged point, like a crudely made stake for vampire hunting. She gripped it with both hands.

At least now, she could protect herself.

The sound of squealing hinges caused her to stumble backward. Her back collided with a fifteen-foot tall stack of the coffin-like crates. The entire stack wobbled. Christine had to clamp her hand over her mouth to hide her gasp of alarm as she darted away from the shifting edifice. Two of the top crates canted to the left, slipping off the stack and crashing by her feet, missing her by inches.

This time she couldn't hide her shrieking.

A pair of bodies, brown and rotted and smelling like overripe fruit, tumbled from the crates. The head of one broke loose, rolling until it bounced against her feet, wild white hairs sprouting from its beef jerky skull. She reflexively batted the head with the wooden slat and ran into the depths of the storage room, no longer caring about who might now be in there with her.

When Tank and Stephanie made it to the clearing, they followed Sam's frozen gaze to the strange spot on the ground.

A perfect circle of ice, the diameter large enough to encircle three people, lay at their feet.

"What the hell is that?" Stephanie said.

"It's like a crop circle in the snow," Kelly replied. Tank noted that she was holding fast to Sam's arm.

Sam knelt by the circle. "I've been looking at all of the prints, trying to trace where they started and ended. It looks like Nicky and Christine were walking by the trees over there. After stopping for a while by that tree, they came here, right where the circle is."

Tank tapped the ice with the tip of his boot. "It's solid, Sam. But this is where the grass is, not water. This doesn't make any sense."

"Give me your ice pick," Sam said.

Tank handed it over. His friend hacked at the circle. Shards of ice flew in the air.

"Keep your hands and knees off the ice," Kelly warned him.

Sam hammered away, grunting with the effort. He stopped for a moment, pushing the edge of the pick under the ice and using the handle as a lever. He pushed on the handle until veins popped out along his temples.

Tank knelt by him. "Here, let me try."

Sam let go with great reluctance. His breath came in short gasps. "I think I hit bottom. If we can pry a good chunk up, I'll know for sure."

Tank threw all of his body weight into the handle. The ice groaned at first, then started to crack, sounding like the blast of a starter's pistol. A two-foot long wedge of ice popped free, sending Tank sprawling into the ice circle's center.

Stephanie cried out, "Tank!"

He felt her hands tugging on the cuff of his jeans, pulling him away from the center.

Sam shouted, "It's okay! He can't fall through. Look, it's all dirt underneath." She cast her light to the newly exposed ground.

Tank got up, brushing snow and ice from his clothes. "If that's solid ground, how the hell did that circle come to be? And where did Nicky go from here?"

Sam tugged at his chin with a wild look in his eyes. He turned to Kelly. "Where could it have taken them?"

"I...I don't know, Sam."

Tank recalled how the strange footprints around their houses just seemed to have appeared, with no entry or exit trails. It was eerily similar to this.

"You have a whole fucking room filled with stuff like this. How can you stand there and tell me you don't fucking know?" Sam blurted.

Tank gripped Sam's shoulders. "Take it easy, Sam. This isn't Kelly's fault."

"How do we know that? Maybe she brought the whole thing to us! You, me, Steph, we moved on, lived our lives. But Kelly couldn't let it go. Maybe it could sense that, and that's why it's come back here!"

Stephanie said, "I know you're upset, but that doesn't make any sense. Just calm down and we'll go to the police."

"Do you think what we saw makes any sense? Does what happened earlier today make sense? If we tell the police this, they'll throw us in a fucking drunk tank."

"What we need to do is report Nicky and Christine as missing. They don't need to know about all this other stuff, which we don't even know is at play here," Stephanie said.

Sam pointed an accusing finger at Kelly. "She sure as hell knows it. I want my son back. I don't care if it's just one of your bourbon-addled theories, tell me now where you *think* he is."

Kelly looked at them with wide, shimmering eyes. Her mouth opened and closed but she couldn't get the words to come out. Tank saw how badly her hands shook.

Finally, she said, "I wish I knew but I don't. No one does. When people connected with this thing go missing, they don't come back. They just don't."

Sam looked like he was going to hit her. Tank kept a tight grip on him. The wind was picking up and howling like a pack of wolves. If they stayed out much longer, they were going to get a serious case of frostbite.

Kelly started to cry. Stephanie put an arm around her.

"It's time to go to the police," Stephanie said. "They'll start a search party."

Tank wasn't so sure. If anything, they'd wait until morning, not wanting to endanger the searchers on a dark, freezing cold night.

"You said we were marked, Kelly," Sam said. "Marked for what?"

"For a return, like this," she said, each word quivering from her lips.

Tank was about to tell her to stop feeding into Sam's frustration when they were enveloped by a blinding white light.

Raising his hands over his eyes to shield them, Tank said, "What is that, a helicopter?"

Stephanie huddled next to him. "I don't hear anything."

She was right. Other than the wind, the night was devoid of any unnatural sounds, mechanical or otherwise.

Sam shouted at the light. "I want my son, you bastards! Come down here and face me! Come on!"

Kelly yelled, "No, don't look at the light. That's what they want you to do."

"What the hell does that even mean?" Tank said.

"It's a distraction," Kelly insisted.

He thought he saw something huge moving above the trees. It was a long, dark shape that blotted out the stars.

"There's something up there," Tank said. "Look, just past the light."

All four looked up and saw the rectangular object rotate around them. The beam remained steady, a cone of brilliance that seemed to dare them to break its boundary.

"I'm scared," Stephanie said.

Tank pulled her close. He couldn't believe the size of the thing. It could almost be mistaken for a blimp, except for the utter absence of sound. They marveled at it. Even Sam had grown silent.

They were caught in a beam of light emanating from a goddamn UFO. Tank couldn't come to grips with the absurdity of it. Was Kelly right? Were appearances of creatures like the Dover Demon associated with the whole UFO nut job phenomena?

And if she was correct, they should probably heed her warning.

He looked to her. Kelly's head was turning in every direction, searching for something around them.

"Kelly, that thing up there is real," he said.

"They want us to think that, yes," she replied.

"If it isn't real, what's going to happen next?" Stephanie asked, her hands wrapped around her husband.

"Nothing good, I suppose."

Tank watched as Sam pulled the gun out of his pocket, aiming it at the source of the light. "Sam, don't!"

"Let's see how they like it when someone turns the table on them," Sam said, squeezing off twin shots. The bullets whined high into the air.

The light suddenly shut off.

"I guess they didn't like it," Sam said with a dangerous edge to his voice.

Tank heard something moving within the trees. It was much too dark to see among the densely packed trunks, even with the handlamp.

"You shouldn't have done that," Tank said to Sam.

"It stopped their little game, didn't it? Kelly was right. It wasn't real. I mean, how could something that big just disappear like that?" Sam kept the gun in his hand, though he was smart enough to point it at the ground.

"We just need to keep our heads," Tank said. "We don't really know what we're dealing with."

Sam staggered to the ice circle.

"This probably isn't real either."

He shot two more bullets into the center of the circle. The ice shattered like glass.

Tank yelled, "Damn it, Sam! Cut it out!"

"They have my son! They need to know I'm not here to play their game." He faced the onyx woods. "You hear me? Give me my son!"

Tank hadn't seen Sam like this in decades. His friend had a lion's share of anger issues when they were growing up. A lot of therapy had channeled that misplaced anger into a focus and drive that made him a lot of money in very little time. Retiring early seemed to be the final polish to all of his hard edges.

The Sam Brogna before them now was the same one Tank had to save from taking on the Waltham varsity hockey team—alone. At the time, Tank wasn't sure who needed the help more, Sam or the team.

"Give me the gun, Sam," Tank said.

Stephanie added, "Please, before you hurt yourself."

Kelly stayed silent, eyes wide, looking beyond them.

Sam held up his hands. "Look, I'll put it back in my pocket. I've made my point."

Tank was worried. Sam looked one step away from madness. He had to get them back to the SUV, if only to warm up. It didn't look as if Sam would go quietly.

"Guys," Kelly said, barely above a whisper.

"Come on, let's get back to my truck so we can talk things out," Tank said.

"I'm not leaving here," Sam said. "You saw it. Whatever it is knows we're here. I'm ready to face it."

"Maybe you scared it off when you shot at it," Stephanie said. "We're going to freeze to death if we stay out here much longer. I promise we won't go far. Just to the truck for a little while."

Sam looked skyward, shaking his head.

Tank fell backward when Kelly barreled into him.

"Run!" she shouted.

They came out of the trees. There must have been ten of them.

The first thing Tank thought was *albino aliens.*

Pale creatures with enormous heads and orange-tinted eyes burst from the trees like a pack of panicked deer. One tackled Sam from behind. As they fell to the ground, they disappeared into the snow. Sam never even had a chance to shout in surprise.

"Oh my God!" Stephanie screamed.

Tank fumbled for his gun. Three of the creatures swarmed over Kelly, driving her into a snow bank until they, too, vanished.

Stephanie was ripped from his side, wailing for him to help her.

Turning to grab for her outstretched arm, he was smothered by several of the terrifying monstrosities. It felt like the entire world was pulled from under him. His head spun so hard, he blacked out, the last sensation to take with him being the oily feeling of their naked flesh on his exposed skin.

Chapter Twenty-One

Nothing was adding up. With plenty of time to think, Nicky couldn't piece together any relationship between the Dover Demon and where he was now. This solid steel prison of a room was something out of a sci-fi movie. The demon was, at best, some undiscovered animal that may or may not still be alive in the copious wooded areas of Dover. Animals didn't make places like this.

No, this had to be something else. Were the demon stories something concocted to keep people away from Dover? Like the way people said Area 51 was intentionally made into a cultural phenomenon to keep people looking in the wrong place. And if that was the case, what exactly were they, whoever *they* were, trying to hide?

"You watch way too many conspiracy shows," he said, sitting on the edge of the bed. The only positive was that his head finally felt clear. He could stand without feeling the world spin off its axis.

He got off the bed and walked to the wall, placing his ear against its cool surface, listening. If someone were on the other side, maybe he'd be able to hear them. He stayed that way for several minutes. Confronted by silence, he went to the next wall, repeating the process until he'd tried all four walls.

This room is probably soundproofed. I can't hear them and they can't hear me, unless they have the place bugged.

Why was he here? He was beginning to think he'd been placed in some kind of government quarantine. Why they would play with his head by threatening to turn out the light before was anyone's guess. There were plenty of assholes in the military, just as there were in any walk of life. He was in high school. He knew all about assholes in power. Right now, he was just glad they'd decided to turn the light back on.

What was worrying him most of all was not knowing what had happened to Christine.

Might as well try it again, he thought.

He slammed both fists on the wall. "Hey, wake up out there! Tell me what you did with my friend. You can keep me here if you want. Just tell me where she is."

This time, the light didn't flicker or dim.

There was a loud click, and he felt a rush of cooler air waft into the room.

One of the walls slid back, opening enough for him to walk through. Outside the room was total darkness.

Nicky hesitated. This could be some kind of trick. What if there was nothing on the other side of that wall? He could step into thin air and fall into some deadly cavern.

"That doesn't make sense," he said, walking slowly to the opening.

A steady draft blew into the room. Nicky shivered, wishing his coat was near. He hoped he wouldn't freeze his ass off if he left the room.

Maybe that's part of the test. See if I'm dumb enough to risk freezing to death just to see what's out there.

The way ahead was solid pitch. Standing at the threshold, he reached out, fumbling for the walls. His hands swept through chilled air. Gripping the edge of the wall, Nicky took a tentative step. His foot touched solid ground.

He called out, "Is anyone there?"

There was no echo. The air here reeked of mildew. Had he been placed in a room buried deep under the ground?

Nicky remembered his cell phone and patted his pockets. "Thank you," he sighed, pulling it from his back pocket.

Wait, how did it get there? I thought I had it in my coat pocket. Even if I didn't, I never put it in my back pocket.

Girls stuffed cell phones in their back pockets. As a guy, he was always afraid of sitting on it and breaking it in half if he did the same.

It's like they wanted me to find my phone.

He tapped in his security code and thumbed the Flashlight icon. The small, bright light illuminated the first few feet of the hallway leading from the room. Scratch that, it wasn't a hallway in the traditional sense, unless you were a mole living in an underground maze of dirt passageways. The earth here was so pungent, it reeked as if it had been recently excavated. He wouldn't be surprised to find dozens of wriggling worms, torn from their hidey-holes, at his feet.

Nicky took one look back at the room, then stepped into the tunnel. His phone was fully charged. Even though there were no bars, he tried to call home. The display showed CALLING, but a connection was never made.

"Okay, I guess you want me out here for some reason," he said, sure that someone was listening in. He swallowed hard, biting back the fear that waited impatiently to take hold.

He walked down the wide passageway, the phone's light bobbing from the floor to the stygian darkness ahead. The last thing he wanted to do was make a misstep.

"Christine! Christine, can you hear me?"

Maybe she was wandering around just like him, perhaps even just around the bend. There was no sense trying for stealth. Someone put him here. They responded to his hammering on the walls. They knew exactly where he was right now. There could be night vision cameras the size of buttons in the walls of the tunnel, following his every move.

If Christine didn't reply, he only hoped she wasn't anywhere near here. *Please let her be home, telling my father where we went.*

It was a dim hope, seeing as how she was the first to get sucked into the ground back by the pond.

The tunnel's ceiling inclined closer to the top of his head. Pretty soon, he'd have to duck to continue walking. He didn't like that. The closer it came, the more he could feel the weight of the earth above him. His breath came in shorter and shorter bursts. He stopped, closing his eyes, willing the rising panic away. It wouldn't do him any good to freak out right now. Maybe there would be time for that later.

Gotta take a deep breath…hold it…let it out through my nose. Again. Just chill. Stay calm. Breathe…one-two-three-four-five…let it out. Just think of it as walking in the house during a blackout. The walls and ceiling only seem closer because of the lack of light. Just making my way to the kitchen for a little blackout snack. I could go for a dozen pizza bagels right now. Wash them all down with a two-liter bottle of Pepsi. Keep walking. Every step brings you closer to that pizza.

After several breaths, his heart rate slowed.

Nicky opened his eyes, ready to move forward.

A pair of round, orange orbs hovered in the distance, back where the phone's light couldn't penetrate.

Could be rocks reflecting the light, he thought, not daring to take a step just yet. *In a perfect world, I'm back home and those are the lights on the toaster oven.*

He extended his arm, hoping to bring the orange objects into view.

They blinked.

Christine couldn't stop the tears. They blurred her vision, making it impossible to see the details of the rotted corpse beside her. For that reason alone, she saw no reason to stop crying.

If that crate had a body in it, odds are, there were corpses all around her.

What the hell was this place? Why were dead bodies being stored in stacked crates instead of graves?

Maybe this place is *a grave.*

The thought brought an icy chill that locked her muscles and tingled down her spine.

But why would a grave also be filled with a bunch of empty boxes?

Was Nicky in one of those coffin-shaped crates, his skin molting at this very moment?

Stop it! Don't think that. Nicky's alive. We just have to find each other.

Wiping her eyes, she edged around a crate, the corpse disappearing from her sight. She'd search the rest of this room, make sure Nicky wasn't there. And then what? She couldn't even make the door budge an inch.

Maybe there was another door, hidden behind the stacks. She had to keep on checking.

"Nicky," she whispered, on the move again. She would be extra careful not to bump into any more crates and she sure as hell wouldn't be prying lids off anymore.

Christine heard footsteps on the other side of the room. She stopped.

Holding the pointed slat in front of her, she held her breath, trying not to make a noise.

Scritch. Scritch.

It sounded like heavy boots with new soles scraping against the floor.

They were looking for her. She just knew it.

She wedged herself between two high rows of wooden boxes. She'd wait for whoever was in the room to walk by. If they spotted her, she'd thrust the makeshift stake at them and hope to hit something vital. If any shred of luck were on her side, they would simply walk past and leave the room.

Something foreign and primal in her recoiled at the thought of seeing what was in the room with her. It was as if she had lived through this before in another life, in a time when man was not the top of the food chain. She couldn't explain how or why she felt this way. Her body simply reacted to the presence as if the devil himself were stalking the rows.

The footsteps came closer, stopped for a moment, then resumed.

Christine tightened her grip on the shard of wood. The ragged point wavered in her trembling hands.

A shadow inked its way across the floor.

Scritch. Scritch. Scritch.

The narrow alley between the stacks of crates was filled by a tall, dark shape. Christine's heart slammed against her ribs. She wanted to scream. She ground her molars to keep her jaw from flying open.

The figure didn't move on.

The shoulders turned, now square with her hiding place.

It spoke.

"Nnghh. Nnghh."

A heavy hand swatted the stake from her grasp.

"No!" she shouted, her back banging into something heavy and immovable.

A hand reached for her, swatting at the air, missing her by inches.

"Nicky!"

Flinching from the flailing hands, cornered, Christine thought of the only thing she could do. She had to surprise whoever had come for her, do the one thing that made the least logical sense.

So she ran forward, colliding with the figure so hard, her breath was knocked out. They fell in a pile on the floor.

"Nnghh! Nnghh!"

Trying to rise and gulp fresh air, she saw the figure perfectly. If her diaphragm wasn't cramped, she would have screamed.

A man lay on his back, flailing about as if he were a turtle attached to an impossibly heavy shell. He wore black boots, pants and a heavy, wool sweater. His mouth worked like a fish on land, the only words being varying tones of *Nnghh*. She looked inside his mouth and saw he had no tongue!

His eyes were round with the darkest pupils she'd ever seen. His nose was small, coming to a sharp point. The flesh of his face was waxen, free of blemishes or any sort of character. It was like looking into the face of a mannequin.

He lashed out, trying to grab on to her ankle. Christine jumped back, unable to tear her gaze from the mannequin man. Why couldn't he get up?

The wooden stake lay on the floor by the man's flopping feet. She had to get it. She wouldn't make the same mistake twice and let him take it from her so easily.

Christine jumped over his torso. She felt his fingers graze her calves. She scooped up the stake and ran to the main entrance. With any luck, the mannequin man would have forgotten to close the door behind him.

Sam was shocked to realize that his face wasn't buried in snow.

Feeling a tremendous pressure at his back, his open mouth tasted the moldy earth.

What the hell?

Struggling to get up, something pressed hard on his back, shoving him down.

It was those things, the demon creatures that had attacked them. How had they ended up here?

It didn't matter. Right now, it was of paramount importance to get them off.

He thought of his son, felt his rage boil. If they had attacked Nicky like this, he would make them pay. Questions of what they were and where they came from could be asked later.

He felt blood and adrenaline flow into his legs and arms. With a heavy grunt, he started to rise.

Frantic hands pushed at his back and legs. He fought against them. Whatever they were, they made no sounds. They were merely phantom points of resistance.

"Get the hell off me!" he shouted, now on his knees. He heard something hit the floor behind him. The grasping at his body ceased and he was suddenly free.

Jumping to his feet, he saw that he was in some kind of underground tunnel. It was quite wide with a ceiling of close to seven feet.

He turned to face his attackers.

"Fuck me sideways," he said, fists clenched.

Three utterly alien creatures stood in a tight line a few feet from him. They were exactly what he had seen back in 1977—pale-bodied bipeds with unnatural orange eyes and heads that looked too big for their thin necks to support. They were covered in filth from their struggle in the tunnel.

It had taken nearly forty years, but he had found the Dover Demon once again—three, in fact. Their stomachs pumped in and out like tiny bellows.

He heard Stephanie scream, followed by Kelly. He couldn't see them in the spare light, but he knew they had to be close.

Why are there lights?

He spotted a couple of low wattage ceiling lights. What the fuck was this place?

Sam made a sudden movement toward the demons. They flinched, taking several steps back. Confidence swelling, he took two big strides toward them. The three scampered down the tunnel, wanting nothing more to do with him.

"Help!"

It was Kelly. Sam dashed toward the sound of her voice.

Rounding a bend in the tunnel, he spotted both women struggling with a pair of the demons. Sam grabbed one by the back of its neck, biting back the repulsion of coming in contact with its waxy flesh. He ripped it from Stephanie, tossing it at the wall. The demon was remarkably light. It had to weigh no more than a five-year-old child. It hit the wall and came to a tumbling stop. When it rose, it narrowed its coral eyes at him then dashed away, just like the others.

Before he could ask Stephanie if she was all right, he had to free Kelly. She was rolling along the tunnel floor, shrieking at the demon, its long fingers wrapped in her hair. Her gun, Betty, was on the ground, just out of reach.

"Kelly, stay on your back!" he shouted.

Their rolling came to a stop. Kelly locked her hands around its throat. The demon kept one hand in her hair, using the other to clamp over her mouth and nose.

"Oh no you don't," Sam said, rearing his leg back and kicking it as if he were going for a fifty-yard field goal in the Super Bowl. He caught the demon right in the ribs. It didn't so much as make a whimper. It did roll off Kelly, though its hand was still stuck in her hair. It pulled its legs up to its chest, in obvious pain.

"Get it off me," Kelly said, struggling to get her hair free.

"Hold still," Sam said, trying to work its thin, tapered fingers from her hair.

He froze when Stephanie said, "Sam, step back."

She had the ice pick over her shoulder.

Kelly's eyes went wide. "Wait, Steph, don't!"

Stephanie went to a knee and heaved the ice pick into the creature's wrist, severing it from the arm. A thick, milky fluid that smelled like rotting garbage oozed from the wound. Its fingers unfolded. Sam had no trouble extracting it from Kelly's hair.

The demon's body relaxed and it closed its eyes. It chest rose once, then settled for good.

They watched whatever color it possessed leach from its flesh until it almost became translucent. The opaque liquid continued to flow, its body deflating.

Sam nearly retched from the stench. As curious as they were, they had to step away as its death odor overwhelmed them.

"Thank you, Steph," Kelly said, breathless, hanging on to Sam. She reached down to retrieve her gun.

"That's one less to worry about," Sam said.

Stephanie looked at them with tears welling in her eyes. She said, "Where's Tank?"

Chapter Twenty-Two

Tank may have been disoriented, but he still knew how to point his gun and shoot.

Blam!

The bullet tore a chunk off the shoulder of the creature tugging at his left arm. It spun away, white froth spewing from the wound. Tank drew his knee into the creature by his legs. The demon tumbled to the other side of the tunnel.

How he went from the snowy night above to this underground lair was of no consequence. The five Dover Demon-esque things that were scrambling over him, trying to get him down, merited all of his fuzzy concentration.

It was high school all over again, Tank beneath of pile of rabid defensemen on a crisp Saturday morning, the chanting of the cheerleaders a distant hum, hands scrabbling at him, trying to punch the ball from his grip. And somehow, Sam's voice could always be heard in the scrum, 'You got 'em right where you want 'em, Tank! Don't drop that fucking ball!"

Except Sam wasn't here now, and he was pretty sure if he could see beyond these nightmarish creatures, there wouldn't be any pretty co-eds in short skirts waving their pom-poms. Somehow, this week's game was being hosted in hell and the away team was out of time outs.

It seemed like more had joined the fray. He couldn't tell where they were coming from because the spider-like fingers of a demon behind him kept raking at his eyes.

Tank threw a wild elbow, hoping to knock it off. He hit something, but it wasn't the one at his back.

One of them attempted to tackle him at the waist. He placed the barrel of the gun against its slimy flesh and pulled the trigger. The head gave way as if it were made of a thin-coated candy with a reeking, gelatinous surprise in the center.

The one on his back slid off, as did the other three.

Tank turned on them. "Come on! You want some more?"

The absurdity of the situation couldn't hack its way through his addled senses.

Flipping the gun in his hand, he loosed a roundhouse punch, pistol-whipping the nearest demon. He felt the crackle of its eye socket, watched the orange glow dim as it hit the ground.

Where's the whistle? That has to be a personal foul!

He guessed that was enough. The ones that could still stand turned tail and ran, fleeing into the darkness.

The two demons he'd shot were dead. He could tell just from their ghostly pallor, not to mention the copious amount of fluid that was leaking out of them. Two others lay still, eyes closed, but chests still moving.

Tank hovered over the one he'd kicked, nudging it with his boot.

"What are you?" he said, though he wasn't entirely sure he was speaking to the creature. He'd be damned if it didn't look exactly like the Dover Demon he'd encountered all those years ago, which in turn looked just like what people called a gray alien, though this thing's skin was many whiter shades of pale. He recalled cave paintings found in Charama in India that had caused a recent stir. The 10,000 year-old images looked like traditional large-headed aliens alongside some kind of craft. They were far from the only ancient depictions of what modern man would deem extraterrestrials. Cave art and petroglyphs depicting alien-type creatures could be found all over the world, some of them thousands and thousands of years old.

Jesus. Are these things related to that?

The sudden collision of science with science fiction made his head ache.

In the melee, he hadn't had time to consider the high strangeness that none of the creatures had made even the slightest sound as they fought, and died, against him. Now, it chilled him.

Looking at the lights, he said, "What is this place? How did you get us here?"

The demon opened its eyes to narrow slits. Its lids operated like a lizard's, the bottom and upper lids meeting in the middle.

They hadn't felt like lizards, which were typically dry and scaly. These things felt as if they were coated in cold pudding, which was pretty much what the stuff seeping from them looked like. The thought turned his stomach.

His adrenaline levels subsiding, he also finally noticed the horrible odor coming from their wounds. If he had to go by smell alone, he'd swear they were made of toxic sludge. Spatters of it covered his coat and pants. He removed his coat and kicked it away. It wasn't very cold down here and he didn't want to be in the vulnerable position of being on his knees, throwing up.

Looking down each end of the tunnel, he shouted, "Stephanie! Sam! Kelly! Hey, are you down here?"

His cries were swallowed up by the absorbent soil.

Tank's vision wavered, and for a moment he thought he might pass out. Whatever the demons had done to get him down here had really fucked with his head. He wiped at his nose with the back of his hand. Blood smeared across his calloused flesh. He imagined this is how it would feel to be dragged through a wormhole.

Sitting as far from the rotting bodies as he could, he called out again.

"Steph! Are you down here? If you can hear my voice, just say anything. I'll come to you. Stephanie!"

He knew he had to get his head in order before attempting to walk. Arms resting on his knees, he kept his gun tight in his grip, waiting for the little creatures to return.

"Do you hear that?" Stephanie said.

"What is it?" Sam asked, keeping his voice low as possible.

"It sounded like a voice. I couldn't make out what it said."

Kelly rubbed her back. "Do you think it could have been Chris?"

Stephanie turned on her. "His name is Tank. I know you liked to call him Chris to bust his balls when we were kids, but enough's enough."

Kelly backed off. "I…I'm sorry. I'm just not used to calling him by his nickname. I haven't called him anything for over thirty years."

Stephanie sighed and she shook her head. "I'm sorry. I'm just scared."

Sam put his arm over her shoulder. "Come on, let's keep moving. Maybe we'll get closer to the source of the voice. If it's Tank, that big mouth of his will lead us right to him."

He gave her a squeeze and smiled. She could see he was frightened, but not so much that he couldn't try to lighten her mood. She also figured he thought the voice might be Nicky's and he wanted to get moving as fast as he could.

There was a sharp pop, followed by the distinct sounds of a struggle.

"That has to be Tank!" Stephanie cried, running headlong down the tunnel. She heard Sam and Kelly keeping up right behind her. Her focus was so narrow—find her husband—that she couldn't take in where they were or the fact that she'd just hacked the hand off a creature from her nightmares. She wouldn't dare do that until she was back in Tank's arms.

"Steph, slow down. We don't know what could be waiting for us," Sam pleaded.

Stephanie ignored him, as well as Kelly's urgent request to at least take it to a slow jog.

Cold droplets of sweat rolled down her back. Pumping her arms and legs, she pressed as hard and fast as she could.

"Steph, are you down here?"

It was Tank!

If her heart wasn't beating so fast and her breath wasn't bursting so hot and furious, she would have been able to answer him.

Something gnarled and unforgiving snagged her left foot, sweeping her legs out from under her. She went down hard on her back. Dazed, she saw Sam reach down, black specks clouding her vision. She tried to move her left leg but it was held firmly to the floor.

She panicked, kicking and struggling like a drowning woman.

"Hold on, Steph!" Sam said, kneeling at her feet. "Stop kicking."

Kelly stopped alongside her, pale-faced and out of breath. She looked like she was about to pass out.

"Just follow the sound of my voice," Tank said from somewhere nearby.

Sam said, "You're caught up in the thickest root I've ever seen. I think it'll be easier if we slip your foot out of your boot."

"But...Tank," she said, the act of speaking feeling like darts thrown into her lungs.

"He sounds like he's all right. We can't do anything until we untangle you, though." Sam grabbed the bottom of her boot. "Okay, now slowly see if you can pull your foot out."

Wriggling back and forth, she angled her foot so it could slide out of her heavily insulated boot.

"I'll go ahead and find Tank," Kelly said, regaining a small measure of color in her cheeks.

"No, wait for us. We have to stick together," Sam said. Stephanie's foot was almost out of the boot. The roots were jagged. Pinpricks of fire erupted on the exposed skin of her ankle as she rubbed against them. It was like petting a shark against the grain of its dermal denticles.

"He can't be far," Kelly said, stepping away from them as if she were in some kind of trance.

"Kelly, don't," Stephanie said. "I'm almost there."

"He's just around that corner," Kelly said.

"Kelly, just hold still, I mean it," Sam barked, guiding Stephanie's foot through the brambles as best he could.

Their old friend kept walking.

"Hurry, Sam. I think something's wrong with her," Stephanie said.

Before she turned round the bend, Kelly cast one look back at them. Stephanie gave her foot a final tug and she was free.

"It's all right, Kel, I'm coming," she said.

Kelly pointed down the unseen passageway. "I think he's just down there." Her voice sounded like someone emerging from a deep sleep.

"Let's all see, together," Stephanie said, holding onto the boot Sam handed her. She could put it back on her foot once they caught up to Kelly.

Kelly's head rolled downward. "I feel funny," she said.

Stephanie and Sam were only a dozen or so feet from her when the air between them grew hazy. It was like staring at the waves of heat rising from baked asphalt. She reached out, her fingertips grazing the odd disturbance. Her arm pulled back, fingers frozen.

"Sam, don't," she warned when he tried to move past her.

The haze shifted like flowing magma. They could barely discern Kelly's still form on the other side of it.

And then she was gone. She hadn't moved. She hadn't slipped out of view down the next passage. One second she was there, swaying as if in a trance, and the next she simply disappeared, along with the mystical miasma.

Sam shouted, "Kelly!"

Instead of Kelly, they heard Tank reply, "Hey, where are you?"

Stephanie was more reluctant this time, wincing as she passed through the space where the vapor had been. There was no sign of Kelly, but also no glacial sensation.

"Tank!" she said. She didn't even feel the icepick as it slipped from her grip, hitting the dirt with a barely audible *thwap.*

"Down here," he answered.

She tugged Sam's sleeve to get him to go with her.

"What happened to Kelly?" he said, unable to move from where she'd been standing just a moment before.

"I don't know. Let's get Tank and we'll look for her together." Sam reluctantly followed, looking over his shoulder for Kelly to reappear.

Stephanie found her husband leaning against the wall at the end of the long tunnel. He looked ragged but unhurt. She noticed the gun in his hand, resting against his leg.

Pulling her to his barrel chest, he said, "I got a couple of 'em. The others ran off." She could hear the steady thud of his heart.

He said, "Sam, where's Kelly? I thought I just heard her."

Sam shook his head as he walked around the demon corpses. "They took her someplace else," he said. "I have a very strong feeling we're being played with."

Nicky retreated back to the sterile room the moment he realized the orange orbs were eyes and that those eyes most likely belonged to the Dover Demon. What else could it have been? He couldn't think of any animal that had orange glowing eyes the size of saucers.

He pulled up just short of the steel wall that prevented his access to the room.

Kicking at it, he shouted, "Open the damn door! Let me in!"

The irony of begging to get back inside the room wasn't lost on him. Casting a quick look behind him, he saw nothing, but he could hear the steady approach of the demon.

Now punching the solid wall until his fists both tingled and throbbed with waves of agony, Nicky cursed like never before. Any second now, those alien hands would have him in their grip. The muscles of his back twitched with unholy anticipation.

"I'm sorry," he said, snot running freely from his nose. "Please...please let me back inside. I won't bother you again. I promise!"

Kicking and punching and begging did no good. The wall remained in place.

Terrified of facing the creature, but even more so of being taken from behind, Nicky turned to face the pitch passage, his back pressed against the cold steel wall. The light from his phone was pointed at the floor. It danced along his shoes, his hand trembling as if he had palsy.

He didn't even have keys in his pocket he could use as a weapon.

Its eyes are so big, maybe so it can see in the dark, Nicky thought. *It stayed back in the shadows before, even though it could've jumped out and gotten me. Maybe it's afraid of the light. It might even hurt it.*

That was pretty much the rule with nocturnal creatures. What the laws of nature had to do with this place was yet to be determined.

Something scraped across the dirt floor in front of him.

It was there! Probably close enough for him to touch it if he could will himself to take one small step.

If a bright light was his only form of defense, he knew he was fucked. It was like bringing a feather duster to a boxing match. But hadn't David defeated Goliath with a slingshot and a well-aimed rock?

Oh Jesus, don't let them be giants like Goliath, he thought, cursing the one time any of his Bible school lessons had popped into his head outside of church.

Just do it!

Tightening his grip on his phone, Nicky swung it upwards, stopping when it was at chest height.

The creature hissed, a foul odor that made Nicky's diaphragm hitch uncontrollably.

It had a large, pale, hairless head. In the harsh light, it clamped its too-large eyes shut, covering its face with a hand that defied explanation. The palm was small in comparison to the five long fingers that extended from it. In that brief moment, Nicky thought the fingers were so elongated, they had to possess extra sets of knuckles just to function properly.

All that really mattered was that he was right. The demon shrank away, backing up to where it had come. Nauseated but emboldened, Nicky stepped toward it, the phone's light outstretched like a crucifix in an exorcism.

"You don't like that, huh?" he said.

The alien beast was all of four-feet tall with a scrawny body dotted with goose flesh. It stood and moved like a human, and if he only saw its body, he would have believed it to be a child. But its face defied classification, and the feet were very much like its hands. Tubular, skinny toes scratched furrows in the dirt as Nicky drove it deeper into the tunnel.

For as long as he could remember, Nicky had wanted to have his own sighting of the town's infamous cryptid. He wished he could go back in time and take back all of that wasted time spent dreaming of this moment.

This wasn't the stuff of wishes fulfilled by a genie. This was every child's nightmare, the boogeyman living just beneath your feet, breathing in your ear as you burrowed your head deeper into the pillow, too scared to turn.

He kept moving forward just as the creature continued to back away. If he had to walk for miles in this underground maze while keeping it at bay, he would. Along the way, he had to find Christine, then locate the exit to this hellhole.

The creature's eyes dared to open a crack. Nicky responded by thrusting the light closer to its face. If he'd actually touched its flesh, he was pretty sure his resolve would crumble. He'd have to be more careful.

It hissed again and another wave of noxious fumes washed over Nicky. For a scary moment, he almost doubled over to puke, thereby taking the light off the demon. Searing bile splashed the back of his teeth but he held his ground.

"You'd like it if I got real sick, wouldn't you?" he said to the mute creature.

He looked for other passageways or doors, any break in the monotonous earthen warren that might lead to Christine.

"Christine, can you hear me?" he shouted. Vile smelling spittle poured over his lips onto his shirt.

I can't stop puking on myself!

Just over the demon's narrow shoulder was a sharp turn. It must have sensed it, because it was able to slither around it without a misstep. Nicky was quick to make the turn himself and keep it captured in the beam of light, lest it try to attack him.

Rounding the corner, his knees turned to jelly.

Every square inch of the tunnel was filled with demons, some clinging to roots sprouting from the walls and ceiling.

"Holy shit," he muttered, his feet tripping on themselves as he tried to stumble back. The light only affected the trio of demons in the front. The rest opened their slits of mouths and unleashed a dozen toxic hisses. It was like being hit in the face by the gangrenous bowels of a festering landfill.

There was nothing he could do to hold back his insides. Nicky's shoulder keranged off the wall and his vision went out of focus.

The demons approached him.

"Get back!"

Despite the heaving of his stomach, he waved the light in their faces.

It was dimming!

With quick, jerky movements, the posse of demons surrounded him.

"No, no, no, no!"

Nicky watched with increasing dread as the battery indicator on his phone flat-lined to empty. The light winked out.

Acting with a hive mind mentality, the demons pounced on him. He screamed so hard, no sound escaped his throat.

Kelly was on her hands and knees, shivering in snow that was up to her elbows. The cold air snapped her back to her senses.

What the hell just happened?

She was back in the woods, though not by the pond. She'd come out of the tunnel into a circle of trees. The moon looked as if it were just overhead, casting its silvery glow on her like a spotlight.

Getting to her feet, she yelled, "Sam! Stephanie! Tank! Hello!"

How had she gotten here? The wooziness she'd felt before the air got all fuzzy and strange in the tunnel was wearing off. It reminded her of how she'd felt riding the rollercoaster at Dorney Park. While she was on it, her insides were a jumbled mess. Hitting the loops and sharp turns, she was sure she was on the verge of an out-of-body experience. Once she was off the ride, that electrical sensation would gradually subside and she'd be back to her normal self.

Going into the tunnel and then back out was just like being on that rollercoaster, only her brain felt crispy around the edges, as if one of her senses had shorted out.

Nothing in all of her focused research had prepared her for this. This was more along the lines of people who'd had alien encounters while in the midst of transcendental meditation. During deep TM, people had reported seeing strange beings while weaving through rips in the fabric of reality. There were no laws of physics in these cases, just the fleeting moments of mind-altering *experience*.

It was absolutely freezing out here. With no idea where she was, Kelly knew time was running out fast. If she didn't find shelter soon, she'd die. It must have been ten degrees without the wind. If she went the wrong way, she could be lost in the woods.

She looked around. There were no prints in the snow. Somehow, she'd just appeared here, just like the demons that had walked around her house and entered her living room.

"Wormholes," she said, teeth chattering.

Her muscles were starting to cramp up. A tiny chisel banged away at the inside of her skull. It was her body's way of warning her that if she didn't get a drink soon, there would be dire consequences.

Damn it, how can I help myself or anyone else if I can't even go a few fucking hours without a drink?

For the first time in years, she regretted ever picking up that first bottle—a fifth of Jack Daniels the night after they'd come across the Dover Demon. She'd taken it from her father's overflowing liquor cabinet, scurrying up to her room and downing a quarter of the bottle while sitting on her floor and staring out the window. It was the only way to clear the disturbing images from her head. From that night on, sleep, wonderful oblivion, came at a price.

She felt like crying, but for whom? Herself? It had been a long time since she'd cared enough about herself to even consider shedding a tear. Was it Sam? Yes, she'd loved him at one time, but that was a lifetime ago. They were different people now, and even without the drinking she was sure they could never be more than passing acquaintances. Tank and Stephanie had become strangers.

No, it was for Nicky and Christine. They were down there, somewhere—lost, confused, terrified. Even if they somehow survived this night, their lives would never be the same.

Kelly wept because she knew what they would become. Many nights, she prayed for it to end, to take her in her sleep.

A powerful light swept over the trees to her left.

She looked up, scanning the sky for more phantom ships. Only the stars blinked back at her.

Where did that come from?

Another beam of light stabbed *through* the trees, capturing her in its jaundiced glow.

"Oh!"

That out-of-body feeling engulfed her again. Her stomach dropped as if she were barreling down the steepest decline of the rollercoaster.

The snow at her feet swirled up in a tight cyclone, stinging her face with tiny icicles. She watched in horror as the moon raced down to squash her. It slipped onto the snow's cool surface, riding the undulating hills until it passed under her feet! Kelly's eyes rolled painfully in her head as she followed its ascent back into the night sky.

She closed her eyes to stop the vicious spinning in her brain.

When she opened them, she was in a dark room.

She lay on a table, her wrists and ankles bound by heavy straps.

Struggling to free herself, Kelly kicked and shook her arms as much as the restraints would allow.

A voice behind her said, "It will be painful if you don't sit still."

Christine's heart leapt when she spotted the open door.

I have to get out of here!

She burst out of the room, pushing the heavy door until it closed. From this side, she couldn't find a way to lock it. There was no time to look for something, a rock or thick root, to wedge under the door. She didn't want to be anywhere near it if and when the mannequin man regained his senses and came back after her.

Running down the dimly lit tunnel, all she wanted to do was put as much space between her and that waxen-faced man as possible.

She wanted to cry out for Nicky, but thought better of it. She doubted there was just one person down here. All of this wasn't the work of a solitary man, especially one that didn't even look like he should be alive.

Instead, she ran as silently as possible down passageway after passageway, her fear of being lost forever increasing with each frenzied step. Her parents would never have peace, wondering if she was alive or dead, even after going through the motions of a funeral, the centerpiece an empty coffin.

It felt as if she were running in a circle, though she hadn't come upon the steel door to the storage room…yet.

We should have gone back home with Roy! But I wanted to do something with Nicky and be close to him. He was so dead set on going to the Dover Demon site. How could I turn around when we were so close?

Your crush may have cost you your life.

Both your lives.

Roy had to have alerted their parents by now that she hadn't come back. She didn't know what time it was, but it felt like she'd been trapped here for hours, if not an entire day. It was hard to tell with all the blocks of missing time. They could be standing right above her head at this moment, calling for her, and she had no way of hearing them.

A bass heavy, warbling sound pulsed through the tunnel. Christine stopped. The ominous note rattled her insides. Clutching her stomach, she bent over, watching the dirt sway beneath her feet. She almost toppled over, blasted by vertigo.

The sound ceased, as did the gravitational pull of dizziness.

Exhaling the breath she'd held, Christine stared down the gloomy tunnel. Something seemed different. It looked longer than it had before, stretched into a terrifying infinity.

She took a tentative step, finding she could move without falling on her face. Walking, not running now, one hand stayed in contact with the earthen wall, her fingertips grazing over wet dirt, ragged roots and the blunt edges of buried rocks.

Why does it feel like I've been moved somewhere else?

The lights were a bit brighter, the wooden support beams that popped up intermittently seemingly made of fresher wood.

She choked back a gasp when her hand came in contact with a solid, metallic door. There was no handle, no visible hinges. Maybe it wasn't a door, but some kind of support plate. Gathering her courage, she made a fist and rapped lightly on the door. It sounded hollow, as if there was an open space on the other side.

Looking up and down the tunnel with rabbit glances, she knocked again, louder. When there was no answer, she pressed her ear to the door.

Was that an electric hum?

"He…hello," she said, her lips inches from the door.

She knocked once…twice…was about to ask if anyone was on the other side when the slab of metal flew open as if a hurricane wind had shattered it from the frame.

"Oh my God, no!"

A trio of pasty creatures squatted around a man's body lying on the ground. They looked almost exactly like the few pictures of the Dover Demon she'd seen in books, websites and TV shows.

All of them turned to her, their impossibly large, cantaloupe eyes burning a hole right through her soul.

The man on the floor was unconscious. He only wore an undershirt and boxers. He looked to be middle-aged, with a potbelly and salt and pepper mustache. She didn't think he was breathing.

One of the demons had its hand snaked up the pant leg of his boxers, reaching for what—his penis?

The other two had their long-fingered hands on his chest. She had definitely interrupted them from doing something very wrong to the unconscious man.

Christine backed away, colliding with the wall behind her.

The demon with its hands in the man's underpants rose, stepping to the door. Its long, flat feet made disturbing squishing sounds when it walked.

"No, no, please, just leave me alone."

Her mind screamed for her to run but her legs were locked in place. Those alien orange eyes kept her rooted to the spot. Within them she sensed something both feral and intelligent, a primal force that studied her like an X-ray.

When it reached a hand to touch her, she lashed out with the wooden stake. It caught the creature across its chest. An angry wound opened slowly, weeping a thick fluid that looked like liquid fabric softener, except it smelled like death itself.

The demon's mouth opened but no sound came out, merely a strangled hiss that spewed horrid breath in her face.

Seeing what had happened, the other two demons were on their feet, charging from the room.

Christine ran, feeling them close behind.

Chapter Twenty-Three

Sam felt time slipping through his fingers. Nicky had to be down here somewhere. So was Christine. And now Kelly was missing.

The kids were the priority. Kelly had spent her entire life looking into the whole Dover Demon thing and the strange phenomena she was sure was related to it. If anyone could keep their heads and have an inkling of what was going on, it would be her. In fact, without her, he felt they were slightly disadvantaged.

He, Tank and Stephanie jogged down the tunnel, stopping at a fork.

Tank said, "Do we split up?"

"No way," Sam said. "I have a feeling that would be a very bad idea."

"Let's go left then," Stephanie said.

They had just made the turn when they were dropped by an onrush of lightheadedness.

"Crap, I think I'm gonna pass out," Tank said, taking a knee.

"I can't see. Everything is blurry," Stephanie said.

Sam felt it in his gut, turning end over end. Back in college, he and some guys from his fraternity had found an old truck tire at the dump, where they'd been looking for a replacement wiper motor for Sam's Chevy Nova. They brought the tire back to the frat house, and after many beers, twenty of them rolled it to the hill atop which Dormley Hall stood. Sam took the first turn, slipping into the tire and hollering at them to let it go. He spun end over end faster than he believed possible. The tire spit him out before it hit the bottom of the hill, speeding across the empty parking lot until it smashed into the fence by the cafeteria. After Sam had thrown up every beer he'd possibly ever drunk, he declared he was going to try it again.

That spinning sensation in that tire that had turned his stomach to mush had been exactly like this.

As suddenly as it began, it stopped.

They were back at the fork. Only, to Sam, it felt as if they were now facing the opposite direction.

"What the hell was that?" he said.

Tank helped his wife to her feet.

"It felt like we just stepped onto the Tilt-a-Whirl while it was in full swing," Tank said.

"Does this look right to you?" Sam asked.

Stephanie shook her head. "This doesn't even look like the same fork. See, the support beams are different, darker even."

Before Sam could answer, the feeling returned. He had to clamp his eyes shut to stop the tunnel from spinning out of control.

When he opened them, the stars stared down at him.

"Huh?"

He lay atop a tremendous mound of snow. It was deathly cold.

"Tank? Steph?"

"Down here," Tank said. They were struggling to get out of the snow at the base of the mound.

Sam slid down the mound on his ass. He glanced around, unable to discern any familiar landmarks. It looked as if they were in plot of snow-covered farmland. "Goddammit." He kicked the snow.

If he thought he was miles away from finding his son down in the tunnels, he was a world away now. It took everything in him not to succumb to utter helplessness.

"Where are we?" Stephanie asked her husband.

"I have no idea. If there was a road or a house or any kind of structure nearby, I might be able to tell you. This looks like the literal middle of nowhere."

Sam tapped the side of his head. "What is the possibility that we're actually still down there, that this is all in our heads?"

Stephanie shivered. "I can feel my toes going numb, Sam. It hurts to even breathe out here. I don't think that's in my head."

"A person's mind can be manipulated into believing anything, right down to experiential events of all five senses. I told you I think we're being played with. This is all a game to them."

Tank said, "Them? You mean the alien-fairies that Kelly talked about? I don't think we should be buying everything she said, man. Whatever this is, it's beyond her. It might be beyond anyone."

"How the hell are we supposed to find Nicky when we can't even walk a straight line without being turned upside down?" Sam's blood rushed in his ears like a tsunami tide, deafening him to Stephanie's reply.

He did see a wave of pain wash over her face. She faltered against Tank.

"I don't feel good," she moaned.

Tank held her up by her elbows. "I've got you, honey. Just lay right into me. I won't drop you."

Sam's eyes grew large as he watched the snow around his friends undulate. Tank and Stephanie started to sink into it as if it were quicksand.

"Sam, grab Steph!" Tank yelled, trying to lift her out of the sucking snow.

"Tank, what's happening?" Stephanie said, her eyes rolling up until all Sam could see were the whites.

"Take my hand," Sam said, kneeling at the edge of the eddying snow.

Tank made a flailing attempt and missed. He and Stephanie were now chest deep in the snow.

"Run and get help, Sam!" Tank said.

Sam knew how futile that would be. No one would believe him. He'd be the main suspect in the disappearance of five people, time wasted when everything the police and military had possession of should be focused on this place.

Just as the snow was swallowing Tank's head, Sam leapt into the center of the quicksand snow. Plunging headlong, he was dragged into a dizzying vortex where light and sound held no sway.

Sam next found himself strapped to a table.

Tank was bound to another one on his right. His large friend fought the thick bindings wrapped around his wrists, ankles and chest.

"I'm done asking what the hell," Sam said, trying to raise his arm.

"We have to get out of this," Tank said, his voice tinted with desperation.

Sam struggled, barely able to move an inch. The table swayed with his exertions.

"Gnnnnggghhhh!" Tank groaned, the leather cuffs creaking.

When that didn't work, he thrashed about like a man being electrocuted.

"Take it easy, Tank!" Sam said. "You're not going to free yourself by freaking out."

Lifting his head as much as he could, Tank motioned across the room. Sam noticed that they were in something akin to a medical exam room, though without the eye charts or scales. The white walls were tattooed with scuffmarks and there was a moldy smell that seemed to come from everywhere. He followed Tank's level gaze.

Stephanie and Kelly were tied down to tables or gurneys as well. Their eyes were closed, their breathing steady. They looked to have been drugged.

"I'll snap my fucking wrists if I have to," Tank said. A thick vein popped up in the center of his forehead. The flesh of his face purpled from the strain.

"Hold on. The girls are on tables with wheels, which means we probably are, too. Try to move your body around so you can bring yours closer to mine. I'll try to undo the buckle on your restraints."

Tank followed his directions, jerking his massive body in Sam's direction. The table started to move, inch by agonizing inch.

"I'm gonna kill the motherfucker that put us here," he said between clenched breaths.

"You and me both, after we find Nicky and Christine."

"I'm afraid that won't happen," a man's voice said.

Sam and Tank swiveled their heads from left to right, searching for the speaker. Of all the things Sam had come to expect, another human was surprisingly not one of them.

"Who are you?" Sam said.

"No one you need to concern yourself with. I instructed your women to remain still but they didn't listen. Luckily, shock from the pain has made them quiet."

"Pain? What pain?" Tank bellowed.

Sam's fingers brushed against the buckle at Tank's wrist.

There's no way I can get him out of that, Sam thought. It was tighter than a drum skin.

"The same pain you'll experience if you don't cooperate," the man said.

"Why don't you at least show your face, you fucking coward," Tank said.

Sam heard the man walking behind them, just out of their sightline.

"What would be the point?" he said.

"At least tell us what this place is," Sam said, stalling for time. It sounded as if Tank was steadily weakening the straps at his wrists. If he kept talking, maybe the man in the shadows wouldn't be able to hear the protesting of the leather. "We have to be here for a reason. What's your acronym?"

"I don't understand," the man said.

"You have to belong to some black ops function of the government. Is it DARPA, the NSA, FEMA? How else can you have underground operations like this?"

Sam's nerves went on edge when he heard steel brush against steel.

If he's sharpening an axe, Tank better break out fast.

"We are not of any government. If we were, this would not be possible. Governments ultimately fail. Every society that's ever been on this planet has eventually burned itself out of existence. We cannot align ourselves with something so fragile. So to answer your question, we have no acronym."

Sam's brain spun. Was this guy fucking with him? He sure as hell wasn't an alien. If he was in charge of this operation, there had to be someone higher up pulling the strings.

Sam's table was bumped. It shifted inches to the right, away from Tank.

"Can I ask you something else?" Sam said.

"I don't know why."

"You have the upper hand here, mister. The least you can do is talk. I'm not even asking you to show your face."

"No. I prefer not to talk to you."

A high-pitched whine assaulted Sam's eardrums. When it stopped, he heard the whoosh of a door opening.

"Prepare them," the man said.

Sam heard people shuffling into the room.

"Prepare yourself," Tank said through gritted teeth.

Lifting his head off the table, Sam spotted three men with their backs to him, standing in front of Kelly and Stephanie.

"Hey, what are you doing?" he yelled. "Get away from them!"

One of the men lifted a solid black case the size of a guitar amp. He opened a pair of latches on the top and stepped away.

"Did you bring the others?" the man behind them asked.

All three shook their heads.

Sam's heart went wild. "Where's my son? I know you have him. Bring me to my son." Finding renewed strength, he fidgeted against his restraints.

"Get them...now," the man said.

One of the men left the room.

*Are they bringing Nicky and Christine here?*A part of him wanted nothing more than to see his son. But not like this. If Nicky was down here, he prayed he was somehow running free, close to finding a way out.

The man said, "Don't wait. We only have a small window."

The room was filled with the sounds of ripping fabric as the remaining men closed in on the women.

"Take your hands off them!" Tank shouted. The table Tank was on began to shudder.

The man trying to tear off Kelly's pants turned, distracted by the commotion.

Sam nearly screamed.

He had a human face, but nothing about it looked real. It was like staring into the blank eyes of a wax figure well before the sculptor had time to finish the intricate work to make its countenance come alive.

It's a mask. It has to be a mask. That's why they're allowed to be in front of us where we can see.

His eyes, solid aqua, with no whites whatsoever, gave Sam a cursory look, then turned back to the task at hand.

"Don't you touch my fucking wife," Tank commanded, bucking against the table.

"I told you to remain calm or we would make it painful," the man behind them said. There was no emotion in his voice. He was just stating a simple fact.

One of the men reached into the case. Slowly, he lifted its contents into the light.

It was an egg.

A large, gelatinous egg.

Sam had seen it before, back in 1977. It looked exactly like the eggs that had dropped from the Dover Demon in the middle of the road.

Stephanie came to and began to shriek.

"No! No! Get away from me!"

The man assigned to Kelly stopped what he was doing and grabbed Stephanie's legs to keep her from kicking.

"Accept the gift!" the man behind them said. "You will become one with a bloodline older than man itself. Take your honor with dignity."

"Don't you dare put that thing near my wife!" Tank barked.

"Tank! Help!"

Stephanie went wild, screaming so hard he thought she'd hurt herself.

Sam said, "What are you doing to her?"

The man didn't answer. Stephanie's legs were spread and locked into metal stirrups.

"Please, don't touch me with that thing," she begged.

"Aaaaaarrrrhhhhhhhh!"

There was a stupendous crash as Tank and the table clattered to the floor. One of his arms had broken free. The two men working on Stephanie didn't so much as flinch. They had their orders and there were going to carry them out like unfeeling automatons.

"I told you to remain calm!" the man said, for the first time showing emotion. Sam couldn't tell whether he was angry or startled. All he wanted was the chance to see the son of a bitch face-to-face before he set to work on him.

Tank quickly undid the ankle and chest straps. When he stood, one of his arms was still lashed to the table. He dragged it with him as he grabbed the two men by Stephanie.

Sam felt helpless, pinned to the table and still unable to see the man behind him. He watched Tank grab both men by their necks, flinging them backward. They stumbled on either side of Sam, crashing to the floor. The egg they had been holding dropped on the table between Stephanie's legs.

"Don't let it touch me!" she screamed.

Sam thought he saw the outer flesh of the egg pulse, as if in time with an internal heartbeat. Tank brought a meaty fist onto the egg, bursting it like an overripe melon.

"No! You mustn't," the man said, still clinging to the shadows.

After Tank freed Stephanie, he got to work on Sam. He was almost done when the two waxen-faced men tackled him by his midsection. Tank and the men slammed into the table Stephanie had been on. Clutching the sides of their heads, he crashed them together. Sam's stomach rolled at the crunch of bone.

Sam fumbled with the chest strap while Stephanie worked to break Kelly from her bonds.

Tank got up and helped Sam with the straps at his ankles.

Sam jumped off the table, eager to see the man who so coldly threatened to hurt them if they didn't cooperate.

"The gift!" he said, shaking as he cowered in a corner.

He was a man, as normal as Sam and Tank. With black hair parted at the side, a sharp nose and dressed in tan slacks and a white button down shirt, he was so unassuming, he could have been lost in a crowd of three. Yet, there was something disturbingly familiar about him.

Sam approached the man whose eyes wouldn't tear away from the demolished egg. He grabbed their captor by the throat.

"Now tell me, where the hell is my son?"

He looked at him with madness in his eyes. "You...you destroyed the gift. You don't understand what you've done."

Sam punched the man in the face. The sharp pain in his knuckles felt good.

"Again, where is my son? I don't care about your sick gift."

"What did you think you were going to do to my wife?" Tank said.

The man looked up at him. "She was going to host her gift. It cannot grow without a host."

"You were going to put that thing *inside* me?" Stephanie said. Sam's eyes shifted. He saw Kelly clinging to Stephanie. She looked dazed.

"Naturally," the man answered. His head snapped back and he momentarily broke free from Sam's grasp when Tank landed a meaty fist in the center of his forehead. He lay on the floor, arms and legs splayed, eyelids fluttering.

Sam turned on his friend. "I need him to tell me where Nicky and Christine are! You can do whatever you want after."

Tank's chest was heaving. "I'm sorry, Sam. I'm sorry. I couldn't help myself. It won't happen again."

Kelly said, "What is that?"

She was looking inside the case. Tank peered inside. "It's another one of those eggs."

"Smash it. Maybe that'll shock him awake," Sam said.

Tank upended the case. The egg plopped out, rolling unevenly until it came to a stop next to the dazed man.

"Get up!" Sam shouted.

His eyes opened dreamily and he tried to push himself up by his elbows.

"We have another one of your gifts," Sam said. "If you tell me where my boy and his friend are, I'll let you keep it."

Sam had spent another lifetime as a ruthless business negotiator. He'd never taken no for an answer, and this would be no exception.

The man struggled to grab the egg. Tank placed his foot in the center of his chest, holding him back.

"Where are they?" Sam asked.

"I…I can't."

"If you can't tell me, I can't let you have your gift."

"It is not my gift. It belongs to her." He pointed a shaking finger at Kelly. She stepped behind Tank.

"So you won't mind if we break it? I think I can speak for her in saying she refuses your little present." Sam picked up the storage case and lifted it over his head.

"No!"

Sam felt his temperature rising. "Yes! You tell me where we can find them or you'll be wearing this damned thing."

"If you harm it, bad things will happen."

Tank applied more pressure to the man's chest. "Bad things have already happened. Talk or you go after the egg."

"I…I can't."

There was real fear in his eyes. Sam made a quick motion, stopping just short of crashing the case onto the egg. The man merely cowered.

"That was close," Sam said. "The next time will be final. So, are you going to tell us?"

The man shook his head.

Sam leered at him. "You will. Tank and I will make sure of it."

With an embittered cry, he smashed the egg, slamming the case on it over and over again. Jellied bits plastered the man's face. A foul smelling white goo smattered clothes. The man cried out as if in great pain.

Sam dropped the case, breathing hard. "We're taking him with us."

He and Tank each grabbed an arm and lifted. The man was a dead weight.

"Where are we going?" Stephanie said.

"Out there." Sam nodded toward the open door. "Nicky and Christine have to be somewhere. We just have to hope they don't drop us somewhere out of the blue."

A runny bit of the egg landed on his hand. It was exceedingly warm. He flicked it away.

"Kelly, you come across anything like this in your research?"

She looked like someone coming down from a very bad trip. He noticed how badly her hands trembled. Kelly shook her head. "No. Nothing like this. Sam, I don't even know what the hell this is."

They were about to step into the earthen hallway when a tremendous, animalistic cry reverberated throughout the tunnel system. It was like nothing Sam had ever heard. The closest he could compare it to would be the wailing of damned souls in hell.

"What the fuck?" Tank said. Stephanie pressed herself to his back.

"I think someone knows what we've done to our gifts," Sam said. "Come on, I don't want to be here when whatever made that noise gets here."

Chapter Twenty-Four

Nicky felt something pulling at him. He took a sharp breath, felt a stabbing pain in his ribs.

He tried to open his eyes, but they were crusted over, his eyelashes fused together as if they'd been squirted with Crazy Glue. He couldn't rub the crust away because his hands were bound tightly to something.

That constant tugging feeling on his body wouldn't go away. There were no hands on him, but he couldn't shake the idea that he was being sucked forward...or downward.

"Dad," he whimpered.

The scene in the tunnel played behind his sealed eyes. Those creatures had overrun him. Their flesh had been cold, wet, putrefying. There were so many, he couldn't fight them off. Their rank odor was perhaps their greatest strength. As he struggled against them, he could sense their physical frailty. For a brief moment, he had thought he could break free. But the horror of their appearance and that pungent smell sapped the fight from him in short order. It was like being thrust into a disinterred potter's field, the rank of death swallowing him whole.

The tears came and he let them flow. He was never getting out of here alive. His parents would never know what had become of him. This is where his bones would rot. He was not only going to die a virgin, but a bawling baby as well. Who the hell went monster hunting and ended up being killed by the creature deep down inside one felt was never actually real? This was all supposed to be fun, right? But Nicky remembered the pain in his head, the ringing. It was as if he'd been poked by a cattle prod, herding him to this place. What was it those Borg things used to say on *Star Trek*?

Resistance is futile.

"Mom, Dad," he spluttered between sobs.

The fight with the demons had unseated his mind. He wanted nothing more than to be five again, sitting between his parents on the couch, watching cartoons before bed, feeling happier and safer than he ever would again.

Thinking of Christine made him feel even worse. If anything happened to her, he was responsible.

The tears came harder.

His left eye slowly began to open, the tears softening the gunk that had held it shut.

Then his right.

Both eyelids rose painfully. His vision was now clouded by tears, but sharpening as he forced himself to stop crying.

"Oh no."

His sensation of being pulled forward had been correct. Nicky stared down into a round chamber of roughly hewn walls and an uneven, rocky floor. Somehow, he'd been lashed to the ceiling of the chamber. His body stiffened, lest he break any of the bonds that held him aloft. Falling from this height would kill him for sure.

A ceiling lamp burned less than a foot from his right shoulder. The light it cast below didn't offer any encouragement.

The chamber was filled with people.

No.

Nicky fixed his gaze on a trio of men leaning against a wall. One was in pajamas, the other two in jeans and T-shirts. From his angle, he couldn't see their faces, just the tops of their heads. He concentrated on their shoulders, chests and backs.

None of them moved.

After staring for a minute or so, he moved to a woman in a dress, something you'd wear to an office, and an old man in shorts and no shirt. They leaned against one another in silent repose.

They're dead.

He looked all around the chamber. There must have been three dozen bodies or more, none of them moving.

There was no sense screaming. It would be even better if those *things* somehow forgot all about him—out of sight, out of mind. Better to die of dehydration up here than be tossed in with the lot of corpses below.

I can't be the only one up here, he thought. Why not just kill him like the rest? What on earth were they saving him for?

A cold slash of light swept over the bodies as a door opened. Nicky held his breath.

One of the demons scampered inside, walking on all fours over the bodies, sniffing the air like a dog. It stopped atop a woman lying on her stomach. Its hands were momentarily entangled in her hair. Pulling hard, there was a tearing sound and its hand broke free, along with a quarter of her scalp. She was dead. She didn't notice.

But Nicky did. He had to bite down hard not to throw up. The demon was right below him.

Please don't look up here.

The demon flicked the hair and flesh of her scalp off its fingers, stood upright and walked on the bodies like an alien Jesus on the waves of an angry sea.

What is it looking for?

It made a full round of the chamber, inspecting a corpse here and there, bringing its face close to the rotting flesh, then moving on. Nicky followed its progress until it came to the open door.

His skin went cold when the demon stopped, looked up and stared him in the eye. There was no way to sense any emotion in those lifeless, orange orbs. It didn't move a muscle as it studied him.

It hissed, opening its slit of a mouth wide. Nicky's muscles shivered.

The demon grabbed hold of the wall and began to scale it.

"No! No!"

When Nicky spoke, it stopped, cocking its bulbous head left, then right.

"Please, just leave me alone," he whimpered.

Resuming its climb, it made its way to the ceiling. For the first time, Nicky saw that there were indeed other people fastened to the ceiling with what looked to be gelatinous webbing. A woman, either unconscious or dead, was no more than several feet from him.

He watched in mute horror as the creature walked along the ceiling as if gravity held no sway. It came directly to the woman, its feet and hands sticking to the ceiling. Carefully clambering over her, it held itself under her body, their faces practically touching. It let loose with another bowel-watering hiss, then tugged at the webbing.

Nicky wanted to yell at the woman, tell her to wake up, to fight the demon as it struggled to free her.

It stopped, raking its long fingers down her face, to her throat.

The demon snapped its face toward Nicky. It opened its mouth. He couldn't see any teeth. Sidestepping away from the woman like a crab, it came to him.

"Get the hell away from me," Nicky yelled, trying to squirm away from the creature. It was hopeless. He was like a butterfly tacked to a board.

The demon scampered down by his legs where he couldn't see.

"What are you doing to me?"

The lower half of his body suddenly swung free. He thought for a moment that he was going to fall and screamed.

The webbing still held the top half of his body tight.

Feeling the demon clinging to his legs, Nicky kicked wildly. The demon rasped. He recoiled at the foulness of its breath.

"Get off of me!"

His knee came up against something soft and yielding. He watched in jubilation as the demon sailed down toward the chamber floor, arms and legs pinioning. By sheer luck, it landed between two corpses, the rocky floor shattering its body on impact.

"Fuck you!" he shouted with an idiot grin.

The orange eyes closed and what little color it had bled from its flesh instantly.

Nicky's triumph was short-lived. The webbing that bound him began to tear.

Something snapped.

He felt himself falling fast, heading right for the prone demon's body.

Christine's lungs were on fire. She'd been running for so long, she thought her heart was going to explode. Somewhere within the twisting tunnels, she'd lost the two demons. She wasn't taking any chances. She had to find someplace to hide, or better yet, a way out of here.

Stumbling to her knees, she dropped the stake, gasping for air.

The tunnel was eerily quiet. She didn't detect any sounds of pursuit.

Exhausted, she rolled onto her back, squinting at the light overhead.

What the hell is this place? It goes on forever. How could everyone above not know this had been built? Wouldn't there have been hundreds of construction machines and workers digging this out for months? Maybe even years?

And who in their right mind would create a place for monsters to live in?

Catching her breath, she pushed herself into a sitting position.

Finding Nicky might be impossible. They were in a maze. It was as if it had been designed so people could be lost forever. When their bodies or minds gave up, the mannequin men or Dover Demons would find their bodies and do whatever it is they did down here.

The thought of being touched by those creatures and the way they had been molesting that man made her shiver. It was one thing to die. It was another, unspeakable thing to be left as a plaything for the beasts that lived down here.

She was about to resume her endless wandering, searching for doorways to rooms that didn't have demons in them when everything spun on its axis. Christine tasted bile, feeling as if she was spinning ass over elbow. Everything grew fuzzy for a moment and she was on the verge of blacking out.

When the sickening sensation stopped, she felt a cold wind freeze the skin of her face. Opening her eyes, the nighttime skyline of Boston was laid out before her.

"What? How?"

She was somehow standing in snow up to her thighs. She was on a hill, alone.

"Hey!" she shouted, her voice echoing back to her. "Help me!"

The city looked to be just a few miles away. She could make it. She knew she could, even despite the cold. The elation of being freed from the underground labyrinth would warm her all the way to the Boston Harbor if necessary.

"I'll ask to borrow someone's cell phone and call Mom and Dad to get me," she said, her teeth chattering. "Then I'll call the police and tell them they have to find Nicky. They probably won't believe me, but I'll make them. I'll make them."

Walking was difficult. Each step was like pulling her legs from quicksand. At one point, she heard laughter, was anxious to see who it was then realized it was coming from her.

Midway down the hill she faltered, pitching forward. She thrust her arms out, prepared to catch herself.

That odd sensation swept over her again. She tumbled down the hill, rolling like a human snowball.

Dazed, she came to a stop, spitting snow from her mouth.

Well, that's one way to make it down.

She wiped the snow from her eyes.

Four mannequin men stood over her.

She was back in a bright room, surrounded by stainless steel shelves and slabs that looked like tables in a mortuary.

A man said, "Put her there."

No. This can't be. I was free. I WAS FREE!

She didn't resist when the mannequin men lifted her onto a table. Nor did she react when she saw one of the demons watching her, its large eyes blinking, with what looked like a doll's smile on its face.

"I was free," she muttered, feeling all of her energy being sucked away.

"Yes," the man said. Where was he? She couldn't even bring herself to turn her head and seek him out.

"There is nothing like freedom lost, is there?" he said. "Prepare her. She's ready."

Christine felt herself going under.

Ready? Ready for what?

She tried to speak but the words wouldn't come.

Chapter Twenty-Five

Sam and Tank carried the man between them, the tips of his boots trailing on the floor. Kelly and Stephanie went ahead of them, searching for a door. It didn't matter where the door led at this point. They needed to get out of the tunnel. The heavy clomp of rushing footsteps was right behind them. Whatever had made that noise seemed to have alerted everyone and everything that lived down in this maze.

"I see one!" Stephanie said, pointing ahead.

An old, wooden door that looked to be made of timber scraps was only twenty feet away.

"I'll kick it in," Tank said, panting. The man they carried was conscious but had gone slack to make their escape even harder.

"I've got him," Sam said, putting the man in a tight headlock.

"Hurry," Kelly said.

Whatever was coming for them was close. Too close.

The door gave way with one savage kick. Tank ushered the women inside while Sam dragged their hostage. When Tank shut the door, they were engulfed by perfect darkness.

"What is this room?" Sam asked the man.

"You will see."

A wave of nausea pulled Sam under and he lost his grip on the man.

The darkness was suddenly gone, replaced by moonlight shafting through the gaps in the boards of what looked to be an old storage shed. Tank, Kelly and Stephanie were on the ground, shaking their heads. Even the strange man appeared dazed.

They were back up top. The cold hit him like a lightning bolt.

Despite his dizziness, Sam grabbed the man by the throat.

"What's going on? How does this keep happening?"

The man said nothing.

Sam shook him, hard.

Tank cocked his fist back, about to introduce it to his face when Kelly said, "Hold on. I know who he is!"

"You do?" Sam said, hoping she could connect the dots that had been floating around his brain since he'd laid eyes on him. He knew he'd seen him before, but he couldn't recall whether it was in town, in the shop or back when he ran his business. Maybe it even went as far back as college or even grammar school.

"He's the one that wrote that article about seeing the Dover Demon. Lando Solo."

Sam's eye narrowed. Yes, she was right! His picture had been small on the blog post because and he wore a hat and glasses, but it was him. And if he wrote the post and was working in tandem with the creatures…

"You fucking lured us here!" Sam cried, uppercutting the man's chin. His head snapped back and his eyes fluttered.

Sam heard rattling chains. Kelly stood by a battered workbench, the scarred surface covered with rusty tools.

"Put him up here," she said. "I think we can get him to talk."

Sam paused. Kelly looked awful. She was a jittery mess. But her eyes were clear. He had an idea what she was thinking, and a part of him was frightened. Once they went down this road, there was no coming back.

He motioned to Tank. "Help me lift him."

"What are you doing?" the man who called himself Lando Solo asked.

"You don't get to ask the questions," Tank said. "At least not until you start answering some."

Kelly and Stephanie cleared the bench, scattering tools and nails and blocks of wood all over the shed's floor. The man tried to put up a fight, but Tank's oppressive weight was just too much. While he held him down, Sam and Kelly wrapped the chains around his legs and chest. They secured them by slipping U shaped irons through the links.

"Maybe we shouldn't," Stephanie said.

Sam said, "We have to. We're running out of time. I have to find Nicky and Christine."

Stephanie backed away to stand by the lone window, the panes grimy with decades-old grit.

"I can't tell where we are," she said. "All I see is snow. Maybe we should leave him here and see if we can find a road or a house and get help."

"They wouldn't let us if we tried," Sam said, huffing with the exertion of immobilizing the strange man. "Right, Lando? What is your real name, anyway?"

He remained tight-lipped, but there was real fear in his eyes.

Kelly hovered over Lando Solo, inches from his face. "Where are we?" she said.

The man shook his head. "I don't know. The doorways are very unpredictable." His eyes danced in his head. He was nervous as hell. He was right to be.

"What doorways? How did we get up here?" Tank pressed.

"They...they move all the time. We can't control the access points. Only they can. We're not allowed to know how they do it. We wouldn't understand even if they tried to explain it. Movement is merely a slippage through dimensions."

"Who are *they*?" Sam asked, digging his fingers into the man's forearm. He winced.

But he wouldn't answer.

"Are you talking about those alien things?" Kelly spat, practically shouting. "Those things that ruined my life?"

A smile crept across his face.

"Answer her," Tank said, grabbing his kneecap. He started to twist. The man went rigid. But he remained silent.

Sam took a breath, deciding to take a different approach. "To be honest with you, I don't care much about whatever secrets you have going on down there. I want my son and his friend. Now, you either tell us how to find them, or it's going to get very painful."

The man tittered, despite Tank's increasing pressure on his knee.

Kelly nudged Sam aside. "You're going to tell us everything! Now!"

She pulled a screwdriver from her pocket and drove it into his hand, impaling it to the bench. He howled like a feral animal. Blood spattered her coat.

"Who...are...they?" She twisted the screwdriver. Tank let go of the man's knee.

"What are you doing?" Stephanie said, near tears. "You can't torture another human being."

Kelly whipped around to face her. "I'm not even sure he is human."

Sam looked at the pool of blood making a halo around the man's hand. He sure bled like a human, unlike those Dover Demon things.

"My son," Sam said, now that Kelly had wiped the smirk from his face. "Where is he?"

"The boy…he can't get the gift. They will have taken him…elsewhere."

"Stop talking in circles," Tank shouted.

"He was never prepared. His body cannot accept the gift."

"You mean those eggs?" Kelly said.

"Yes." The color had drained from his face. His breath came in shallow gasps.

"Prepared how?" she said.

His eyes locked on hers. "As you were. As you all were."

Sam's impatience came to a boil. He screamed, "Where the fuck would they take my son?"

Spying a jar of nails on a narrow shelf, he grabbed a sharp carpet tack and jammed it under one of the man's fingernails. He pushed it in slightly, just enough to elicit a groan of agony.

"There are…are too many places," the man said. "It's impossible to know."

Stephanie sobbed behind them.

"Then take us back down there and lead us to some of these places," Sam said.

When the man didn't answer, he shoved the tack all the way under the nail bed. The nail broke free with a small pop.

"How were we prepared?" Kelly asked. It was obvious to Sam that they were at odds with what they wanted from their captive. Kelly was searching for answers to the madness that had plagued her all her life.

The man shut his mouth tight. Kelly fumbled for a hammer on the floor.

"Kelly, no!" Sam barked.

She brought the hammer down on the man's knee with a loud crunch. The man nearly levitated off the bench.

"I'm going to break pieces off you in short order unless you tell us everything, you hear me?" she said, spittle flying into his face. The hammer shook wildly in her hand.

Tank tried to place a hand on her shoulder to calm her down but she pulled away. He looked to Sam.

"Let her try," Sam said.

Kelly tapped the hammer softly on the tip of the man's nose. "Now, you're going to start with how we were prepared, what those things are and how to find the kids. I'll even let you keep your real identity to yourself. You hesitate once, and you can say goodbye to your nose."

Nicky managed to land on his feet, driving them into the body of the creature and tucking into a hard roll. He heard and felt the thing's bones shatter from the impact. He tumbled over a row of dead bodies, settling in a spare gap between a heavy man with red hair and a big beard and a young woman in a nightgown.

He lay on his back, inspecting the damage. His hips and legs throbbed and his ankles felt as if someone had stuck needles right through the bone. Slowly, carefully, he tried to move each leg. They hurt like hell, but it didn't appear that anything was broken. It took some doing, but he was able to eventually get to his feet.

Nicky looked around the chamber. Corpses were everywhere, but none of them appeared to have decomposed. There was no malodorous smell of death or decay. It actually looked like he was surrounded by dozens of people in a deep sleep. He wasn't going to touch one to feel for a pulse to see if they were truly dead. He'd trust his eyes and instincts.

Were all of these people just killed?

It would explain their appearance. If that was the case, this was mass murder on a terrifying scale. The chamber was cold. It reminded him of a butcher's meat locker.

He looked up.

Several other people were still on the ceiling, secured in the webbing. There was no way he could get up there to free them. The only way to help them was to find a way out of this nightmare and bring the cops, National Guard and whomever else he could drag to this place.

The creature had deflated. Even its skull looked smaller, flatter. Nicky stepped over it, his hips barking. Both ankles felt like they were sprained. He carefully wove his way around the bodies and out the door.

The passageway was empty. No sign of more creatures.

Walking was going to be a bitch, but he couldn't just sit here and wait for another demon to come check in on the chamber of corpses.

What were they doing with them? Worse, what were they planning to do with him?

If that was a meat locker, then we all must have been meat. Were they actually going to eat me? He shivered at the thought.

As strange as it seemed, he was lucky to still be alive.

He thought of Christine and limped back into the chamber. As much as it repulsed him, he looked to the face of each body, praying Christine's wouldn't be among them. His body sagged with relief when he realized she wasn't there.

I could walk for days and not find her, he thought. *It's like a nightmare that just goes on forever.*

He'd have to keep going. His stomach cramped from thirst. It was a stark reminder that he couldn't, in fact, wander around without ceasing. Sooner or later, his body would give out.

Remembering all of the horror comics he'd anxiously read over the years, he regretted every moment spent being thrilled by the sinister images and chilling words.

What he wouldn't give for a superhero right now.

Shuffling one foot after the other, he continued down the tunnel.

He didn't notice the tall figure creeping up behind him.

What is that?

Christine felt something heavy and warm inside her. She'd never had sex before, but the full sensation in her vagina was exactly how she imagined it would be like when she let a man make love to her.

Reaching between her legs, she realized she had once again blacked out and was now in a different place.

She held her breath. There was window beside her. There were no blinds or shades. She was on a bed, in a room decorated with posters of young farm animals. The black eyes of a dozen horses, sheep, cows and pigs stared down at her.

"What are you doing to me?" she whispered, rising from the bed. It was as if her mind was melting away, leaving her with missing time and frayed bits of images and emotions. Was any of it even real? Something was very wrong. Jesus, did she have some kind of serious brain injury? And where was her family?

Her vagina throbbed.

"No."

Christine shook her head.

"You keep making me loop back," she said to the empty room. "Every time you change things up, you make me doubt everything. But I know this is real. I know you're trying to break me down."

Planting her feet on the floor, she expected the room to spin or the door to fly open. Weaving to the window, she looked out at an empty, snow swept landscape. She could be in Siberia for all she knew. It sure as hell looked like it out there.

"What do you want from me?" she said, leaning her forehead against the icy pane of glass.

She jumped when a voice said, "To live."

Christine looked around the room. Other than the bed and posters, it was completely empty. There was no closet, no place for a man to hide.

Unless he was under the bed.

She dropped to her knees, checking the narrow space under the box spring.

There was no one there.

"Where are you?" she asked, using the edge of the mattress to pull herself up. She felt so tired. Every muscle ached.

"Are you comfortable?"

Biting her lip, she said, "Where is this place?"

There was a long, silent pause, then the man replied, "It is where you will live, until it's time."

Letting loose with a primal scream, Christine grabbed the poster of a pair of ponies in a field, tearing it from the wall. She did that with all of the other posters, crumpling and tearing them to long shreds.

There has to be a camera or microphone behind one of them, she thought as she shredded each poster.

All that was left were four bare walls and a floor littered with scraps of paper.

"Are you comfortable now?" the voice repeated.

Christine pulled at the bed board. Tugging like a woman possessed, she broke it free from the bed.

"Let me out of here!" she bellowed, launching the board at the window. It bounced off the glass, clipping her shins. She howled in pain.

Through the tears in her eyes, she saw that the glass wasn't even scratched.

She was about to attempt it again when a sharp pain in her abdomen made her see stars. Reflexively cupping both hands between her legs, she felt a tremendous heat on her palms. Her fingertips brushed against a lump that shouldn't have been there.

Frantic now, she fumbled with the button and zipper on her jeans, desperate to get them off. When she pushed her thighs together, there was a wet, squishing sound along with resistance as something pushed her legs back apart.

Unable to control her terror, tears and snot painted her face as she kicked her jeans off. Tucking her thumbs under the elastic band of her panties, her entire body trembled as she removed them, taking them as far as her knees.

What was wrong with her? What was *in* her? She tried to remember a prayer, any prayer, as she reached between her legs.

Pushing a finger inside, it came against something hot and spongy.

"Oh my God, no!"

Using the fingers on both hands, she probed as best she could. Her vagina was filled by something too slick to grab hold of and too far inside to see.

She wanted to throw up, to shout until her voice box gave out.

"What did you do to me?" she cried, curling into a ball on her side. "What did you do to me?"

The heat radiated to her stomach and chest as she shouted, her body tense as a board.

The thing inside her moved, burrowing deeper.

Chapter Twenty-Six

Kelly admired her handiwork. Tank and Stephanie had backed away from the table. Though no longer begging her to stop, they seemed to want to remove themselves from what had to be done.

Sam remained by her side, demanding answers.

Kelly had been searching for the creature they'd called the Dover Demon most of her life. She never dreamt she'd end up torturing a man to get to the truth. Her right hand shook so much, she had to shift the hammer to her left. They may have thought she had been overcome by emotion, but the truth was, the DTs were riding hard on her. She was at the point where she might trade the answers to everything that had plagued her for a bottle of whiskey.

Stay focused. This fucker knows more than he's saying.

She jammed the pry-end of the hammer under the man's armpit, applying enough pressure to make him hiss with pain. His nose was already a flat disaster and two of his teeth had been whacked off, leaving jagged shards embedded in his bleeding gums.

"The armpit is a sensitive place," she said. "More than you'd think. Women know because we have to shave there all the time. You haven't built up that tolerance. Answer me with the truth or I introduce you to a brand new pain."

Sam applied his weight to keep the man's arm steady.

"How were we *prepared*?" she asked, her voice shaky.

When the man didn't respond, she applied more pressure.

"Wait!" the man cried, blood from his nose burbling into his mouth. "I can't tell you exactly what happened to you, but I can tell you how it works."

"Go on," Sam urged.

Kelly saw a burgeoning madness in her old boyfriend's eyes. If he didn't find out where Nicky was soon, he would kill the man.

"You had an encounter when you were younger," the man said. "Because of the sowing now, it had to be when you were teenagers."

Kelly eased off with the hammer. The man was starting to hyperventilate. Now that he was talking, she didn't want him passing out.

"Do you even remember your encounter?" he said, chest heaving.

"Yes," Kelly said. "We saw one of those things laying eggs, then men came and took them. How did that prepare us?"

"Then you don't remember everything. You can't. Even your regressive hypnotherapy can't unlock those memories. We've seen plenty try. At some point, you were touched by one of the Ennuki. It imprinted you so it could find you when the sowing began."

Tank said, "What are the Ennuki?"

"What your town called the Dover Demon. What many call aliens, intruders, visitors. Others think them ghosts, or creatures by more names than can be counted throughout the ages."

Kelly pressed him. "Are you saying they put some kind of tracking device in us?"

The man shook his head. "No. Nothing material. Their touch can alter your DNA, so imperceptibly that modern science would never detect it. But to them, you become something that can never be lost...or the same."

Growing bolder, the man smiled.

Sam grabbed him by the throat. "Where did you and your Ennuki take my son?"

The ground under the cabin rumbled. Tools clanged against the walls.

Sputtering, the man said, "There's no need to hurt me. I will tell you everything. It's too late anyway."

"What were we marked for?" Kelly said.

"For this moment. For the gift that we tried to implant in you. When the sowing begins, the Ennuki return to the ones that have been imprinted. Your DNA, left to evolve for over three decades, is now ready to accept the gift. You may have destroyed the two gifts earlier, but there are many more waiting for you."

Kelly gripped the table, feeling overwhelmed. "Wait, you planned to put those eggs *in us*?"

"Yes," he said, matter-of-factly. "Your body has been altered to incubate the gift."

"That's some goddamn gift," Tank huffed.

"To feed and grow the oldest living species on the planet with your own body? I would call that the best gift you can receive," the man said, coughing, blood seeping from the sides of his mouth. "You've been given the highest honor. Better that than the feeding rooms."

There had been times when even Kelly thought her theories had gone too far, stepping beyond the boundaries of sanity. Nothing she or any of the wildest conspiracy crackpots dreamt up came close to what he was saying, if it was true. She was suddenly uncomfortable in her own skin. What had those DNA changes done to her? What now made her so different that she could grow one of those foul-looking creatures inside her?

"My son never saw one of those things or was imprinted," Sam said. "What do you want with him and his friend if they haven't been prepared?"

"They have divergent purposes. The girl you speak of, her womb will play host to an Usher. They are the men without clear faces or tongues. Think of them as your equivalent of a lab assistant. The Ennuki, though far more evolved than we will ever be, are frail. They need the Ushers to conduct menial and physical tasks. I understand they come from a genetic strain dating back tens of thousands of years, when the Ennuki attempted to mate with man. The result wasn't a success as far as special propagation, but they have an incredible purpose."

Sam shook him. "And my son?"

The shed rocked again. It sounded and felt like the ground was readying itself to swallow them up. Kelly stiffened, waiting to be dragged into another one of those doorways, ending up wherever the Ennuki and their handlers wanted them to be.

"The sowing is happening all over the planet at this very moment. Some, like yourselves, will be gifted and cared for to nurture the Ennuki until the reaping. We also need to restock our food stores. You cannot sow without nourishment."

Sam lashed out, punching the man's face again and again, raining blows until his face was unrecognizable.

"You…are not…feeding…my son…to those…fucking things!"

Kelly tried to pull him away and he hit her in the head by accident. She fell into Tank. The big man was able to wrestle Sam away from the semiconscious man.

The ground vibrated and Kelly almost lost her balance. Stephanie had to hold her up.

Through his ruined mouth, the man sputtered, "You can't…fight it. Just accept it. This is bigger than…the human race." His chest heaved, his breath sounding like milk gurgling through a straw. "And far more important."

Kelly's head wobbled. It was happening again. She stumbled forward, desperate to grab hold of Sam. She didn't want to go through it alone. When the shed came out of focus, she held on tight, his sobs of rage blowing against her neck.

A pair of strong hands latched on to Nicky's shoulders, tugging him backward. He landed on his tailbone, the pain ricocheting from the base of his spine to the top of his head.

One of the demons stared down at him.

This one was different.

It was tall, with a broader chest and muscular arms. He couldn't help but notice, gazing up at the creature straddling him, that it had no visible genitals.

Nicky didn't move. Something told him that if he resisted, there would be terrible consequences. This demon exuded power, as if the others he'd seen were nothing more than children.

Its thin-lipped mouth was pressed into a tight line. The bulbous, orange eyes didn't so much as blink. Nicky could smell its foul breath leaking from the slits it had for nostrils. His only hope now was that whatever end it had in store for him was quick and painless.

The demon crouched down, its oval head moving from left to right, inspecting him.

I could kick it right between its legs, but would that even do anything?

His own ankles and hips hurt too much to make a good run of it even if he was successful in bringing the creature down. It could easily catch up with him.

Whatever was going to happen would happen right here, right now.

What I wouldn't give for Batman's utility belt, he thought, feeling entirely helpless. Reading comics, he always imagined their collective heroism would have naturally exuded from him if and when he faced a moment of extreme crisis.

He realized now it was all just paper and ink, words woven by storytellers who had the same fears and faults of every ordinary man.

Things would be different if his father was here. They may have drifted apart since his mother left, but he knew his father loved him. He'd done everything he'd ever set out to do because he was fearless, just like Captain America or The Flash. At least, that's the standard Nicky had always held him to. He'd heard tales when he eavesdropped on his dad and Tank that his old man had been a proficient brawler, especially in his teens.

Why hadn't that gene been passed down?

"Go ahead, do what you want with me," Nicky said, gritting his teeth. The creature stepped over him so it was now by his left side. It didn't make any sudden or threatening moves. Just looking into its face was enough to make his balls retreat into his stomach.

Its mouth spread into a lascivious, black smile.

Nicky's stoic acceptance of his fate turned to utter dread.

"Get away from me," he said, nearing panic. Those orange eyes held his own like a tractor beam. He desperately wanted to look away or shut his eyes, but the creature wouldn't let him.

When it reached down to touch his face, Nicky tried to slide away, his ankles burning with agony as he pushed himself along the rough floor on his back.

The demon's chest moved in and out, faster and faster, in perfect time with the fluttering of Nicky's heart. It was as if they were somehow connected. But whereas Nicky was imbued with a fear the likes he had never known, the demon seemed to derive great joy. In fact, its pale, glistening body appeared to fill out, become more substantial, as Nicky withered under its alien glare.

Nicky continued inching away, his breath coming in short, painful gasps.

The creature remained where it was, watching him closely.

He stood up, swaying, still unable to look away.

His heart almost stopped when it pursed its thin lips and said, in a shocking baritone voice, "Boo!"

Nicky's body was running before his mind could register that he'd broken the eerie staring contest. Looking over his shoulder, he saw it standing in the same spot, not bothering to give chase.

"Boo!" it bellowed again.

Nicky almost passed out from fright. He managed to keep running.

The sound of laughter was his only pursuer as he forced his body to ignore the fiery pain and just keep running.

Tank and Stephanie ended up in a small cave, the ceiling so low, the top of his head scraped along the jagged rock when he tried to sit up. Sam, Kelly and a very battered Lando Solo were nowhere to be seen. A lone torch, wedged in a fissure in the stone wall, provided flickering light. His wife was still out cold, tucked under his arm.

"Motherfucker," Tank whispered.

Every time they made a shred of progress, they were thrown for a loop. This wasn't all happening by accident. Something was in charge, watching their every move, dropping them into sinkholes of disorientation.

His stomach rumbled. He couldn't remember the last time he'd eaten. His tongue had swollen in his dry mouth. It was impossible to know how long they'd been locked in this madness.

How long until we start feeling the physical effects of dehydration? For all we know, we're at the brink right now. Or maybe it's only been a few hours since we made our way to the pond. This is fucking insane. What are these creatures?

The man had called them the Ennuki.

As an archaeologist, Tank had delved into ancient tales and legends from every corner of the globe. He was fascinated by the rising concept of a lost, advanced civilization that pre-dated modern man, though he never thought it held much credence. People like Michael Cremo and Erich von Daniken had done an admirable job bringing artifacts and archaeological finds that didn't fit into the preconceived notions of man's evolutionary timelines to the light. From ancient Egyptian batteries, to the concept of aliens teaching primitive man to shed their ignorance, it was easy to be sucked in by their suppositions and question everything.

Of course, that was the purpose of science, to question both the known and unknown. He'd never adhered to any of the crazy theories, but the kid that still lived in him liked to read the stories and consider the suppositions.

The name Ennuki sounded so familiar to him. If he could only clear his damn head for a few moments before being thrown in the brain scrambler, he might have a chance of figuring it out.

Stephanie groaned.

"You okay?" he asked.

She looked around the tight cave and clung tighter to him.

"Where are we now?"

"You've got me. Wherever it is, I can promise you someone knows exactly where we are. This time, I'm not running."

Neither could see through the darkness beyond the firelight's reach. Black smoke undulated against the cave's ceiling in black waves.

"Sam and Kelly?" she asked.

"I don't know."

"You don't think they're really going to put one of those eggs in us, do you?"

He rubbed her shoulder. "That's what it looked like they were about to do to you and Kelly. I don't know where they think those eggs are going when it comes to me and Sam."

Stephanie gave a cold chuckle. "I'm just glad I'm with you now. If we get separated again, I think I'll lose it."

"Shhh," he said. "I have a strong suspicion that's exactly what they want. This has all been an extreme version of psychological torture. We never know where we are or where we'll end up. We're chased by creatures that defy logic. That man tells us we've been retrofitted so we can incubate monsters. If this keeps up, we're all going to short circuit. The human mind can only take so much."

They froze at the sound of passing footsteps. Tank held his breath, gripping Stephanie. They faded away, the only sound the crackling of the torch.

Tank's chest expanded when something clicked in his head. He bent close to Stephanie's ear.

"You remember how he said these things are Ennuki?"

"Yes."

"I've heard that name before. It's a take on the Anunnaki. The Babylonians thought they were the gods of the underworld. In the last century, there was a writer called Zecharia Sitchin who proposed that the Anunnaki were actually a race of aliens who came from a planet beyond Neptune. According to him, these Anunnaki were responsible for the advancement of the Sumerian culture and were involved in many of the creation and flood myths. In others words, they're kind of like the fathers of mankind."

"You don't believe that, do you?" Stephanie said.

"No. His stuff was for the masses, a kind of pulp pseudo-science that sold books because it was strange and intriguing. But that man referred to the creatures as Ennuki, which makes me wonder if he and others have attributed a god-like status to these things."

Stephanie added, "Which is why they're being helped along by regular people. Kind of like how Dracula had human assistants to do the dirty work and look out for him when the sun was up."

Tank huffed. "I don't know if I'd call that guy a regular person, but he wasn't one of those demons or those blank-faced Ushers. With everything we've seen and heard, I'm beginning to wonder what's real and what isn't. This could all be an illusion."

"But everything has felt so real."

"This is unprecedented mind-fuck stuff, Steph. I could be wrong. See, I think that's the point. Confusion, doubt, fear. We're riding all three emotions so hard, every second, sooner or later we're going to break."

She lifted herself up and kissed him.

"Nothing to doubt or fear about that," she said. "Just remember, there's something real down here."

Light dust from the ceiling's cave started to sprinkle on them. Tank waved his hand back and forth to clear the air.

"Maybe we should grab the torch and get out of here," Stephanie said.

"That's what they want us to do," he replied. "We're putting too many pieces together."

The sound of heavy stone grinding on stone made them start.

"I think it's going to cave in," she said, scrambling to her hands and knees. She crawled over to the torch and yanked it free. "Come on, if they want us on the move, it's better than being buried alive."

As much as Tank wanted to give a show of defiance, Stephanie was right. If they were being herded, at least there might be a chance for escape somewhere up ahead. If he stayed here, the walls were going to come down on him.

When he tried to move, his back slammed against the wall. Pulling forward, he didn't budge an inch.

"I think my jacket's stuck," he said, tugging on it.

Stephanie said, "Take it off. Hurry."

Bigger bits of rock were coming loose, some heavy enough to knock them out if they fell on their heads.

Tank struggled with his jacket.

They probably want me to leave it behind so they can stick me in the snow and freeze me, he thought.

As he pulled his left arm free, a cold, powerful hand clamped onto his bicep. Before he could look to see what had hold of him, another grabbed the top of his head. Eyes swiveling in their sockets, he watched in horror as long, pale Dover Demon arms sprang from the crumbling rock wall like clutching roots.

"Tank, no!" Stephanie screamed.

They had a grip on his entire upper body, cementing him in place.

"Go, Steph, go!"

Tears spilled down her cheeks.

"I won't leave you!"

"Run. I'll find you!"

The wall gave way behind him and he was pulled through a jagged opening. The fetid breath of the creatures settled on him like a diseased fog as they fumbled with his body. He heard Stephanie cry out before the opening was blocked and he was cast into utter darkness.

He fought hard, fists, feet, knees and elbows connecting with the demon bodies with satisfying cracks and crunches.

But in the end, there were too many, and he felt the adrenaline bleed from his system as they swarmed him like bees.

Chapter Twenty-Seven

The man was gone.

Sam and Kelly were in the living room of an empty house. There wasn't a stick of furniture. The blinds on the windows were broken, bent every which way, letting in the bright moonlight.

They had landed on their feet, in the center of the room, Kelly's hand in his.

"Looks like Lando Solo got away," Sam said, fighting back nausea.

"Just when we were getting him to talk, too," Kelly said. Her hand was warm and wet with the man's blood. She saw some of it on Sam's face and coat, too.

"Care to take a guess where we are now?" Sam asked, letting go of her hand and walking to a window. There was nothing but tall trees surrounding the house. It looked as if a clearing had been made so the house could be dropped in the middle.

Kelly joined him by the window. "Looks like someplace where we can't be seen or heard."

If they were brought here, maybe Nicky had been, too. It felt like the end of the road on a bizarre odyssey. Sam couldn't explain the feeling of finality in his gut.

Bolting for the stairs, he wondered if it was just wishful thinking.

Kelly clomped up behind him, urging him to slow down. There were two rooms on the second floor, both doors closed. He turned the knob on the first, opening the door recklessly. Just like downstairs, it was empty. Even dust wouldn't dare clutter the floors or walls.

"Nicky," he said, loud enough to be heard through the whole house.

Kelly walked ahead of him, ready to open the second door. "You think he's here?" she asked.

Sam shook his head. "I don't know, but I have to try."

The hinge squealed as she pushed the door open.

The room was small, but it did have a bed. The floor was filled with crumpled bits of paper. Sam knelt down, picking up a scrap. It showed a lamb's face.

"Posters," he said. "Like in a little kids room."

"I think I see something," Kelly said. She pointed to the other side of the bed. The shadow of a hunched figure squatted by the wall. Sam leapt over the bed, ready to attack if it was one of those Ennuki or Ushers. Fist raised, he let loose with a guttural growl.

"Aieeee!"

It was a girl. She turned from the wall, eyes unblinking, shimmering with terror.

Sam felt all of the tension deflate from his body.

"Christine?"

"Mr....Mr. Brogna?"

"Oh my God, are you okay?"

Before she could answer, he pulled her head to his chest.

If Christine was here, Nicky might not be far behind. He had to fight the impulse to cry.

He didn't notice Kelly had joined them, wrapping her arm around them both.

"I thought I'd never see anyone again," Christine whimpered. "They were leaving me to die here. How did you get in here?"

"You're safe now," Sam said. "You're with us."

He let the girl cry everything out, her body shaking with sobs.

Kelly raised her hand to his face and said, "Sam, what's this?"

In the scant light, it looked like blood. Their gazes went to the floor. It was covered with blood.

"Honey," Kelly said soothingly, "did they hurt you?"

Sniffling, she nodded.

"Come on, let's get you up on the bed. Sam, can you grab that sheet so I can cover her?"

As Christine stood, Sam briefly saw that the girl was naked from the waist down. He ripped the sheet from the mattress and handed it to Kelly.

When she settled Christine down, she asked, "Can you tell us what they did?"

At first, it seemed as if she hadn't heard the question. Her stare was far, far away. Then she looked down at the sheet and pulled her knees up.

"They put something inside me," she said. Her voice trembled with rising panic.

Kelly took the lead and Sam was grateful. He wasn't sure how well she'd respond to him asking the tough questions.

He thought of those eggs, the gift, but cast it away. If what the man had said was true, the young girl hadn't been altered to receive it.

"It's still there," Christine said. "I can feel it. Moving."

She suddenly sucked in a great breath, grunting with pain.

"It's going further inside," she groaned. "Please, help me. Get it out."

Kelly looked to Sam, unsure what to do.

"Get what out?" Sam said.

"The *thing*! I don't know what it is," Christine spat.

She kicked the sheet away and spread her legs. Sam whipped his head away, staring out the window.

"Good Lord," Kelly mumbled, taking a faltering step back, away from the bed. She bumped into Sam. "She's right. There is something in...in her..."

Sam couldn't bring himself to look. He'd known Christine since she was five, tagging along with Nicky and Roy when they walked home from school. The thought of looking...down there...was too much to bear.

"Then she'll need a doctor," he said, numbness flooding through him. After everything, was this his breaking point? He hoped to hell not because he still had a long way to go to find his son.

Kelly shook him. "There are no doctors, Sam. We have to help her."

"Get this fucking thing out of me! Ahhhhhhhhh!"

Christine's back arched and Sam could swear he heard something moving inside the girl. Kelly flew to her side.

"Okay, I'm going to see what I can do," she said. "Sam, I need you to hold her still. Can you do that?"

He shook himself from his fugue. "Yeah."

"Good, hold on to her arms."

Sam sat on the bed behind Christine, putting her head in his lap while he grabbed hold of her arms, keeping them flush with the mattress. Sweat was pouring out of her, slickening his grip. The look on her face was a mask of unadulterated horror.

"I've got you," he said, trying to maintain a level of calm. He was, after all, the adult and she was still just a child. Seeing her this way was breaking his heart.

Kelly said, "I can see a little of it. I'm going to see if I can get a handle on it. When I say go, I want you to take a deep breath and push. We're going to treat this just like you're having a baby. Can you do that?"

"Y-yyes," Christine said, on the verge of sobbing.

Kelly positioned herself between Christine's legs. Sam watched with quiet revulsion as she reached both hands to the edge of Christine's vagina.

"Okay, Christine, go."

Christine swallowed a mouthful of air and pushed. Kelly reached inside her. She grimaced as her hand went deeper. Christine's body went rigid as a girder. For a moment, Sam felt she might break free from him and hover over the bed.

"I almost got it," Kelly said.

The squishing sounds made Sam woozy. It looked as if Kelly was digging for clams at a Cape Cod beach, her hands deep in the soft muck.

"Holy Christ, it's slippery," Kelly said.

Christine let loose with an earsplitting scream.

"You're making it move deeper!" she wailed.

Kelly shook her head. "Just push some more. I have it. I have it!"

Sam pushed down as hard as he could on Christine's arms. Her head thrashed in his lap.

There was a loud pop, and Kelly was splashed with a pink froth that smelled like sulfur. She flinched, pulling her hands free.

"Oh God, oh God!" Christine screamed. Her eyes rolled up until all Sam could see were the whites. Her body went limp as she passed out.

"Keep her awake!" Kelly shouted, wiping the goo from her face and reaching back inside.

Sam tapped her cheeks, shouted her name, but she was out. Her mind had had enough and shut down to avoid the madness.

"It's gone," Kelly said.

"What?" Sam said.

"I can't see or feel it anymore. It's so deep inside her, there's no way I can get it."

"Jesus. What the hell is it?"

"I...I don't know. It was like a kind of sack. I could feel something inside it, but it was so slippery, I couldn't hold on long enough to get it.

It's like it knew what I was trying to do and found a way to stay where it was."

Sam handed the sheet to Kelly. "You might want to get all of that off. There's no telling what it is. I know it didn't come from Christine."

Kelly wiped at her face, arms and chest. The sheet absorbed the froth until it was sodden.

"What do we do?" Sam said, pushing the wet hair from Christine's face.

Kelly sighed with exhaustion. "For now, we let her sleep. Maybe it'll move again if it thinks it's safe. I can always try again."

"Or maybe it's now exactly where it wants to be."

"I'll stay here with her. Why don't you look through the rest of the house, see if you can find any sign that Nicky was here. I'm sure if he was here now, he would have heard all this and come running."

Sam rose from the bed. His knees buckled, but he managed to stay upright.

This is a fucking nightmare, he thought, looking at Christine. He cupped Kelly's face in his hand. "I'll be right back."

Her eyelids slowly closed and opened halfway. "Don't be gone long."

Nicky stopped running to catch his breath. His ankles screamed bloody murder. He worried that one misstep might snap them entirely. Then he'd be royally screwed.

"I'd kill for some adamantium," he said, his hands gripping his knees.

The demon back there spoke! It may have only said the one word, but Nicky sensed it knew far more than that. It was playing a part back there, the role of the boogeyman. He felt the delight it took in scaring the shit out of him. Why didn't it come after him?

"Because it knows this place is full of others to do its dirty work," he said.

One thing he was sure of. He couldn't run anymore. Not only was his body done in, but mentally he'd had enough. This whole thing was starting to feel like the mother of all spook house rides.

What he needed was a weapon. If he had something, even if it was just a pointed rock, he'd feel better standing his ground. He may not win, but he could take as many down with him as possible.

The biggest free rock around him only qualified as a pebble. For the first time, he noticed how sanitized the tunnel system had been. It looked roughly hewn, but there were no signs of debris. Either someone, or something, took great care in maintaining the passageways, or it was all some kind of hologram. Or maybe even some kind of post-hypnotic suggestion. Nicky had read enough science fiction to have an open mind to anything, especially at this point.

Taking a painful, staggering step, he walked slowly down the tunnel.

"Now's the time if you wanna come and get me," he said, but not as loud as he would have hoped. He may have grown weary of running, but he was still very much afraid. "I'm not running from you anymore. I won't play your games."

His hope of ever finding Christine in this constantly evolving maze had faded. If he couldn't even tell where he was from minute to minute, how could he possibly find her?

He was so thirsty. His mouth felt as though he'd licked a beach.

Nicky hobbled onward. He was tempted to just sit down and wait for the creatures to do whatever it is they ultimately wanted with him. If their goal was to wear down his resolve, mission accomplished. His muscles were starting to cramp from dehydration.

The tunnel shook, raining granules of dirt on his head.

The familiar rush of disorientation made him lose his balance. He reached out for the wall to steady himself, swiping at air. Bracing for impact, his legs gave way as if he'd been shot at the knees.

I hope I hit my head, he thought as he fell, preferring the oblivion of unconsciousness to this.

Instead, he landed in a pile of soft snow. He opened his mouth, greedily chomping on the snow, savoring the icy cold as it melted and sluiced down his throat. For the moment, he didn't care where he was. Every fiber of his being was focused on the snow, taking in as much as he could to still the ache that gripped his body.

Ignoring the creeping numbness in his hands and face, he ate snow until his stomach hurt. When he rolled onto his back, the luminescence of the moon made him squint. The triangular tips of tall, swaying fir trees danced in the sky, brushing against the edges of the moon.

"You want me to run now, don't you?" he said. Jamming his hands under the waistband of his pants to warm them, he settled deeper into the snow. Mustering what little strength he had, he shouted, "Well, fuck you!"

The words echoed amongst the trees until they were swallowed by the whistling wind.

They weren't going to let him freeze to death out here. He didn't know how he knew that, but he was absolutely certain of it. If he stayed right here, they would bring him someplace else.

Won't they be surprised when I do the same thing there? Nothing.

The sound of crunching snow to his right caught his attention. It hurt his neck to turn and see what was making the noise.

The pale, oval head of one of the demons poked out from behind a tree. It blinked rapidly, as if its eyes weren't accustomed to the drying wind.

Nicky struggled to sit up.

Other heads started to appear, until he was pretty sure every tree hid a curious creature.

If this had happened just a day earlier, Nicky was sure the sight of all these Dover Demons surrounding him would have given him a fatal heart attack.

Now, he was too damn tired to even react. He focused on the one straight ahead of him. It was no more than ten feet away. At most, it was a little over four feet tall. A hand gripped the trunk, the fingers wrapping around it like a lizard's tail. It had no clothes or hair or fur. It must have been cold.

"Hey!" he shouted at it. The creature pulled back, slipping behind the tree until only one eye was visible. "Come over here. I can't hurt you."

There was something different about these creatures from the tall one that had spoken to him. Were they children? The tall one had a menacing air that nearly stopped his heart. Not so with these.

Nicky waved a hand, speaking softly. "Come on. Don't be afraid. Let me see you."

The creature took one side step, fully exposing itself. Its flat stomach puffed out with each breath. The others stayed mostly hidden.

Is this what they wanted all along? To break me down until I could accept them without screaming my head off or running away?

Nicky tried to urge the creature on. "Cool. Come closer."

The creature took a few tentative steps, then stopped. Its mouth opened and closed, but no sound came out.

He marveled at the strange being. It was the Dover Demon and an archetypal gray alien and so many other things. And he was actually making contact with it, not running from it or struggling against it.

"My name is Nicky. I came out here looking for you. Can you talk? Do you understand me?"

To his surprise, the demon nodded its bulbous head.

"Holy shit. You know what I'm saying."

A chilling wind snaked through the trees. The creature closed its eyes while spreading its arms out, as if to catch the wind.

"Are you here to hurt me?" Nicky asked.

It opened its eyes, and the orange tint seemed to grow brighter.

It slowly shook its head.

Nicky's pulse galloped.

I can't believe I'm talking to it!

"Can you help me? All I want is to go home. And find my friend Christine. Do you know where she is?"

It must have been too many questions at once, because the creature merely stared at him.

"I'm sorry. I'll do them one at a time. My friend is a girl. Do you know where she is?"

It shook its head no.

Nicky's spirits dwindled. If he couldn't find her, the least he could do was make his way back home and bring others to search for her.

"Okay. Do you know how I can get out of here?"

With that, it gave a small smile.

"Does that mean yes?"

The others came out from behind their protective trees, scrunching the freshly fallen snow as they approached him.

Nicky tensed.

"Will you help me get home?"

Swiveling his head back and forth, he counted at least fourteen of the creatures. Some were as tiny as three feet. They were all so close now. He could smell the sickening odor of their breath as it wafted from their mouths in spiraling plumes.

The air was charged with an emotional shift. Suddenly, they didn't seem so innocuous. There was nowhere to go. Even if he managed to slip between a pair of them, his ankles would give away before he made it ten feet.

"You said you weren't going to hurt me," he said, balling his fists.

The demon nodded once more.

When Nicky opened his mouth to speak again, they rushed him as one. The weight of their bodies expelled the air from his lungs as he struggled, his screams swallowed by the moon.

Chapter Twenty-Eight

Stephanie clawed at the fallen rocks until her fingers bled, shouting her husband's name over and over. Exhausted, she collapsed onto the floor.

For the first time since they had all been sucked into this hell, she was alone. The thought paralyzed her. Tank had told her to run, but she had no desire. Her husband was on the other side of this rock wall. If she left, she'd only be distancing herself from him.

"Goddamn you, Sam and Kelly," she said, sobbing.

If they had just let everything go, maybe none of this would have happened. Stephanie had spent a wonderful, full lifetime putting that night out of her mind. There were times she'd actually convinced herself it had never happened. After the initial reports were made public, the Dover Demon fell into the cracks, becoming a little known blip on the radar of the unexplained.

Then the paranormal craze came in the early 2000s and interest was rekindled. Sam wrote that book under a pseudonym and encouraged people in that comic book shop to explore the mystery. Why? Why couldn't he just leave well enough alone? He should have known better.

And Kelly, she'd been trying to kill herself with booze for decades. Little did they all know how her obsession had ruled her life.

Their deep yearning is what brought the demon back. Monsters exist only when you believe in them.

She had to find Tank.

Maybe there was a way to get behind the wall. This place was littered with winding passageways.

Wiping her tears with the back of her hand, she retrieved the torch and set out on unsteady legs.

She was bone weary. What she wouldn't give for a large coffee with a protein shake chaser. That and about three days of uninterrupted sleep…in Tank's arms.

Stephanie realized this was a very different place than the tunnel system they'd been in before. Venturing from the cut in the earth where she'd lost Tank, she stepped into a cave. Stalagmites, some taller than her, sprouted from the cave floor. They were slick and jagged, like old, rotted teeth. The soft *plink-plink* of dripping water echoed around her. The torchlight did little to expose the hidden crannies of the prehistoric space.

Her heart did a triple beat when she spotted a circle of hazy, white light at the other end of the cave.

It was an opening!

Careful not to lose her footing, she edged around the tightly packed stalagmites, her eyes never leaving the illuminated entrance. As she came closer, she could feel the gentle caress of the night air on her face.

Because of a slight incline, she had to take the final approach to the entrance on her hands and knees. The flesh of her palms was flayed open by the sharp, rocky floor. Her kneecaps felt close to popping off as jagged edges dug into the soft tissue beneath the caps. Stephanie didn't slow down, despite the pain. Even if what was outside was on the other side of the world, she had to get out of the darkness and the oppressive weight of the earth above her. All avenues in this strange place led to even odder twists and turns. There was a chance Tank could be outside waiting for her. More likely was the possibility of being dragged down the rabbit hole once again. The key was to keep moving. Stephanie feared stopping. Once they did, the game was over. The finality terrified her. What, exactly, would be their end?

Slipping several times, her hands buried themselves in snow, numbing the pain. She pulled herself to her feet, walking free from the cave.

The cave's mouth was on a ridge. Walking to the edge, she looked down at an endless cluster of evergreens, their verdant needles bathed in white. The ground was, at best, only twenty or so feet away. There looked to be enough crags in the rock face for her to make her way down without falling to her death.

She froze when she heard someone shout, "No! You promised!"

Oh my God! That's Nicky!

She yelled, "Nicky! Where are you? Nicky!"

The pained pleas of her godson staggered her. She had to find him. She looked everywhere, but could only see trees. He was down there, in those trees. And he was frightened.

"Nicky!"

He didn't call out again.

Stephanie tossed the torch into the cave, needing both hands to make her way down. Her foot missed an outcrop of stone and she started to fall. Flipping onto her back, the wind was knocked out of her. She watched the stars whiz by as she slid down the hill. She screamed.

To her relief, there had been so much snow that she sailed down the hill as if she were sleigh riding in the park. She came to a stop not far from the tree line.

Her head spun and she prayed that didn't mean she was about to be thrown into another place.

No! You're just dizzy from sliding upside down and backward. Keep moving. Find Nicky.

"Nicky! It's Stephanie! Can you hear me? Where are you?"

She trudged through the knee-high snow, entering into the darkness of the trees.

"Nicky!"

Stopping for a moment to listen for any sign of her godson, she thought she heard something moving off to her left. It could have been the settling of a tree branch, laden with snow. Either way, she had to find out.

It was freezing and snow was falling into her boots and creeping up her legs, but she didn't care. Nicky was close. She just knew it.

Running in the snow was far from stealthy. She wasn't concerned about sneaking up on someone. She had to find Nicky.

She thought she saw something, a diminutive shadow, pass between two trees up ahead. She stopped, keeping close behind a wide evergreen. Another shadow darted from left to right. Then another.

What the hell is going on over there?

Moving slowly, she crept closer, careful to hug the trees so she could easily duck behind one if needed.

There was a clearing up ahead.

Stephanie had to cover her mouth to muffle the sound of her gasp.

Nicky was on the ground, his arms up, covering his face. He was surrounded by tiny demons, their heads and shoulders bopping up and down as if to the beat of some unheard tune.

One of the creatures stood over Nicky, one hand on his arms. What was it doing?

Nicky's arms fell to his sides.

The creature bent closer, its alien face hovering over Nicky's.

Before Stephanie could stop herself, she shouted, "Stop it!"

All of the demons turned to her.

"Get away from him!" she screamed, emboldened now to approach them. She was going to get Nicky or die trying. He looked utterly helpless. He moaned a bit and even though his eyes were open, she could have sworn he was in some kind of trance.

To her shock, the demons backed away from her. All except the one standing over Nicky.

"Don't you touch him," she said.

With a lightning fast jerk, the demon wrapped its hand over Nicky's face.

"No!"

Stephanie ran, hurtling toward the demon. Nicky's body convulsed.

It felt like both hot lava and brittle electricity. Nicky's body and brain were on fire. The pain was quickly replaced by a soothing numbness. His body went limp, though his skull buzzed. Nicky couldn't speak, couldn't move.

The childlike demon had bullied itself into his brain. Nicky felt himself, the pure essence of everything he had come to be over seventeen years, being pushed into a dark, empty place. No matter how he struggled for control, he couldn't stop the interloper from taking full control.

Get the hell out of me!

The demon pushed harder. There was a pinprick of pain at the top of his spine. A straight wall of flame ran down his back, spreading to his extremities. Then that too quickly ebbed.

Nicky opened his eyes, saw the creature on top of him. But it was as if he was looking down a long tunnel with eyes that weren't his own.

Oh God, I'm dying.

He could easily picture his body floating away. He was still here, his back frozen in the snow, the demon's weight pushing down on his chest. And in a way, he wasn't. It was impossible to describe. Nicky felt like one of the Jaegers from the movie *Pacific Rim*—a mechanical humanoid controlled by two humans. Inside his Jaeger head were two beings, struggling for control.

Help me, Stephanie! I don't know how much longer I can fight this thing.

With only a few yards between them, Stephanie left her feet, driving into the creature with all of her weight. It rolled off of Nicky. She felt its bones crunch under her as they tumbled in the snow. When they stopped, she pushed herself away from it, desperate not to touch the alien creature any longer than she had to.

She hurried on her hands and knees to Nicky, scooping him into her arms.

Tapping his cheeks, she tried to bring him out of whatever hold the creature had him in.

"Wake up, honey. Wake up. You're okay, Nicky."

He felt like a dead weight in her arms.

She turned to see the other creatures scoop the broken one from the snow and carry its body into the trees and out of sight.

Why didn't they attack her? If she wounded one of their own, why would they just leave her be?

Nothing about this night was making any sense.

Nicky's eyes fluttered.

"Stephanie?" he croaked.

"Yes," she said, tears splashing his face. She wiped them away, kissing his forehead. He seemed so young, so helpless, just like when he was a baby.

"Are you hurt?" she asked.

"My ankles. I fell. I don't know if I can walk anymore."

If he couldn't walk, she didn't know what they were going to do next. She felt weak as a foal. There was no way she could carry a seventeen-year-old boy, even on her best day.

"We have to find Tank and your father," she said, more to herself.

He attempted to lift his head from her lap.

"Dad is here?"

She sighed. "I don't know where here is. We all went looking for you and ended up in...in."

Nicky nodded. "The world beneath our own."

"What did you say?"

"It...it told me. I know what this is and what they are. Stephanie, it's unbelievable."

His eyes were glassy. He had the look of someone on a real bad trip. Stephanie worried that he'd either hit his head or just checked out, overwhelmed by everything he'd been through.

"Tank! Sam! Kelly!" she shouted as loud as she could.

She may not be able to bring them to anyone, but she hoped to hell someone could make it to her and Nicky.

Christine had mercifully passed out. Kelly checked her pulse. It was ragged, but strong.

What did they do to you?

Something living, sentient, was deep inside the poor girl. If they made it out of here, where could they possibly take her? The first hurdle would be belief. She couldn't imagine any sane doctor taking them at their word. And even if they did find that one in a million person willing to accept their wild story, would they be able to handle what they saw? What could they do to get that thing out of Christine? Even if they did, was it possible to rehabilitate her back to any semblance of normalcy?

No, that ship had sailed. None of them would emerge from this night the same.

"We're not getting out anyway," Kelly said, stroking Christine's hair.

Things may not be as she had envisioned them, piecing everything together over the years. But one thing held true—people did not return. Whatever these demons and their human helpers had in mind for them, letting them back into their normal lives was not one of them.

Kelly could accept that. Life hadn't exactly been a picnic. She'd stared so long and hard into the abyss, it had finally stared back. She didn't like what she saw, but she hadn't liked much of anything for years now.

I would like a tall glass of whiskey and soda on the rocks right about now.

For the moment, the DTs let her be. They'd be back, though. And each time they came trembling into her limbs, she felt worse. Her stomach was a tight knot of fiery pain. Her mouth and eyes felt like dry desert sand. It hurt to blink.

Lying back against the wall, she closed her eyes.

Sooner or later, those things were going to come back for them. It could be here, in this tucked away fairy tale house, or back underground.

There were gifts waiting for them. She pushed away the image of what it would be like to have one put inside her.

No. Right now, all she wanted to do was sleep. It might be the last nap of her life. Best to try and forget everything and let go, even if it was only for a few minutes. Whatever dreams came, there would be waking nightmares to follow.

Tank used his bulging forearms to smash several of the creatures off his chest. They flew into the cave walls, knocked unconscious.

If he could somehow thin the herd of these bastards!

They weren't strong and from everything he'd seen, built with all the durability of crystal decanters. But when they enveloped him with sheer numbers, it was hard to break free.

A pair of fingers, tasting of wet soil and ammonia, pried his mouth open. He bit down hard. The tips of the fingers rolled in his mouth. He spat them out, along with the horrendous fluid that leaked from them. In the middle of his struggle, searing vomit exploded from his mouth. It was as if his body was protecting him, pushing out whatever poisons had leaked from the wounded Ennuki.

There was no way to tell how many there were. Every time he flicked one away, two seemed to take its place. There must be reinforcements waiting in the dark to take their turn like it was a tag team wrestling match.

Tank raised his knees, catching a couple of the creatures in their midsections. As they rolled to the side, there was a loud hiss and two more leapt from the pitch to take their places.

Grunting like an angry, wounded bear, Tank somehow managed to get to his feet. The demons crawled all over him, clinging to his shoulders, arms, legs, torso and neck. One even pulled on his hair, trying to wrench his neck back and upset his balance.

"You're starting to piss me off!" Tank yelled.

He swung his arms together, cracking two Ennuki bodies against one another.

Pedaling backward, he heard the satisfying crunch of Ennuki bones when he introduced them to the cave wall. Keeping his back to the wall, he continued to punch, kick and tear at every demon that made the foolhardy choice to attack.

By the meager light in the cave, he saw a floor littered with broken bodies.

Now that his back was protected, he was gaining the upper hand. He and Sam had been in a real knock-down, drag-out bar fight in New York when they were in their early twenties. He remembered the euphoric rush of adrenaline when he'd realized they were about to turn the tables on the five frat assholes who had decided to brawl because they didn't like their Massachusetts accents.

That old feeling was back again.

He punched one square in the face, elbowing another in the throat as he pulled his arm back.

They were down to their last six or so. He was having a tough time shaking the ones that had wrapped around his ankles.

It was then that he remembered the pistol in his pocket. A demon latched on to his arm when he tried to pull it out. He reflexively pulled the trigger, shooting into the ground, just missing his foot. It didn't spook the creatures in the slightest. The blast was deafening.

Jamming the barrel to the face of the one on his arm, he watched its head explode in a pulpy mist. Fat droplets of its alabaster blood got in his eyes, momentarily blinding him.

Eyes closed and burning, he lashed out, grabbing one by the neck. He smelled the sizzle of flesh as he stuck the smoking barrel somewhere on its body. The body jittered from his grasp when the bullet tore into it.

When he could see again, the picture before him wasn't as promising as he'd hoped. The cavalry had arrived as more spilled into the tunnel like rats from a sinking ship. He fired into the mass until the hammer clicked on empty chambers.

Through everything, he still hadn't managed to dislodge the creatures from his legs.

"Damn it to hell!" he hollered, trying to kick them free.

What's the fucking use? he thought. There were too many to count waiting for their chance to take a crack at him.

Suddenly, he felt as if he'd been swept up into the eye of a hurricane. The demons clung to him as he left his feet.

Not again!

He came out of the hurricane in a snow-covered field. He wondered briefly if it was the same one they'd all been dumped into earlier.

Landing on his knees, he crushed the two Ennuki attached to his legs.

The others peeled off him the moment the world stopped spinning. Tank watched them dash into the trees fifty yards away. They moved so fast, so much like upright lizards, they barely broke through the upper crust of the newly fallen snow.

Backing off the two dead demons, he sat in snow that went up to his chest.

"Now what?" he said, watching his breath trail away.

It was so tempting to lie back in the snow and close his eyes. The fight had bled him dry of any strength he had left.

Maybe it's better to just freeze to death. I won't even know it's happening. All I have to do is sleep. I'm so damn tired, that won't take much.

As long as Stephanie was out there, he couldn't let himself do it. He may not be much help to Sam and Nicky and Christine now, but if he had enough in him to stay conscious, he had to find his wife.

They'd been together almost forty years now and he loved her more than when they'd gotten hitched straight out of college.

"Uunnnggghh!"

His knees went off like gunshots as he got to his feet.

There was nothing as far as he could see. Just snow and trees. The snow had stopped falling and the breeze from earlier had ceased as well.

I may not even be in the same state right now.

The snow was deep. It took Herculean effort just to make one step. He wished he could scamper like those things, unaffected by the snow.

Breathing hard, his chest hurt.

So damn cold.

He walked in the direction of the trees. At the very least, their canopy of evergreen branches should have made for less snow, which would mean easier walking.

Now if I only knew where the hell I was going. I don't even know what fucking day it is, much less where I am.

Tank scooped up some snow, filling his mouth so he could at least get some hydration.

Drink now before those bastards flip you somewhere else.

He'd spent a lifetime controlling his environment and destiny, both with his hands and force of will. He may not have graduated at the top of his class at Fordham University, but he knew what he wanted and stopped at nothing to obtain it.

This experience had laid him low, reduced him to munching on snow that had probably been pissed on by a passing bird, staggering to God-knows-where, separated from his wife and friend and sick with worry over the fate of his godson.

"If you're going to kill me, do it now," he said, his attempt to shout failing as he simply didn't have the strength.

There goes Big Tank, too weak to even yell.

Coming upon the first tree, he leaned his chest into it, letting it support his weight for a while.

"I'll just wait right here until you come fetch me," he said, his heart palpitating dangerously.

Tank's forehead pressed into the sharp bark. He couldn't keep his eyes open. He wondered how long he'd remain on his feet if he fell asleep standing.

A voice, whispering through the trees, jarred him awake.

Stephanie?

It came again, an urgent cry whose words were lost, absorbed by the woods and snow.

He had a choice. He could stand here, calling back, or he could walk. If that was Steph crying out, she could be hurt. He'd have to go to her.

Gripping each tree he passed, Tank weaved like a drunk through the woods, locked on to the phantom voice in the night.

The house was empty. It looked as if no one had lived in it for decades. Sam kicked a block of wood across the living room floor.

Why an abandoned house? And who would put a house here, in the middle of nowhere?

Of course, with the snow cover, he couldn't get a true lay of the land. There could be a road out there, with civilization not far behind.

But the place just felt...*removed*. It was like an artist's full scale rendering of what a hermit's cabin would look and smell like. There was as much substance here as on the faux street of a Hollywood set.

Nicky wasn't here. As his father, he could just tell. The separation from his son was killing him. Nicky was everything to him. The only thing that kept him focused, from losing all hope, was the need to find his son and the hunger for retribution. These things and the people that worked in tandem with them had taken his sole reason for living away.

Sam promised himself that he would not waste his next opportunity should he face another Ennuki or Usher or what he could best categorize as a human handler or protector. What he and Kelly did to that man in the shed would be the stuff of playtime at a daycare.

How long until we're ripped out of here? he thought, opening the front door to let the cold air sharpen his senses. *When it happens next, where will Kelly and Christine end up? It's not likely they'll keep us together. This was just a tease. They know I want my son more than anything. This is their way of saying, 'Close, but not cigar. Pay a buck and try your luck!'*

He swooned, standing in the doorway, and had to latch on to the doorknob to stay upright. It passed quickly, and he realized they weren't jettisoning him just yet. It was simply exhaustion making itself known.

Looking up at the stars, there wasn't a sign of a passing plane. If they were still in or near Dover, Logan Airport was just twenty miles away. There were always planes in the sky.

"Tank! Sam! Kelly!"

Hearing his name swept away every cobweb in his brain. Was that Stephanie?

"Stephanie!"

His voice echoed back to him as it drifted into the pitch.

He thought he heard something else. Not quite a reply.

"Kelly, come down and hear this," he called.

She didn't reply. Sam raced up the stairs. Kelly and Christine were fast asleep. After what he'd witnessed with the girl, he was grateful that she wasn't conscious.

Should I wake them?

He paused at the foot of the bed.

He couldn't leave Christine alone. And he and Kelly couldn't drag her out into the snow searching for who was calling out to him. It sounded slightly like Stephanie, but it could also be a trick.

Let them be. I'll come back for them, if this place is even still here.

Sam covered them as best he could with the bottom sheet, untucking two corners from the mattress. Darting back down the stairs, he had to stop before he blacked out.

You're really riding the edge. Take it steady and slow.

Exiting the house, he thought he heard his name again.

He hollered, "Stephanie!"

It sounded as if it was coming from the forest to his right. For the voice to carry this far, the person behind it couldn't have been too deep in the woods.

He trudged through the snow, hoping like hell this wasn't some way of luring him to an even worse ordeal.

Chapter Twenty-Nine

Sam's spirits were buoyed when he spotted a trio of figures emerging from the cover of trees in the distance. They looked too tall to be the Ennuki.

Of course, they could be those strange Ushers. Or maybe the goon squad sent to make us pay for what we did to that Lando Solo bastard.

If they were, he was finding a hard time giving a shit. Keeping conscious long enough to find out who was approaching was hard enough.

One of the figures waved their arms.

"Hello!" Sam shouted, waving back. He stopped to catch his breath.

"Sam?" a woman's voice cried.

Holy Jesus, it was Stephanie!

"Steph! Who's with you?"

When she spoke, a wicked breeze tore across the field, snatching her reply.

"What?" Sam yelled.

Again, the wind kicked up when she replied.

Are they controlling the fucking weather, too? he mused. Then again, for all he knew, they weren't actually outside. This could all be a huge mind game, like being trapped in the Matrix, even though the deadly cold felt pretty damn real.

One of the figures stumbled, and the other two paused to prop him up.

He couldn't just stand here and wait for Stephanie. She might need his help, no matter how meager it might be. Ordering his legs to resume walking, he pushed on. The muscles in his thighs burned as if someone had injected them with acid.

Losing his balance a time or two, the sideways fall into the soft snow didn't do any damage, but wasted energy trying to get up. When he was less than thirty yards from the staggering figures, his eyes burned with tears.

"Nicky!"

Forgetting all of the exhaustion and pain, Sam ran as best he could in the deep snow to his son. A pale and shaky Tank and an exhausted Stephanie walked on either side of his son.

Nicky beamed at him. "Dad!"

No more words were spoken when Sam pulled Nicky into his arms. Both wept, locking in an embrace that felt like forever. Tank and Stephanie gave them some space, then embraced father and son.

When Sam finally pulled his son away to see his face, he said, "I thought I'd never find you." He couldn't control the quivering of his lower lip.

Nicky was more stoic, though his cheeks were stained with tears.

"That's what they wanted you to believe," Nicky said.

Tank said, "Am I crazy, or is that a house over there?"

"Yeah, it is," Sam replied, not able to take his eyes from his son. "Kelly and Christine are inside. Or at least they were when I left. How…how did you find Nicky?"

Stephanie said, "I found him in the woods, surrounded by those creatures. His ankles are hurt bad. There was no way we could walk, so I just started calling out for help. Next thing I knew, Tank was there, too."

"A little worse for wear," Tank said.

He wasn't kidding. Sam's oldest, strongest friend looked as if he'd been drained of all his blood.

"Let's all get back to the house," Sam said. "At least it's warmer in there."

He unburdened Nicky from his friends. Tank leaned into his wife as they faltered their way to the house.

Despite his elation at finding Nicky, Sam was wary. All of the players had been called to the stage. What would the next act entail? He shuddered as a fragment of a distant memory came roaring to the surface of his mind. For a split second, his spine went rigid, burning as if someone had spit a line of gasoline down his back and dropped a match. In that moment, he had the odd impression that his body was no longer his own.

When Nicky dug his hands into his shoulder, nearing collapse, the pain and the memory were gone.

"You think they'll let us get there?" Tank said.

Nicky nodded. "Yes. They've been herding us here all along. We won't be slipping through those weird black holes anymore."

"How do you know this?" Sam asked, barely letting Nicky's feet touch the ground.

"We're going to have a lot to talk about," Stephanie said.

It took a while to make it to the lonesome house. The flash of strength Sam had felt when he saw Nicky burned out by the time they walked in the front door. He did his best to let him down gently onto the dusty floor.

Tank collapsed in a heap, shaking the walls. Stephanie sat, resting against Tank's side.

"Please tell me there's something to eat or drink," Tank said, his voice raspy.

"Just the snow outside," Sam said. "I'll get you some." He wasn't sure how he made the three trips, bringing back handfuls of snow for each of them, forgetting to get any for himself.

After packing the snow in his mouth and letting it melt, Nicky said, "I thought you said Kelly and Christine are here."

"They're upstairs," Sam said. "Christine…she went through a lot. I think they're both asleep. At least I hope they are."

"We need to wake them up," Nicky said.

"We'll wait down here," Tank said, his eyes closing. "I just need to take a breather."

"No!" Nicky barked, shocking Tank wide awake. "From now on, we all have to be together."

Stephanie wearily shook her head. "Hon, I don't think Tank can make it up the stairs. That fight with those things nearly killed him."

Sam said, "Wait, you had to fight the demons?"

"You mean those little Ennuki fuckers? Yeah. It was like being thrown into a pit of pissed off monkeys. But do you know what's weird? There were so many of them, now that I think about it, they could have at least knocked me out. I had to be outnumbered twenty to one. They kept coming and coming. When I'd used up all my bullets and every ounce of strength, I ended up topside, not far from Steph and Nicky."

The house groaned as a strong gust battered the old wood siding. Sam wondered how many more blasts the weathered place had in it before it collapsed on itself…and them.

When he turned around, Nicky was holding on to the railing, making his way up the stairs. His face was spotted with sweat. He hissed in pain with every step.

"Come on," he said. "They need us."

"Wait, let me help you," Sam said.

"Bring Tank," his son replied. "I'll be fine."

Why is he so insistent we all go upstairs together? Sam thought. *Maybe he'd been alone for so long, he fears anything less than being surrounded by all of us.*

He couldn't begin to imagine the hell Nicky had been through. If safety in numbers was what he needed, Sam would carry Tank if he had to.

It took Stephanie's assistance to get Tank on his feet. The big man's head lolled forward as they made their way up the stairs.

"Stay with us," Sam said. "Just remember the game against Waltham when we were down by ten and you'd broken your arm but refused to tell anyone but me. You threw two TDs in under a minute and partied your ass off after the game. Didn't even ask anyone to take you to a hospital until the next day. You can walk through walls, brother. Stairs is baby stuff."

Tank chuckled, his eyelids fluttering. "So what's the score now?"

"I'll be damned if I know. I'm not even sure of the game."

Stephanie said, "But Nicky does. One of those things touched him. I don't know what happened, but it changed him somehow."

Sam wondered what kind of touch Stephanie was referring to. What had it done to him? And how did she mean it had changed him? Hadn't they all been changed since coming upon the pond?

If one of those Ennuki appeared right now, he'd pummel it until it was just a memory.

"Just a few more steps, baby," Stephanie said to Tank.

They heard Nicky hobble down the hallway. "Christine?"

There was a loud thump. Sam almost dropped Tank, eager to get to the landing.

He craned his neck to see around the banister. A dark shape lay on the floor at the end of the hallway. Nicky leaned against a wall, staring at it.

What now?

Why are you doing this? Nicky railed at himself. His body was bone weary. His heart danced a dangerous beat. He felt all of this at a distance, through a set of secondary senses.

But his mind was blazing with a fire of thoughts and emotions that weren't his own. In taking over his body, the creature had also exposed itself to him, laying bare a fantastical history.

He knew the things he'd thought of as the Dover Demon were called the Ennuki. They'd been here, on earth, longer than recorded time. Though not initially from this planet, they were now *of* the planet, as elemental as water, air and fire. They possessed incredible abilities, like being able ability to transport themselves or other people anywhere they wished.

Trans-dimensional.

It was the best way Nicky could describe them.

That, paired with mind control on both individual and mass levels, made them gods to some. So much so, that there had been no shortage of people willing to devote themselves to their continuance.

Their purposes were the same as man's, though, perhaps, more simplified, more genuine.

All they wanted to do was survive. There were no grander plans, no plot to control the world. If that's what they had wanted, they wouldn't be living in the shadows. Nicky didn't get that from the Ennuki that touched him, but it was easy to fill in some of the blanks.

They were in a cycle they called the sowing. They needed people— those who had been prepared previously to host their gestating offspring, others to be impregnated with Ushers, what Nicky could only think of as lowly servants, while still more to feed the adult Ennuki. When Nicky had been in that chamber of bodies, he'd essentially been locked in their pantry.

I should have stayed there. Then I wouldn't be used for this.

Nicky led his father and godparents farther, knowing what awaited them. And no matter how much he screamed inside, the words to lure them upstairs continued.

Kelly was startled awake when she heard voices downstairs, followed by the front door slamming shut, then opening and closing again. Caught in a kind of sleep paralysis, she could only open her eyes, but her limbs remained frozen, locked in immobile slumber. She could feel the weight of Christine sleeping against her, but she couldn't look down far enough to see the poor girl.

Why can't I move?

She wanted to call out for Sam, but her mouth refused to open.

What if what she heard wasn't Sam? There was more than one person in the house. She could tell by the different voices. But for some reason, she couldn't discern whom the voices belonged to.

Have I been drugged?

The only other option was that she was still asleep, and this was one hell of a nightmare. If she was lucky, this entire night had been nothing but a bad dream brought on by her obsessive nature and too much booze.

If this is a dream, please wake up. Come on, Kelly. Snap out of it!

She couldn't even dream-pinch herself because her limbs were like phantom weights.

Someone was coming up the stairs. Kelly's gaze shifted to the open doorway. Would Sam come walking through, or one of those creatures? Could it be something even worse?

Kelly held her breath.

"Christine?"

Was that Sam's son? She'd never met him, not close enough to hear him talk. That voice though, part boy, part man, searching for Christine, it had to be him. Kelly wanted to shout, "We're in here!" Even her tongue couldn't move, stuck in place as if it had been sutured.

Something crashed to the floor and she definitely heard Sam, followed by Stephanie and Tank.

Thank you, God, thank you!

Her elation was short-lived as her perspective shifted from the doorway to the ceiling.

Something had lifted her up.

Catching fleeting glimpses of furtive shadows all around her, the ceiling came closer…closer, until her nose was almost touching it. Her stomach flipped as she was dropped, hitting what she thought was the bed, though she could feel nothing.

She screamed and screamed in her mind as a long-fingered hand crept from her periphery, covering her eyes, robbing her of her remaining sense.

The Ennuki seemed to melt from the walls, squatting outside the doorway of the room at the end of the hall. Another bled from the wall above it, hitting the floor with a reverberating thud. They were twin gargoyles, leering at Nicky.

He heard his father come up behind him.

"Just stay here, Nicky. I'll take care of them."

Nicky shook his head violently. "Don't. More are coming."

"And that's why I'm going to take care of those two before it gets worse. Kelly and Christine are in that room."

"They're guarding it because of them," Nicky said.

Leaning against the guardrail, Tank said, "If the girls are inside, I say we just walk through them."

"Nicky, what do you know about them?" his father asked.

"Just a little. When they surrounded me out in the forest, for a moment, I could kind of see them in all these different places in time. In between all these images, every now and then, all these different visions came through to me. I know this is going to sound weird, but I almost didn't want it to stop. It was...incredible. Like some kind of virtual reality information stream. I don't know. That's the best I can compare it to."

"So you know that they're planning to do with us?"

Nicky felt his chest tighten. He couldn't take his eyes off the pair of Ennuki guards. He wanted to scream at the top of his lungs, tell them to leave this place, leave him and Christine and Kelly behind. The Ennuki that commanded him wouldn't allow for it.

"I...I'm not sure. I just know that we're all here, now, for a reason. It's like they've been herding us this whole time, showing us things, breaking us down. We could only come to this place after we've been made ready."

Stephanie said, "Like they said we were prepared to receive their *gifts*."

"What do we do now?" Tank said.

As much as he wanted to tell them anything that would give them hope, Nicky realized it would have been pointless. He loved his father too much to lie to him now. "There's nothing we can do. It's happening."

The pair of Ennuki stood straight. A strange odor filled the house, an unsettling combination of cinnamon and bleach.

"What's going on?" his father said, gripping his shoulders. "If you tell me, maybe we can get the upper hand."

Nicky watched a man walk from the wall. It was one of those men with the partially formed faces. The Ushers. Another came striding out of the room, walking between the Ennuki. Stephanie let out a startled yelp.

Ushers and Ennuki were coming from the walls, rising from the floors just like the ghosts on the Haunted Mansion ride Nicky's mom and dad took him on when he was ten. He'd thought it was one of the most awesome things he'd ever seen.

Nothing about this was awesome.

Tank shouted, "They're coming up the stairs!"

Nicky's father pulled him close, a protective arm over his chest. "Get away from us," he shouted at the approaching creatures.

"Please, Dad, don't fight them. It's only going to make it worse."

"Get the hell off her," Tank spat. Stephanie screamed as two Ushers grabbed her arms, wrestling her to the ground. Before Tank could react, another Usher and several Ennuki wrapped him up by the legs. He crashed to the floor with the unmistakable sound of a bone break. Nicky had fractured his leg playing soccer when he was a freshman. That sound had haunted him ever since. He looked at Tank. His godfather and uncle not-by-blood lay unconscious. When Stephanie tried to scream, her mouth was crammed with probing Ennuki fingers, stifling her cry.

"Just let them do what they want," Nicky said to his father.

"I won't let them take you again."

"Fighting against them is exactly what they want."

That part was the one thing he'd been able to slip through. Yes, the Ennuki had reveled in their struggle. And the more they fought against them, the longer the game would be played—a game with a predetermined winner, and it wasn't going to be Nicky and his family.

His father stiffened as an Usher with a broad chest and enormous arms grabbed him from behind. Nicky was yanked backward as his father pushed against the Usher. Ennuki scampered on the floor, grabbing them both by the ankles. "No! No!"

Nicky remained silent, his jaw locked against his will, as they carried them into the room. Kelly lay on a bed next to a sleeping Christine. The room was filled with people and strange beings. The gathering parted as they were brought to the center of the room. A pair of hands forced Nicky to kneel on the cold, hard floor. He turned around to see Tank dragged lifeless into the room, followed by Stephanie who looked as if she'd had a psychotic break. Her eyes were so wide, he thought they'd roll out of her skull. The Ennuki kept her mouth plugged up with their fingers. Her chest heaved with panicked gasps.

A woman's voice carried over the sounds of his father's struggle.

"It's been a long night and I know you're all very tired. You can rest now, knowing you're at your journey's end."

Nicky stared at the stunning blond woman as she separated herself from the crowd of Ushers and Ennuki. Dressed in black pants and a black parka, the tall, pale woman towered over him.

He knew her. She was different now, more, what was the word, resplendent. In her element. Nicky had seen her before. Gorgeous women had a way of standing out in a comic book store.

They'd been tracked and manipulated far longer than he'd first imagined.

Why us?

His father went slack.

"Wh-what?" he whispered.

The woman smiled.

"Sam Brogna. It's been a while, though I knew exactly when we'd meet again."

Chapter Thirty

Sam tried to shake himself loose, but the Usher held on tighter than a thick cord of wet rope.

"How do you know me?" he asked the blond woman. She was strikingly beautiful and so out of place, she seemed more alien than the Ennuki. His son stared at her with trancelike wonder. Something was very wrong with Nicky. It went beyond the fear overload and physical exhaustion they were all feeling.

The woman smiled without a trace of mirth on her face. "I'm not surprised you don't remember me. In your man's world, I was nothing more than a piece of eye candy to you, I'm sure."

One of the Ennuki curled up next to her leg. She placed an affectionate hand on its hairless head.

Sam said, "Look, I don't know what you're talking about. I'm not going to appeal to your humanity because you seem pretty at home with these things. All I ask is that you let my son and the girl go."

She shook her head and said, "If I let her go now, I'd be condemning her to death."

She motioned for the Ennuki and Ushers to stand aside. When they did, Sam saw Christine on the bed. The moonlight glowed on the sweat of her face. Seeing her stomach, bulging as if she were seven or eight months pregnant, he tried again to break free.

"What did you do to her?" he shouted.

"I've made her what all little girls dream of—a mother. I know it looks like she's quite far along, but the gestation time for an Usher is one year. We'll take very good care of her during that time."

"And then what will you do to her, once she's given birth to one of your monstrosities?"

"I'll do nothing to her. The birth is what will kill her. But look what her sacrifice will produce." She waved a hand at an Usher by her side. The man looked as if any defining detail on his face had been airbrushed away. He was a blank slate. Sam was sure that went for his mind and will as well. They used Christine and others to produce a race of slaves—servants for the terrible demons and their human helpers.

Nicky's body shook with quiet sobs. "No, please, not her."

The woman gave his son a look of deep sympathy. "I'm sorry, but it's too late. In time, maybe you'll understand. You already see more than your father or his friends. If you wish, when all is done, I can continue to let you see and grow. Or I can make it all go away…until the next sowing."

Sam's muscles coiled but he knew there was nothing he could do. Whatever meager strength he had left wouldn't be enough to wrestle himself from a child's grasp.

Who the hell is she? How does she know my name?

He racked his brain, a cyclone of images whirling, culling faces from his childhood until now, searching for anyone remotely familiar to the beautiful yet dangerous woman.

"Why are you doing this to us?" he said.

He had to buy time. Get her to talk. Perhaps finding her connection to him would unlock a path that could get them the hell out of this place. It was a remote chance, but it was the only one he had left.

The woman, now covered with clinging Ennuki, sauntered over to him, running her fingers over the lines of his face and jaw. She said, "I knew exactly who you were the moment we met. When you sold your company to my investment firm, I remember you concentrating all of your energies on my partners—older men who could fake gravitas better than a woman does her orgasms when you drunkenly flop yourselves on us. You even shook my hand, lingering long enough to give me a lascivious look before business guided your lustful thoughts to money. We sought you out because of what you had become. You've been watched closely for a very long time, Mr. Brogna."

Sam closed his eyes, calling up the varying days he'd met with the investors, working hard to secure a deal that would extricate him from the rat race and have enough money so Nicky and his own kids would never have to worry. At the time, he'd had two concerns. Getting out with a bundle of cash, and reconnecting with his son before he lost him forever. He vaguely recalled the woman, but couldn't remember her name or the role she'd played in the investment firm. Had they been watching him all those years, waiting to take his success, then his life? A fire burned in his gut.

"Still not ringing any bells?" she said. "Maybe I should extract your memory the way you did to Mr. Solo."

"It didn't have to go that way. He could have cooperated with us," Sam said.

"You killed him, Mr. Brogna. But he had fulfilled his purpose, so we hold no ill will against you. You and your son followed his clues like fairy tale breadcrumbs. Did you think you could torture a man and he'd just walk away as if nothing had happened? His heart gave out. Whether it was the loss of blood or the stress, we'll never know. We don't do autopsies. Now he's in the feeding room. At least nothing of him will go to waste. We'll take care of his family. He was actually a beloved man in his community, just as he was here, in our community."

Feeding room? If she wanted Sam to feel bad, she'd misplayed her hand. He'd kill her and every living thing around them to get his son and friends free. If the man they'd tortured was now food for those demons, so be it. He'd been one of them. Even worse. In his way, he'd been a Pied Piper, leading Sam's family and friends to their doom.

"You still haven't answered my question," he said.

"I like how you think you're in a position to even ask questions," she said. "Normally I wouldn't waste my time, but you've all done your part tonight and the community is thoroughly satisfied. Now first, that man you killed, who we'll continue to refer to as Lando Solo so as not to confuse you, he was a wealthy philanthropist who lived on Beacon Hill. His disappearance will delay the disbursement of his fortune to the numerous charities he was a part of or had created. You and your lady friend have done a great disservice to so many in need."

A thought hit Sam like a blow to the head.

Where is Kelly?

He'd been so preoccupied with the woman, his son and the creatures all around them, he hadn't realized that Kelly wasn't on the bed with Christine.

"Now," the woman continued, "the big *why me?* Call it the wrong place at the wrong time or fate. When you stumbled upon our reaping in 1977, you became an integral part of our thriving yet secretive society. You were taken, just for a small while, and prepared by the Ennuki you saw in the road so you would be ready to receive their gift in due time—the gift of a life more wondrous than you can imagine."

211

Again, the memory of that fiery pain in his spine flashed across Sam's brain. They hadn't gotten away as he'd remembered. No. After those men took the eggs, they returned for them, dragging them off the road. Oh, how the girls had screamed. Sam had been pushed face first into the dirt, unable to help Kelly or Stephanie. That creature from the road had stood over him. It bent down, its slimy hand wrapping around his head. And then came the pain, followed by a dullness that somehow made everything all right. The next thing he knew, he was back on the road, running to the car.

That's when they did it! They prepared us then, but were able to wipe it from our memories.

"I won't let you put those, those things in us!" Sam shouted. The Usher applied more pressure around his chest, constricting his lungs.

She wagged a finger at him. "This is exactly why you were chosen for tonight's hunt. We don't give everyone the same freedoms that were allowed to you. I knew you were a fighter, in every sense of the word. Which is why we lured your son and his friend here. We didn't want to just take you as we do so many others when it's their time. No, you were going to provide some sport to the evening. Your fear and anger and struggles have been like an elixir to the Ennuki. They feed on it, just as much as they feed on human flesh."

Sam spat a gob of phlegm and blood on her feet. A tiny Ennuki flattened itself to the floor, lapping it up. Sam had to look away.

"You're sick," he said. "What kind of a person feeds people to monsters?"

"Monsters? You're failing to understand our place in this world. The Ennuki aren't monsters. We protect them because they are ancient, full of fascination and wonder. Do we tear down the pyramids because they're old and of no practical use? No, we treasure them. For eons, the Ennuki have lived here, and for just as long, select bloodlines have worked in tandem with them, protecting them, preserving them, helping them thrive."

"Thrive? For what? So you can live underground like rats, stealing people from their homes so you can implant them with their sick eggs or leave them for food? What twisted government agency do you work for?"

The woman sighed. "It's so much more than that. You can cast any government conspiracy theories aside. We are greater than any country's government. We have existed long before contrived political or social systems. There's a symbiotic relationship that must be maintained, both sides benefiting so much from the other, even if one side is ignorant to the greater plan." She squatted so she could look him in the eye. Sam saw no remorse in her crystal blue eyes, but a fevered conviction in all that she had said. "Sam, we need the Ennuki. They feed man with mystery! Without mystery, there is no faith, no yearning for greater truths, even emotion will slide away into a state of apathy. A world without mystery is a mundane existence. Strip it away, and mankind will be nothing short of living, breathing automatons that will grow, eat, shit and procreate until their hearts run out, knowing the grave is just an extension of the banality of life. Sam, the Ennuki keep man truly *alive*." She turned to Tank. "Of all of you, I would think you would understand the most, Mr. Clay. Please tell me I'm right."

Sam turned round to see Tank stirring. His friend used his forearms to push his head from the floor.

He grumbled, "The only thing I understand is that you're insane."

Tank hadn't let on that he was conscious the entire time. He listened to every word in the exchange between Sam and the woman, gathering knowledge and strength in equal measures. Sam did right to keep her talking. First, it gave them a better idea of what they were dealing with. Second, every minute spent talking gave his body much needed rest. He may not be able to take on the world, but he'd recharged enough to put up some kind of fight.

He remembered seeing her in the bar the night he went to talk to Stephanie. Now he realized his bumping into her had been no happy accident. She was merely sizing him up, maybe wanting to get a close look at her future prey. Had they all run into her at some point these past few months? He felt naked, exposed and raw. They'd been under a microscope this entire time without knowing it.

The woman said, "You study ancient archaeology, do you not? You've seen how past civilization depended so much on mystery. It formed their basis for religion, society and political and economic structures. If ancient people weren't afraid, they would have never gathered as one, building great societies that advanced the human mind and condition. We as a people would have never advanced as we have without the underlying plethora of enigmas that the Ennuki provide. Our mission is to provide for their every need, to keep them strong so that we can not only survive, but thrive!"

"So tell me," Tank said, "your little pets, do you care for them, or are they as much a prisoner as we are? It looks to me like you've tamed them pretty good, like hairless dogs. How much can a pack of dogs change the course of human history? I think you're looking for a way to justify your actions and the ones of every damned fool before you."

The woman's cheeks reddened. Her air of cold superiority noticeably dissipated.

While she pondered her retort, Tank glanced at his wife. Stephanie was there in body, but he could see in her eyes that she was gone, far enough to protect herself from what was happening. She'd never been comfortable with what they had experienced, spending three decades convincing herself it had never happened. She wouldn't even be here if it weren't for Nicky. Tank prayed that she could come back to him once they made it out of here. He eyed the Ennuki that held her in place.

I'll make you bastards regret you ever laid a hand on her. That's right, keep staring at me, buddy. I'm going to rip your fucking eyes right out of your head.

"Talking to you is pointless," the woman said. "Your mind is too narrow. Just know that the mystery of your disappearances will strengthen us, both above and below." She turned to an Usher. "Show them."

The Ennuki hissed like feral cats, flitting about the room. Sam continued struggling to get free while Nicky remained on his knees, immobile.

When the Ennuki and Ushers shifted, the farthest corner of the room became visible. Tank had to control himself when he saw their latest move.

Sam cried out, "Kelly!"

She was held to the wall by a slick-looking webbing. Her eyes were open, dilated with terror. Even though her legs were free, she didn't move. Her boots hovered several inches off the floor.

An Usher carrying one of the wet, leathery eggs placed it on the floor before her.

The woman said, "Strip her."

Four Ennuki scampered to the corner of the room, busily working at her clothes, tearing buttons and ripping fabric. Her gun fell from her pocket, skittering along the floor. Kelly's mouth hung open in mute horror. Tank stayed as still as possible.

"Let her go," Sam demanded. An Usher grabbed his hair, jerking his head back.

Kelly's body was completely exposed. Fat droplets of sweat danced between her heaving cleavage.

The woman picked up the egg. Its flesh pulsated in her hands.

"Kelly never wavered in her belief in the Ennuki," she said. "She knew there was more than what you remembered. She wanted to see more, to know more. You thought she was unsettled when she was, in actuality, awakened. For that, we've rewarded her beyond the gift that she is about to receive. All physical sensation has been suppressed. She won't feel a thing, at least not at first. Inside her will grow a new generation of Ennuki. Her body will provide decades of nourishment. As will yours."

As the egg was brought in contact with her bare stomach, Kelly winced.

"You don't have to do this," Tank said.

His blood went cold when Nicky turned to him and said, "They do. She's right. It was always going to come to this, Uncle Tank."

Sam cried out, "Nicky, stop. They did something to your mind— brainwashed you or something. This isn't right."

Twin trails of tears poured from Nicky's eyes. "I love you, Dad. But there's nothing we can do now."

"That's not you talking," Sam said, his voice trembling with rage and sadness.

Tank watched as the woman stepped away from the egg that was now attached to Kelly's stomach. His own gut lurched as the egg was slowly absorbed into Kelly's body.

Kelly's eyes flew open, attempting to look down and see what was happening.

Taking several deep breaths, Tank drew up whatever he had left and sprang to his feet.

Chapter Thirty-One

If Kelly's cries could have escaped her lips, they would have deafened everyone in the room.

She watched the egg worm itself into her stomach, but she felt nothing.

How is it going to fit inside me?

That woman had said her body would nourish it for decades.

Please just let me die.

Kelly prayed her heart would simply give out. She heard its frantic thrum. If it galloped anymore, it would have to break. If there were a merciful God, he would take her now.

Looking down, the egg was gone, every cell now one with her—*in her.*

She saw Tank throw his captors off him like rag dolls, freeing Sam next.

Pandemonium broke out.

Kelly looked over at Christine—her distended stomach harboring yet another creature in this menagerie of madness. Would the girl ever regain consciousness? Or would she remain like this, a sleeping beauty for the next year until it was time to make her fatal delivery?

She shouldn't even be here. They used her for sport, wasting nothing. They'll make monsters any way they can.

She suddenly felt very sleepy as some sensation came back to her.

Kelly was full, so crammed inside that she felt something would have to give. Organs would pop, the flesh of her stomach would have to rupture to make room for her uninvited intruder.

Unable to keep her eyes open any longer, Kelly let herself be pulled in by the hungry tide of oblivion. Her last thought was how full of love and hope she'd felt that night in 1977, driving home from the movies. Sam was the love of her life, and she'd been sure that they had a long, wonderful future ahead of them.

That life had been robbed from them.

And now this one, too.

"Aarrrrhhhhh!" Tank bellowed, rising up with determined fury. Sam watched him grab an Ennuki by the ankles and swing it into an Usher.

Once Tank was free, he pulled the Ushers away from Sam, who now joined in the melee.

In the midst of the instant chaos, Sam heard Nicky scream, "Stop, you're only making it worse!"

Sam couldn't imagine what they had done to his son's brain. He'd make them pay for it now and hope it could be reversed later.

The Ennuki were easy to fend off, but the Ushers, full-grown pseudo-men, were a different story. Sam fought with renewed vigor, clawing his way to Kelly. He saw that Nicky was left alone, Ennuki running past him to get to Sam and Tank.

The blond woman shouted, "Don't let them leave here!" She was swarmed by Ennuki as they formed a protective shield around her.

Right now, Sam didn't give a shit about her.

"Kelly!"

With an Usher tugging at his back, he stumbled into her. His face came in contact with her stomach, her flesh cold as the grave. He saw her chest move, so she was still alive.

How was that enormous egg inside her?

He tore at the webbing around her wrists. It remained in place, as solid as strips of iron. Ennuki and Ushers pulled him away. Sam punched and kicked wildly.

Tank blurted, "You want to touch my wife?"

Sam watched his friend grab the pair of Ennuki that held Stephanie and drive his fists into their eyes. He yanked the orbs free, flicking wet gristle from his hands as he went for the next. The demons hissed hysterically, flopping on their backs as if they'd been electrocuted.

The entire house shook with their struggle and the sounds of hurried footsteps coming up the stairs.

Damn reinforcements!

He looked to Kelly and saw the terrified pleading in her eyes. If she could speak, he knew what she would say.

Kicking an Ennuki aside, its body rolling into another, he found Kelly's gun, Betty. Turning to her with the gun, the relief that softened her face told him he was right.

"I'm sorry, Kel," he sobbed.

Sam pulled the trigger, aiming for the very spot where the egg had been placed. Her abdomen exploded, spilling pus and flesh that was not her own. The Ennuki hissed like a den of vipers, recoiling at the mortally damaged gift.

Recovering from their shock, the Ennuki redoubled their efforts to subdue him. The woman shouted, "Make him pay, but don't kill him!"

Sam held his own, but his strength was fading fast. He used up the last few bullets Betty had to offer, taking down an Usher and a pair of Ennuki. When it was empty, he used the handle to pistol whip as many as he could. The gun fell when he felt the bones in his hands shatter.

Bellowing with rage, he pulled an Ennuki from the floor, flinging it at the woman. Its body was repelled by the shield of Ennuki.

"Dad! Uncle Tank! Stop!" Nicky screamed, over and over.

He reached over and grabbed his son's arm. There was no way they could continue fighting in here. He had to get them out of the house. Sam eyed the window, wondering how far the drop would be. It was the only way out. If he could cushion the blow for Nicky with his own body, he would.

"Come on," he said, bashing an Ennuki in the face with his elbow.

Nicky refused to move.

"You're feeding them," Nicky said.

"Then let's stop by getting the hell out of here!"

As Sam dragged him through the scrum to the window, Nicky tugged back on his arm.

"They won't let you leave. If you go out there, they can easily bring you right back."

The woman said, "Listen to your son, Sam. You can't fight your way out of this. You've let your wife go. Now you need to let yourself go as well."

Lacy.

Despite how things had ended, he hoped she was left out of this. What would become of her when he and Nicky never returned? So many lives were being destroyed tonight. He'd failed everyone.

And just like that, his body gave in. He lost his grip on Nicky as he was pulled away from the window. He turned his head in time to see Tank disappear under a pile of Ennuki bodies. Stephanie lay on the floor, immobile and frozen in fear.

"Nicky, I'm so sorry," he blurted.

His son sniffed back tears. "You have nothing to be sorry about, Dad. None of this is your fault. It has to happen. There was nothing any of us could have done to stop it."

Sam forgot about the Ennuki and Ushers wrestling to take him down. He couldn't fathom the sudden role reversal. His son was giving *him* comfort in the face of a long, painful death.

Now that he and Tank were once again restrained, the woman emerged from the protective ranks of the Ennuki. Sam said to her, "I'll stop. I promise I'll stop. Just please, let Nicky go."

The woman flashed a chilling smile. "We have every intention of returning your son."

"Don't believe her," Tank said. He'd been laid out on his back, an Ennuki resting on each limb to hold him down.

"What choice do you have, really?" the woman said. She then turned to Nicky. "The Ushers will take care of you. I'd prefer you not see this."

When Nicky opened his mouth to protest, one of the demons ran to him, pressing its forehead against his own. Sam's heart was crushed as Nicky's eyelids drooped and he was led away by an Usher.

"Nicky," Sam blubbered as he slipped out of sight.

The woman looked to him. "Shall we begin?"

Stephanie was the last to receive the gift. She saw everything as if it were on a movie screen, far removed from her. She sat in the very last row of an impossibly long theater, viewing a horror movie that was more snuff than anything else. Sam and Tank were affixed to the wall, next to Kelly's ruined body. She'd watched the Ennuki tear off their clothes and the blond woman press an egg to each of their stomachs. The way they screamed and thrashed about, it must have hurt worse than any pain she could have imagined.

It only got worse when the eggs were fully absorbed. They screeched in agony until their voices blinked out. They lost consciousness soon after.

The woman approached her. "At least with the Ennuki, men can experience the pain and pleasure of carrying a child."

Stephanie didn't react—couldn't and wouldn't give her the satisfaction of pleading for her life.

She watched the egg touch her stomach, felt its cold sliminess. Something inside her burned as the egg merged with her. It felt like every nerve ending was on fire. Stephanie could tell the Ennuki, watching her with their large, unblinking eyes, were waiting for her to cry out, to beg for the pain to stop.

You'll get nothing from me!

Enduring pain that would shatter the strongest will, Stephanie looked to her slumbering giant of a husband and said goodbye.

Chapter Thirty-Two

From the *Boston Herald*—

A seventeen-year-old Dover student was found this morning outside his family's comic book shop, twelve hours after disappearing along with a friend, his father and several others. He was hypothermic and in an extreme state of shock. The disappearance had been reported by the parents of Christine Woodson. Ms. Woodson, a close friend of the missing boy, Nicholas Brogna, had gone snowmobile riding with him and her brother earlier in the day. Her brother returned home, expecting them to be close behind.

"I thought something might be wrong when Nicky's dad asked me where he was. It wasn't like either of them to take off without telling anyone," Christine's concerned brother, Roy, told reporters.

It's believed that Nicholas's father, Sam Brogna, enlisted the help of Chris and Stephanie Clay to search for his son as well. Both disappeared around the same time yesterday. So far, Nicholas has been unresponsive to questioning. A search party is being organized.

Anyone with information pertaining to the missing persons is encouraged to contact their local police or this newspaper.

Yesterday's blizzard is said to be responsible for a dozen deaths so far throughout the Boston metropolitan area. It may go down as the deadliest in over one hundred years.

Spring

Chapter Thirty-Three

Nicky Brogna saw the woman once while walking home from a bar in downtown Boston.

It had been five years since the night he lost his father and friends. Five years of silence, of moving to the city with his mother, forging a new life while harboring secrets so terrible and strange, he knew there was never going to be a way to unburden himself.

He was taller than when they'd last met and he'd grown a full beard to go with an unruly head of hair. He was pretty sure she hadn't recognized him.

But it was her. Dressed in high-end clothes and carting one of those little toy dogs that seemed to be bred solely for the rich and famous.

Would she be there when it was his time?

He wondered how old she was now. Maybe forty? Odds are, she would still be alive when the next sowing came for him. He'd accepted that fate, long ago gave up fighting its inevitability. They had let him go, but not without altering him just as they had done to his father and Tank and Stephanie and Kelly. He was pretty sure they'd tried to wipe his mind clear of that night but for some reason, it hadn't taken. It was both his miracle and his curse. Either way, he was sure they hadn't cared. They'd already demonstrated that there was no escaping your fate once you'd been marked.

By his count, he still had another twenty-five years left of mock freedom. The sowing seemed to come every three decades. He wondered what was changing in him daily on a sub-cellular level.

Some nights, sleep rarely coming until he was beyond exhaustion, he contemplated how he would kill himself. Should he do it now, save himself from a life of having this dark cloud hanging over him? Or should he wait until it was just about time, when they thought he was ripe for the plucking? It would be fun, if you could call such thoughts fun, to snatch away their prize just when they thought they had it in their grasp.

Five years removed, the things the Ennuki had flashed into his brain made less and less sense. Everything became a massive jumble. That clarity that came with contact grew fuzzier and fuzzier with each passing day. They had not only shown him their history, but had controlled his words and actions. In the end, he couldn't shake feeling that he'd been his own father's executioner. Perhaps that, too, was part of their game.

Most days, it was hard to tell who he hated more—himself or the Ennuki and their twisted community.

This is what they want. They're tracking you, like a stolen car. They eat up doubt and fear like it was mother's milk. Don't give it to them. Let them fucking starve.

He'd tried college but he could never concentrate long enough to grasp anything being taught. He had money, but never peace of mind. On his nineteenth birthday, he announced to his mother that he was moving to an apartment. It would only be seven blocks away from hers in downtown Boston, but he needed the space.

For her part, his mother never seemed to grasp how to handle him when he returned. She was devastated by the loss of his father, not that she'd ever speak it aloud. He'd heard it enough in her quiet sobs late at night when he was supposed to be sleeping.

Their connection had been forever changed. He knew he was the problem, but she still blamed herself. He refused all of her requests for joint therapy. There was nothing a head shrinker could do for him. They didn't exactly cover this in their training.

PTSD in the wake of Ennuki encounters that will end in certain death thirty years in the future.

Nope. That was definitely not part of the course material.

The Dover Demon legend grew the night they were taken, as several other people in town were said to have spotted the strange creatures dashing through the snow. Nicky fumed at the satisfaction it must have given the hidden community. Those poor witnesses, most of them teens like himself at the time, had no idea what was in store for them.

At least in the city, the Ennuki didn't dare to enter. Too many people, too much potential for exposure. Here, Nicky was safe.

At least for twenty-five years.

"Sorry, excuse me," he said, bumping into a guy in a yellow jogging suit.

The man paid him no mind, lost in his iPod.

Nicky wouldn't find any Ennuki or Ushers here, not even hiding in the dark alleys on the south side. Though he knew they could take him at any moment by opening one of those mind-bending doorways.

Not that they would grab him now. He wasn't ready for them. The gift wouldn't take.

The woman's blond hair bobbed several yards and pedestrians, ahead of him.

She walked this route every day from her office to her ritzy apartment. In a way, he wished she'd recognize him. How would she react? Surprised? Or would she have known he was near all along?

As she turned the corner on the last leg of her walk, he hurried past a posse of teens carrying shopping bags and taking pictures.

Nicky grabbed her elbow hard enough to make her gasp.

"Remember me?" he said, low enough so only she could hear.

Her eyes narrowed in genuine confusion. He continued walking with her, his beard hiding the tight line of his mouth. Her dog pranced along as if nothing was happening.

She brushed a lock of hair away from his eyes and smiled knowingly.

"I'd thought they'd spared you," she said. "It really is the humane thing to do. I followed your story, saw how you spoke of nothing. I honestly believed you didn't remember."

Nicky tapped his temple. "I guess I didn't want to forget."

"So you wanted to deny yourself peace?"

They stopped at the entrance to her building. The dog started yapping.

"I have a different kind of peace in mind."

Nicky pulled the screwdriver from his pocket, driving it into the soft flesh of her throat, pushing until it hit the tip of her spine. She staggered backward, choking on her own blood, arms searching for something to hold on to.

"That's for my dad. I hope the others get my message."

He slipped into the crowd before anyone noticed the woman bleeding out. The first scream came as he walked down the subway stairs.

He'd been preparing for the trip to Dover for weeks now. He'd wished he could have stashed his motorcycle at Roy's, but his old friend had never forgiven him for letting Christine disappear without so much as a clue where she'd went. He knew the truth wouldn't offer one ounce of consolation.

Instead, he'd had to hide the motorcycle in back of Kelly Weather's abandoned home. People had bought his parent's house as well as Tank's within a year of their disappearance. Not so with Kelly's. Nothing good had ever happened to the people who'd lived there. It wasn't cursed, but it was tempting karma to live there.

Securing his backpack to the seat, he drove out to Upper Mill Pond. It was a beautiful day. He felt lighter today. Just one more stop before he could finally move on.

Luckily, there were no joggers or nature lovers about. He stopped the motorcycle at the pond's edge and sat in the grass, waiting for night to come.

The forecasters were calling for a storm tomorrow. The clouds rolled in at dusk, obscuring the moon and stars. The temperature dropped considerably. Nicky put on a leather jacket he'd brought.

Rustling in the grass put him on high alert.

Flipping on his flashlight, he spotted two pairs of orange eyes staring at him from across the pond.

"I took care of her," he said, standing. "She's dead. You're free if you want to be."

The Ennuki blinked, heads tilting to catch his voice on the wind.

"If you choose to stay, I'll be ready for you. I'll know when you're coming. I can sense you as well as you can me. When the time comes, if you want it to, I won't go easy."

There was a dull hum overhead. He looked up and saw three red lights drift overhead.

"I'm not falling for that."

The humming ceased and the lights blinked out.

"Just want to make sure we understand one another."

The Ennuki rushed from their cover, disappearing into the night.

Nicky hopped on his motorcycle. The roar of the engine was followed by the sounds of scurrying in every direction. He'd been surrounded.

Driving away, he knew there was no way to stop them. They had survived for more centuries than he could count and would continue long after every Brogna was gone. He considered them manipulators and scavengers—monsters perhaps no worse than man. Did the fear they instilled really force man to unite, to evolve? Perhaps.

Maybe he'd have the chance to ask them one day.

The End

Subscribe to the Dark Hunter Newsletter!

Become one of Hunter's Hellions and subscribe today to get your free story, special access to upcoming books and more!

http://tinyurl.com/h5fufn2

About the Author

Hunter Shea is the product of a misspent childhood watching scary movies, reading forbidden books and wishing Bigfoot would walk past his house. He doesn't just write about the paranormal – he actively seeks out the things that scare the hell out of people and experiences them for himself. Hunter's novels *The Montauk Monster* and *The Dover Demon* can even be found on display at the International Cryptozoology Museum. His video podcast, Monster Men, is one of the most watched horror podcasts in the world. He's a bestselling author of over 16 books, all of them written with the express desire to quicken heartbeats and make spines tingle. Living with his wonderful family and two cats, he's happy to be close enough to New York City to gobble down Gray's Papaya hotdogs when the craving hits.

Follow his dark travails at www.huntershea.com.

Look for these titles from Hunter Shea

They Rise
Loch Ness Revenge
Savage Jungle : Lair of the Orang Pendek
Swamp Monster Massacre
Megalodon in Paradise
Fury of the Orcas

CHECK OUT OTHER GREAT HORROR NOVELS

DEATH CRAWLERS
by Gerry Griffiths

Worldwide, there are thought to be 8,000 species o centipede, of which, only 3,000 have been scientificall recorded. The venom of Scolopendra gigantea—the larges of the arthropod genus found in the Amazon rainforest—i so potent that it is fatal to small animals and toxic to human But when a cargo plane departs the Amazon region an crashes inside a national park in the United States, muc larger and deadlier creatures escape the wreckage to roan wild, reproducing at an astounding rate. Entomologist, Frank Travis solicits small town sheriff Wanda Rafferty's help and together they investigate the crash site. But as a rash c gruesome deaths befalls the townsfolk of Prospect, Fran and Wanda will soon discover how vicious and cunning these new breed of predators can be. Meanwhile, Jake and Nore Carver, and another backpacking couple, are venturing up into the mountainous terrain of the park. If only they knew their fun-filled weekend is about to become a living nightr

THE PULLER
by Michael Hodges

Matt Kearns has two choices: fight or hide. The creature in the orchard took the rest. Three days ago, he arrived at his favorite place in the world, a remote shack in Michigan's Upper Peninsula. The plan was to mourn his father's death and figure out his life. Now he's fighting for it. An invisible creature has him trapped. Every time Matt tries to flee, he's dragged backwards by an unseen force. Alone and with no hope of rescue, Matt must escape the Puller's reach. But how do you free yourself from something you cannot see?

ECK OUT OTHER GREAT
RROR NOVELS

BLACK FRIDAY
by Michael Hodges

Jared the kleptomaniac, Chike the unemployed IT guy, Patricia the shopaholic, and Jeff the meth dealer are trapped inside a Chicago supermall on Black Friday. Bridgefield Mall empties during a fire alarm, and most of the shoppers drive off into a strange mist surrounding the mall parking lot. They never return. Chike and his group try calling friends and family, but their smart phones won't work, not even Twitter. As the mist creeps closer, the mall lights flicker and surge. Bulbs shatter and spray glass into the air. Unsettling noises are heard from within the mist, as the meth dealer becomes unhinged and hunts the group within the mall. Cornered by the mist, and hunted from within, Chike and the survivors must fight for their lives while solving the mystery of what happened to Bridgefield Mall. Sometimes, a good sale just isn't worth it.

GRIMWEAVE
by Tim Curran

In the deepest, darkest jungles of Indochina, an ancient evil is waiting in a forgotten, primeval valley. It is patient, monstrous, and bloodthirsty. Perfectly adapted to its hot, steaming environment, it strikes silent and stealthy; it chosen prey: human. Now Michael Spiers, a Marine sniper, the only survivor of a previous encounter with the beast, is going after it again. Against his better judgement, he is made part of a Marine Force Recon team that will hunt it down and destroy it.

The hunters are about to become the hunted.

 SEVERED**PRESS**

CHECK OUT OTHER GREAT HORROR NOVELS

MONSTROSITY
by Tim Curran

The Food. It seeped from the ground, a living, gushing teratogenic nightmare. It contaminated anything that ate causing nature to run wild with horrible mutations, creating massive monstrosities that roam the land destroying town and cities, feeding on livestock and human beings and on another. Now Frank Bowman, an ordinary farmer with n military skills, must get his children to safety. And that wi mean a trip through the contaminated zone of monster madmen, and The Food itself. Only a fool would attempt Or a man with a mission.

THE SQUIRMING
by Jack Hamlyn

You are their hosts.

You are their food.

The parasites came out of nowhere, squirming horrors that enslaved the human race.They turned the population into mindless pack animals, psychotic cannibalistic hordes whose only purpose was to feed them.

Now with the human race teetering at the edge of extinction, extermination teams are fighting back, killing off the parasites and their voracious hosts. Taking them out one by one in violent, bloody encounters.

The future of mankind is at stake.

And time is running out.

Made in the USA
Columbia, SC
25 February 2018